NEVER

Andy Christopher Miller

Andy Christopher Miller is a poet, author and psychologist. He is a winner of the Yeovil Poetry Prize and has been placed in a number of national competitions. His memoir of growing up in 1950s Weymouth, 'The Naples of England' (Amcott Press), has been widely praised by a range of established writers. A diarist for over fifty years, he has also published 'The Ragged Weave of Yesterday' (Amcott Press), a reflection on the psychology of this strange pastime and a personal history of British life as the 1960s became the 1970s. He has served as an honorary professor of educational psychology at the Universities of both Nottingham and Warwick and his ten books in this capacity include 'Child and Adolescent Therapy' (Open University Press) and 'Pupil Behaviour and Teacher Culture' (Cassell). With Vally Miller, he is currently preparing a book about the west of Cornwall, 'Way to the West', which matches original water colour paintings and poems.

'Never: A Word' is his first novel.

Praise for Andy Christopher Miller's writing

'... a wonderful book ... anyone yet to read it has a real treat in store' John Lindley, Poet Laureate for Cheshire

'...a distinctive voice' Daisy Goodwin, Poet, television writer ('Victoria') and Yeovil Literary Prize judge

'... can shift from lovingly recalled detail to moments of powerful experience' Tony Jones, Winner for best radio drama, Writers Guild of Great Britain

'... the writing is lovely; lyrical, subtle, original and surprising' Chris Thompson, Radio and television writer ('The Archers', 'Heartbeat', 'Emmerdale')

'... moving, funny and compelling' Megan Taylor, Author, 'The Lives Of Ghosts'

'... vivid and touching' Frances Thimann, Author, 'November Wedding'

' ... an honest author' Judi Moore, Author, 'Little Mouse'

'... pulses with life and energy' Aly Stoneman, Left Lion, Nottingham

'... an intimate and immensely readable book' Dr Phil Stringer, University College London

' ... self-effacing, honest and with a gentle humour' Prof Tim Crook, Goldsmiths, University Of London

'... powerfully moving' Dr Nathan Lambert, University Of Nottingham

'... may already be a collector's item ... for there is a breath of humanity in this book' Ed Drummond, Poet, activist and legendary British rock climber

'... the best writing I've read for ages ... climbs through the important things in life' Prof Terry Gifford, Director, International Festival of Mountaineering Literature

NEVER: A WORD

Andy Christopher Miller

Amcott Press

Published by Amcott Press
68 The Dale
Wirksworth
Derbyshire
DE4 4EJ

*This novel is a work of fiction and the characters and
incidents portrayed in it are imaginary*

Andy Christopher Miller 2021

www.andycmiller.co.uk

CONTENTS

1. AS LONG AS EVERBODY IS ALL RIGHT

'Dad says I shouldn't have told you. I mustn't say anything else'.

It was December 27th, 1984. Sue and her mother, Avril, were back in the kitchen doing the dishes after tea while the others settled in the living room to the television and the new toys. Callum's new computer, the Sinclair Spectrum, was dormant now, disconnected and inert on the kitchen table. Sue had been wondering all day when she might get the next opportunity to speak with her mother. Down in Ilkley's Riverside Gardens that lunchtime, the children had raced around the park, disappointed that there had been no snow over Christmas, Callum shouting to his grandparents to watch him swing on trees or career down a slippery bank. Grace had attempted to keep up with her brother but retreated to Sue's side tearful and frustrated when Callum purposely chose challenges beyond her capabilities.

Sue might have very little time alone with her mother. The pull of the computer on the children had been intense, there had been hardly a moment when the rubber keys were not being stabbed or when the slow connection to the cassette player was not flickering away, downloading. Tomorrow would all be taken up with Cinderella at the Alhambra in Bradford and then her parents would be off on their long drive home the morning after that.

'Dad says it was wrong to tell you. You mustn't say anything to your sister. She's not as strong as you'.

It had been the same the evening before, an explosive flash flood with events and memories careering past as she stood with her mother in the kitchen washing up after Boxing Day tea. It was only supposed to have been a casual enquiry to tidy a few footnotes in her curiosity before the real work, if there were subsequently to be any, could begin.

There had been two recent television series about tracing family trees, and both took a diligent and reverential approach. Like Songs of Praise, wholesome and reassuring. It was said to provide a fascinating insight into the unwritten history of ordinary life down the ages. For those with the will and aptitude, here was an invitation to the famous, huge archives in London. Or, age-weathered parish records could be accessed in out of the way village churches, with a system of charges constructed around half crowns and guineas and turn-around times for correspondence stretching into many months.

Sue had decided that it couldn't be for her, at least not until the children were that bit older. She could see the appeal of securing her family and herself within the branches and twigs of the centuries, but this was a world of cardigans, old books and a slowed-down appreciation of the delicately savoured fact. She was already up to her eyebrows with her job and family and now her growing involvement in the campaign against nuclear weapons as well.

Not yet, except for the one injunction:

'If you are thinking of doing this, talk to your oldest surviving relative today. Don't wait until tomorrow, do it today!'

So she told her mother that she was thinking of tracing their ancestors.

*

Ever since Sue could remember, her parents had been entertaining her with tales from their earlier times in Weymouth before their recent move, relatively late in life

8

and with her father's job, to the dockyards at Portsmouth. Stories about larger than life relations and neighbours, mean or sadistic teachers, hard toil during Saturday and holiday jobs, picture shows, dances and swimming galas.

Les sometimes reminisced about his childhood with a sense of worldly resignation. Like as a small boy having to carry a metal bucket of faggots slopping about in gravy all the way along the harbour side in Weymouth from Mitchells butchers shop to the restaurant up on the seafront. The bucket so heavy it cut onto his hands, the instruction that he was not to keep stopping, his payment of threepence divided into one penny for his mother for the housekeeping, one for sweets and then one to save.

Avril tended more towards character descriptions, sometimes complete with gestures and vocal mannerisms, and great, florid evocations of time and place. Giggling and attempting to get changed in bathing machines for school swimming lessons in the sea. Hiding under her bed as a child as the rag and bone man creaked his cart along their road with his cry of '*Raaaaayg .... Po*!'. Cousin Dora, poor, silly Dora, who used to clean for a doctor out at Upwey and who got disastrously taken in by him.

Sometimes Les and Avril seemed to be in competition for the audience of their two daughters, not that Sue or Janet particularly minded. Whichever story triumphed after the series of alternating openings, it had already by that stage escalated into something half magical and compelling.

On other occasions, her parents seemed to pool their contributions, each looking to the other for a cue or a pause for breath in the rushing narrative.

'That delivery man from the brewery – '

'You'd see him loading up first thing – '

'You could smell that brewery all over town, especially where we lived, we – '

'They used to say his horse knew the way. It used to stop at every – '

'A big thing it was, it used to frighten me if it came – '

'The man was drunk by mid-morning, used to have a drink at every stop, completely blotto he was by – '

'And it was right by the harbour, no bollards there in those days, just a straight drop – '

Sue was easily returned to the thick, green water from her childhood, a weathered pontoon with a skirt of swaying weed on the surface, an occasional shoal of tiny fishes mouthing at the air, curious about the world beyond theirs. Her unsettling contemplation of its probable depth.

'You'd see that horse in the afternoon, straight as a die, inches – '

'The man, fast asleep, keeled over on some sacking, snoring – '

'Knew the way back along the harbour side, the wheels almost – '

'But you knew it would never – '

'It was a lovely old horse. Even if it was a bit – '

'I used to love that horse.'

Avril would often lose herself in the stories, becoming gruesomely vivid and engrossing to Sue as a child. She relived the parts, sometimes became one character after the other, the events tumbling out beyond her control. Lost in another place, time and body, she would eventually be pulled back into the present by Les.

'Steady on now, mother, come on'.

It seemed to Sue like a kindly, family joke. Well, almost.

'You were getting a bit carried away with yourself there'.

Avril's animated account would then die away and she would ease back into the room, returning far more subdued, offering perhaps a parting comment to her companions – 'a great big thing it was, that horse' or 'poor silly Dora'.

*

'Family trees,' said Avril, clearing a space for the dried dishes on the surface beside the sink. 'That's a funny thing to want to go doing, isn't it?'

'I don't think so,' replied Sue. 'We'd all like to know a bit more about where we came from, wouldn't we? Tell me about who you remember.'

'Well there's my Dad,' said Avril, rather briskly. 'I don't know if you remember him?'

'Of course, I do,' said Sue. 'He used to live with us when I was very little?'

Grandad Pritchard was there among Sue's earliest memories. Smiling, lines in a handsome weathered face and with thick grey hair inked in with black. Returning from work, he stored his wellington boots away in the under-stairs cupboard, Sue's beside them. At that time, a small table had somehow been fitted into the kitchen and Sue remembered sitting with him, at three or four years of age, as her mother gave him his tea. 'Thank you, our Avril,' he said and then, to his granddaughter 'What are you having, – bread and sops?' Sue ate this sat beside him, bread torn into pieces with sugar and hot milk, and rehearsed saying beneath her breath 'Thank you, our Avril' as her mother placed hers down before her.

Grandad Pritchard had been a sailor in the Royal Navy. In photographs, he wore a peaked cap and complex uniform, more precise and tidier than any clothes Sue had ever seen. He had apparently once brought back a parrot for

Avril when she was a little girl from the other side of the world.

'My Dad was a proper matelot, if you know what I mean,' Avril said. 'If he had a bit of money then everybody had to have a drink on him'.

At other times Avril had talked about the sense of responsibility she felt for her father's future.

'After my mum died, they were all after him. Aunt Margaret fancied her chances and others were making eyes at him. He used to like to go to the dances and they were all there. He was a bit silly, you see, and I used to worry myself sick about him. He wanted me to have a look at these women, to see if I thought they were suitable'.

Sue knew this story well and how it culminated in her grandfather marrying a snobbish and totally unsuitable old spinster. He had only lived for a few years after that, dying when Sue was eight or nine, and the acrimonious matter of where all his money ended up was a subject that surfaced unexpectedly on occasions all through her growing up.

'Your other grandad, Grandad Roberts, was different,' Avril explained. 'He was merchant navy'.

Sue remembered him as well, a thin, wiry man who said little. Tiny movements of his mouth constantly suggested that he was biting back some witticism or ironic comment even in the absence of any ongoing conversation.

'He wasn't daft, not by a long chalk,' Sue had sometimes heard her father say. 'Just kept himself to himself. Couldn't see the point of talking just of the sake of it.'

Sue had once seen a photo of Grandad Roberts in the local paper showing a huge model ocean liner that he had made entirely from match sticks.

'He had a lot of patience, Dad's dad,' said Avril. 'All those nights at sea, I suppose. They had to find something to do.'

Grandad was married to Granny Roberts and they often visited on Christmas Day. Avril became noticeably agitated before these visits and Granny Roberts seemed a harsh judge of the Christmas dinner and very sparing in her thanks or appreciation. She was Grandad's second wife and to Sue, as a child, this seemed unremarkable. Some people had parents and others step parents. Her father had one of the latter.

But the television programmes had helped her realise that, despite all the stories that she had been regaled with so regularly during her growing up, stories that in turn she had relayed to Giles as they were getting to know each other, there were also relatives who were never mentioned.

'I never knew Dad's mum, did I?' she asked. 'I've always assumed she died before I was born?'

'Oh, your dad's mother died a long, long time before you were born'.

'I knew Granny Roberts wasn't Dad's mother, but I don't seem to know anything about his real mum,' said Sue. 'When did she die?'

Avril held up the dinner plate she was drying and stared hard into its empty face.

'Oh, it was years ago. Our Dad was only a little boy. He never talks about it'.

'Gosh, I hadn't ever realised, in all these years'.

'Well you wouldn't. He never talks about it, your dad'.

'So, what did she die of?' asked Sue as she too stopped her slow circular drying.

Her mother stiffened and stared down more intently.

'She done herself in. In the sea. Off the Nothe, I think'.

The Nothe! Where Sue had scrabbled as a child along the thin sunless strip of rock exposed at low tide, lifting black, smelly stands of weed in search of a mouthful of winkles to take home to boil for tea. The Nothe fort, a little beyond the tourist magnets of the beach and town, with ramparts and a sea wall, tunnels and heavy gates, there as a lumpen defence, so she had been told at school, against sea-borne invaders across the centuries.

Avril turned her head away towards the table, still holding the plate. Granny Roberts had to somehow become a less established figure for Sue, who was struggling to fit another woman, faceless and nondescript, into parts of her dominion. Somebody in a cart-wheeling trajectory against the sky, propelled from the top of the fortification onto the rocks.

So much of it couldn't be right. Sue could not be learning about such happenings for the very first time at thirty-five years of age. She struggled to find any words to say. This violent, dramatic death was out of kilter with her whole sense of the past, with the pattern of people in a landscape, the threads and connections of family circumstance.

But there was no time for any further questions. Callum had bounded into the room full of restless enthusiasm followed by Giles carrying Grace.

'Is it still switched on?' he said, pointing to his new computer. 'Come on Grandma, we're all going to play'.

*

'Our Dad says I shouldn't have told you. I mustn't say anything else'.

Avril came straight out with it the following evening as soon as Sue had managed to engineer some time alone with her in the kitchen and raise the matter again. All that day, when they had driven in convoy to Bradford for the pantomime, Sue had been burning to ask the host of questions that built each upon the other in her mind, while also trying to ensure that the outing was a success for the whole family. She had briefly relayed the previous evening's conversation to Giles that morning by locking herself in the bathroom with him while he shaved. He had tried to follow his wife's hectic, whispered account whilst also keeping one eye on the furrow his razor was ploughing through the foam under his chin. Grace's knocking at the door and pleading to be let in curtailed Sue's account so Giles too spent a frustrated time that day trying to piece together and complete the garbled story that he had heard.

'Dad says it was wrong to tell you. He won't talk about it'.

It did not occur to Sue to wonder when this conversation between her parents had taken place. They had all been together in their holiday bustle almost all the time, with her father and Giles staying up late the previous evening to watch the football on television and drink home-brewed beer. Her mother would surely have been asleep by the time Les and Giles made their whispering way upstairs. Sue knew that she and her mother could be interrupted again at any moment. A queasy awareness was growing in her that moments when she could initiate the exchange of intimate family information had, in her life, been isolated between periods of silence, somehow rigidly enforced over months and even years.

When the opportunity did arise, clearing up on that second evening after the matinee and a late tea, Sue could think of no obvious or immediate questions. There was so much to re-configure, points of detail seemed potentially distracting and unhelpful. Instead, she wished for the broad sweep of an account – pictures, words and colour – and, particularly, some explanation as to how she had never heard one hint or slip of the tongue, had never carried through her childhood even the faintest suspicion that, when the adults closed the doors, they communed together with secrets of such disruptive magnitude.

'Why did she do it? When was this, how old was Dad?'

'I don't know. Three children and Grandad away at sea for most of the time, I suppose. Dad was only a little nipper. He won't ever say anything about it'.

Three children and the back parlour, the room with the varnished panels, the stairs up into deep interiors that Sue had never seen and could not imagine. The outside toilet, the squashed-in back yard and the small strip of earth supporting Grandad's rows of vegetables. Granny Roberts fitted there in Newbiggin Road with Grandad in a way that some new, indefinite presence would not. The lens could not focus and no defining outline would emerge from any amount of further facts and figures.

How could any of this be true? All her mother's stories, all the family characters in a loosely formed tableau, all her persistent questions as a child piecing together the links. Sue and her mother had been revisiting them for thirty-five years. How had they managed to weave around this woman, to sidestep her as they galloped or dawdled along?

Sue could not believe that it had never occurred to her to wonder or to ask. If there were stepmothers, then there must

16

have been mothers. It was obvious, but somehow the thought had been inaccessible to her. If this was true, then her father had lost his mother as a little boy, possibly with his own father on the other side of the world, far away at sea. There had never been one reference through all the years, no name, no slip of the tongue – no photograph. The things children shouldn't hear, Sue had never heard. Her curiosity had always pursued every corridor and room it encountered, there could be no locked door let alone a secret wing left unnoticed and unexplored.

Life could not possibly have been so ordinary. Her parents could not have seemed the safe, predictable people they so clearly were, if any of this were true. She and her sister had been insulated from these deaths so completely, by a protection almost chilling in its effectiveness.

'What about your mother, then? I never knew her either, did I? But I do remember your Dad, Grandad Pritchard'.

'Can you remember my father?'

'Of course I remember him, I used to have my tea with him. But what about your mother? When did she die?'

'When you were little'.

'What of?'

The past Sue had never questioned or investigated, even in her fancies, had unrolled a sensational carpet right in front of her.

'She – I can't say it.'

'You can't say it? Whatever – '

'It begins with 'C'. You know what I mean'.

'Cancer?'

'Ooh. Don't say it. I don't like that word'.

'All right, Mum. But you know, nowadays – okay – okay – where was she living when – where were we?'

'In the house in Purbeck Road. When you were a little tot. They lived with us'.

'But – '

And then Callum came back into the kitchen, drawn by the Spectrum.

'Grandad says he wants a rest from Scrabble'.

'Are you ready for a go on the computer yet, Grandma?' asked Callum, ever hopeful that his grandmother would learn to share his enthusiasm for it. 'Grandad's going to read the paper for a while'.

'Oh, I don't think I can do that, my dear', said Avril. 'I can't seem to get the hang of it'.

But there was no more time for Sue to question her mother, even if she could have found any focus and remained out of earshot of the children. Her father had walked into the kitchen carrying a small pile of empty plates that had been missed.

'This is what I like to see, people working. Don't stop on my account,' he said. 'Everybody all right out here then?'

'Oh yes, we're all right,' Avril replied. 'We're just chatting'.

'Just putting the world to rights,' Sue added, the words coming automatically.

'Giles and I think it's time,' Les said, carefully inspecting his home brewed beer in the brown quart bottles with thickened glass necks and tightly secured stoppers.

'I suppose it's a little too early for you, is it Susan? There's also some elderflower wine that's very nice, even if I do say so myself. What about you, Mam, not too early for you, is it?'

'I'm all right for now, thanks Dad,' replied Sue.

'Well, as long as everybody's all right. That's the main thing,' he said.

2. THE CHILDREN OF THE MAY

Three days after the Christmas of Letitia's sixth year, Bertram succumbed to an illness, the course of which she was to remember during her growing up and into her adult years, especially at testing times with her own children. When tiny, Bertram was so often the focus of his sisters' make-believe games, dressed by them sometimes as a nobleman, or an itinerant tinker or any manner of creature, from those familiar in the local farmyards to the fantastical beasts conjured by their storytelling. On this particular day, however, their little brother's enthusiasm for these fancies failed to engage and, after a short period of muddled attempts to do so, he ceased completely to play out the role they had created for him within their excited extravaganza.

Maud and Letitia fussed around him as he began to pull at the long strip of cloth that they had wrapped around his head and fashioned into a turban. They complained that his participation was central if they were to fulfil their destinies as shipwrecked sailor and slave girl. But Bertram ignored their injunctions and continued to tug half-heartedly at his disintegrating headgear. He lowered himself onto the flagstone floor of the living room, falling against, as much as seeking support from, the chair arm. His tears were obscured by the dishevelled material falling into his face. The girls heard him begin to cry softly and recognised his genuine distress simultaneously, Maud pulling away the trailing remnants of the turban while Letitia knelt in front of him, her hands on his small, bony shoulders.

'Bertie, Bertie, don't cry. You can be the sailor. We can play another game if you want. What's wrong?'

Bertram, pale-faced and completely miserable, looked up trying to answer his sister. Instead, his face showed an emptiness of expression, an absence of any of the joyful, although often uncomprehending, compliance with which he usually attempted to follow his sisters' demands and directions.

Maud assumed the nurturing demeanour she sometimes employed with her younger brother and sister and felt Bertram's forehead.

'Let me feel him,' urged Letitia, as Bertram flopped against Maud's shoulder.

'No, fetch Mama, he's unwell, we can't have you fussing around him'.

'Is he cooking up?' asked Letitia.

'No he isn't. Will you just fetch mother please, Letty'.

Ivy hurried in from the scullery at the sound of the girls' raised voices.

'Mama, he's just started crying. He didn't want to be the sultan and he started – '

'Bertie, darling, what's the – '

'Hurts,' he said looking up at his mother.

'What hurts, Bertie? Where does it hurt, darling?'

'Yes, where Bertie?' insisted Letitia, gently shaking his shoulders.

Ivy lifted Letitia's nearest hand from Bertram's shoulder.

'Just let him – '

'Here,' said Bertram raising a hand to his throat as quieter tears, more abject than protesting, broke into coughing.

'What's the matter with him?' asked Letitia.

'I don't know,' said Ivy 'Let's get you up off this cold floor, Bertie. Let's sit you in this chair. Maud, can you clear those things off please and fetch him a cushion'.

Bertram allowed himself to be lowered into the chair, slumping awkwardly against its wooden arm.

'That doesn't look very comfortable, Bertie, let's see what we can do to make it a bit nicer for you'.

But Ivy's ministrations, Maud's patient and obedient assistance with these and Letitia's attempts to cajole her brother into responding, all failed to elicit much by way of a reaction from the boy. Despite the wooden struts digging into his left side, Bertie lowered his head onto the other arm, whimpering, and seemed to drift into sleep.

'I'll make him a cot over by the door where he'll get the warmth from the range. Maud, you can help me by bringing down his blanket and pillow from upstairs. Letty, can you help your sister and carry some of his things too. I'll make him some sage tea for that throat of his,' said Ivy, pressing open the clanking latch on the panelled pantry door and reaching inside.

When Bertram's bed was made, Ivy undressed him with some difficulty as he was barely awake enough to extend an arm or leg, scarcely able to push with his head or draw back a limb. Maud asked to administer Bertram's tea and Letitia to lick any remaining honey from the spoon, but it soon became apparent that Ivy would have to cradle him, to prop him up against her, as the task required an adult strength and reach.

The light from the window illuminated Bertram's face, showing it to be as grey as the flaky ash that spilled into the grate. After testing its temperature by sipping it herself, Ivy raised Bertram's head and attempted to pour some of the tea between his lips. He looked up at her with bleary eyes but seemed to take little of the medicinal liquid.

Leaving him to sleep yet worried by his listless vacancy and increasingly laboured breathing, Ivy attempted to dispel her daughters' concerns and her own by concentrating on their midday meal. She ladled the broth she had prepared earlier from the pan on the range into three bowls while Maud cut irregular chunks of bread from a loaf at the table.

'Has Bertie got what –?'

'Letty, don't speak with your mouth full! Where are your manners? Eat properly'.

'But is Bertie –?'

'Letty! Please, young lady, do as you are told'.

Admonished, Letitia sank behind her soup bowl watching her mother and Maud, neither of them returning her gaze or acknowledging her silent indignation. Then she looked around the room, at the log bucket and the old blue kettle in the hearth, at the narrow shelves up either side of the range with their tins, bowls and pans, and finally at the patterned plates of various sizes, distant and seldom used, up on the high shelf above the chimney breast.

'Come on Letty, eat your soup,' said Ivy in a softer and more encouraging tone.

They all three ate quietly but this only accentuated the impact of Bertram's breathing which escalated from a spluttering wheeze into a more sustained and noisier rasp.

'Girls, I want you to fetch your Auntie Lily, can you?' asked Ivy when they had all finished wiping their bowls with their remaining bread. 'You're good girls, both of you. Go and fetch Aunt Lily and say I need her to give me a hand with Bertie. Everything's going to be all right, I just need another pair of hands for a while, tell her'.

The two sisters were eager to be outside and helped each other with coats, hats and scarves in a ragged scramble. From the front door of the cottage they ran along the raised ridge beside the culvert that channelled the trickle of a stream through the village. Recent heavy rains had caused the stream to flood into the lane outside their house and the subsequent passage of Farmer Triscott's cattle had churned the usual path into an impassable and stinking stretch of ground.

'What do you think's wrong with our Bertie? Has he got what Jimmy Cotten had?' shouted Letitia while ahead of her Maud flicked her toes over the wet grass like a skater.

'Don't say such things, Letty, you mustn't,' shouted Maud, more aware of the discretion with which adults often managed conversations about illness. 'Auntie Lily will know what to do'.

And Aunt Lily received them with open and patient regard despite their competing and disjointed accounts of Bertram's sudden decline. She reassured them, took their small bodies to hers and attempted to quell their racing heartbeats against her skirts and apron.

The two sisters returned home with their aunt at a brisk and purposeful pace. Lily shooed away the small group of Farmer Triscott's geese that were jabbing at the grass alongside the path, marching past them while the girls edged more cautiously around the indignant and tetchy fowl with their lazy but menacing wings stretching and flapping.

'They won't hurt you, girls. Come on, keep with me'.

At the cottage, Ivy was waiting in an obviously agitated state.

'Oh Lily, Lily, he's just come down so fast. One moment he was playing with the girls and the next he couldn't hold himself up. He's got a sore throat and a fever. And his breathing is making an awful noise. He's fallen so weak, so suddenly'.

'Ivy. Ivy, you poor dear,' said Lily taking a gentle grip on her sister's upper arms and pulling her closer, before clasping her in an embrace. At the sound of conversation, Bertram had opened one eye and now watched his mother and aunt in a detached and listless fashion. As he attempted to speak his coughing began again and then his gasping for breath. Lily stroked Bertram's forehead and lifted a damp forelock away from his eyes in attempt to soothe him and hold back his tears and spluttering.

'Ivy, we should take him upstairs, somewhere quieter for him. We must let the fever out. You've got Elderberry Rob somewhere haven't you?'

'I want 'berry Rob as well,' said Letitia, who had remained silently by the front door with Maud, the serious tones of their mother and aunt discouraging them from stepping inside.

The two women lifted Bertram who now made no attempt to take his own weight when upright. Maud and Letitia made an effort to help, the younger sister holding her brother's leg which only impaired the adults' efforts.

'You girls stay down here,' said Lily 'there isn't room on these stairs'.

When Lily returned to the girls downstairs, she suggested they baked some cakes together to lift everybody's spirits. At the kitchen table, they were soon occupied in preparing lardy cake and a fruit cake. The children became absorbed stirring the sticky mixtures and Lily welcomed the responsibility for ensuring their quiet engagement with the task as a distraction for all three of them. Fewer sounds came from the bedroom above.

As the afternoon darkened, a rich smell, sweet and bountiful, grew to fill the parlour and Lily hoped that Bertram and Ivy were drawing sustenance from it in the room above. As the dough blossomed in the oven's heat and their patient wait began, Lily welcomed their vying to be the one to shake the cakes from their tins as a distraction from the occasional whimpering sounds and footsteps in the room above them. Just when it seemed that the increasing calm might herald the peak and subsequent decline of Bertram's fever, the household was unsettled by a small but distinct cry of alarm from Ivy followed by a terrifying, rasping undertow as Bertram fought for breath.

'Stay here, girls,' said Lily, making immediately for the stairs, 'let me just go and see your mother, see what she needs'.

'Is our Bertie going to be better soon?'

'Yes, he's going to be fine, just wait down here,' said Lily, about to go upstairs when the distressing sound of Bertie's breathing again echoed down from the high spaces of the stairwell. The sound severed Lily's attention from the girls and she hurried up to the bedroom with Maud and Letitia following closely, the previous restrictions forgotten by all three.

The girls stopped at the doorway, alert to the unvoiced anxiety in their mother's countenance. Unaware of the children, Ivy turned in her fear to Lily.

'Lily, he's – what shall we do? He's – I can't – '

At the reappearance of his aunt, Bertram's crying began again, at first feebly, but then breaking almost immediately into a convulsing struggle for breath.

'Oh Ivy. Bertie, you poor boy. There, there, settle down Bertie, be calm, just breathe, breathe naturally, be calm'.

Turning to Ivy, she said. 'We must send for Dr Allingham'.

'Will he come? What if we can't afford – '

'He will come. Don't worry on that account, Ivy. George can shoe his horse for him, he's a good man, he'll take that as payment, I know he will'.

'Has he got what Jimmy Cotten had?' Letitia blurted out, the two girls having linked hands as they stood waiting for the women to notice them, to give some direction to their stifled energies.

'Girls, go down stairs, both of you! What are you doing up here? Go downstairs right now!' said Lily. 'Go on, I'll come down straight away,' she added.

And again, as he seemed about to appeal to his mother, another rush of gasping for breath that sounded like a high wind rattling through a coppice of naked willow branches or like Granddad's dominoes in their old metal box being frantically shaken.

'Letty said – ' cried Maud.

'I know,' replied Lily 'Bertram will be all right, we have to send for Dr Allingham. I want you to help me. Your mother will need you to help her too. Get your coats on, we are going to find one of our neighbours and ask them to ride over to Dr Allingham. We'll start with the farm and see if Mr Triscott will allow one of his hands to go. And we have to see whether those cakes are ready to take out yet'.

As they left the house, the cold air awakening them to the outside world, they met Mrs Wakeman, their neighbour, standing to the front of her cottage and Lily quickly poured out an account of the past few hours' happenings.

'Oh Lily, you poor dear – if there is anything – just ask me if you think – '

Lily's relief at finding such an immediate source of assistance threatened to pick apart her composure and she pulled her nieces in against her, their solidity against her legs rekindling her fortitude. Mrs Wakeman readily absolved Lily of the responsibility for contacting Dr Allingham and said that she would see to it straight away.

Back in the house, Bertram's distress seemed to have subsided again and Lily sought to distract Maud and Letitia from their continuing agitation, wishing there was some means by which the mention of the Cotten boy could be obliterated from their common recollection. As she encouraged them to test the readiness of the two cakes, she welcomed the unruly liveliness that broke out.

'Shh, girls, shh. Not too loud now, remember. Maud, you are the oldest, you have to let Letitia help. Letty, you can put the knife in the cake too, just be careful you don't – '

'Let's take Bertie some. And Mama,' said Maud, cutting with a determination more suited to day-old, cold mutton than a crumbling fruit cake not long from the oven.

'I want to take it,' objected Letitia, tears forming in her eyes.

'Let's us three have a piece first to see what it's like,' said Lily, embracing her youngest niece to help her regain her resilience. 'It sounds as though Bertram may be asleep so we should let him rest'.

After another hour or so of this agreeable bickering and munching of thick slices of both cakes, they heard the sound of men's voices outside the house, Mr Wakeman from next door and another they did not recognise. The abrupt snorting of a horse, as if somehow affronted by the front door of the cottage, followed by its whinnying cry indicated that Dr Allingham had arrived.

Lily smoothed dusty remnants of the baking, more remembered than real, from her hands onto her apron as she rose from her chair. The front door opened without a knock and a large man with a brown leather bag, ruddy from the cold and dressed in tweed breeches, woollen stockings and a Norfolk jacket, stepped briskly into the room.

'There's a child ill, not one of these two surely?'

Lily was unable to stifle completely an involuntary curtsey, bending one knee and allowing her head to twist downwards and to one side.

'Doctor, thank you for coming, thank you, it's my sister's boy, Ivy's.

'Somebody's been cooking, there's some nice smells in here,' he said to the watchful children who had retreated to the further corner of the table and moved in closer together.

'Is it you two?'

Neither spoke.

'Girls, answer the doctor properly! Where are your manners?' said Ivy.

'Letty's broken the cake with her – '

'Maud! That's not – '

'No, no, never mind,' said Doctor Allingham. 'Those are the best bits, the crumbly bits. You'll enjoy those. Now where's this little boy?'

'Doctor, it's Bertram, up here,' called Ivy from the top of the stairs. 'We are really – '

'Very well, let me have a look at him,' said the doctor moving towards the stairs. 'And keep these children down here'.

Dr Allingham's movements in the room above were conveyed by a muffled procession of creaking joists across the ceiling. Lily stood at the foot of the stairs, one hand on the banister whilst shooing the children back into the room with the other. The girls, vigilant and with an acuteness of hearing, could discern as much if not more than their aunt, the doctor's voice being clear and measured, their mother's far less distinct and considerably fragmented.

'Three hours or so, you say?'

'Then he just – '

'No drinks at all? Has he been drooling like this all the time?'

'– struggling to swallow – '

'Let's have a look at you then, young – '

And as Dr Allingham was speaking, Bertram emitted a deep and sucking groan, as loud as any injured or dying beast, as if a whole room full of air was insufficient, woefully insufficient, to fulfil the urgent and vital cravings of his lungs.

'Oh my Lord,' said Lily raising her skirt in order to ascend the few stairs even more quickly. As before, the two girls followed automatically, any previous injunctions, even the doctor's, irrelevant and redundant within the maelstrom of panic and emergency.

Huddled low on the top stair, they could see into the bedroom, their aunt holding their mother back from the bed as Dr Allingham attempted to hold still one of Bertram's flailing arms.

'Come on young fellow. Just try to breathe, just relax'.

The doctor sat holding Bertram's wrist, the troubled concentration on his face suggesting that he was unable to locate a pulse. Ivy was leaning forward, restrained by Lily,

30

a hand to her breast and her mouth open, unable to stifle her horror. Dr Allingham pulled from his bag an ear trumpet and, after raising the boy's vest, placed it on his chest. Maud and Letitia lay in silence, their faces even closer to the wooden boards of the landing, both intensely curious about the landscape of sound that might be revealed by the listening device. Bertram moaned only slightly as Dr Allingham pulled at the skin below one eye and then the other, and then fell silent as methodical hands pressed gently on each side of his neck. A trickle of blood-streaked mucus appeared from the boy's nose and Ivy bent forward to wipe it from him with a rag. As the examination of his stomach and then the manipulation of his arms and legs continued, with Bertram offering only a feeble protest at these forced exertions, she dabbed at the dribble from the side of his mouth.   When Dr Allingham extracted a shiny metallic instrument like a large flat spoon from his bag and then attempted to open Bertram's mouth, Letitia raised herself involuntarily as if also to better see inside.

Ivy recoiled noticeably, as if from some foul odour, when Bertram's lips were parted, her son then beginning to resist and struggle and then to splutter and gasp again.

'It's all right young man,' said Dr Allingham. 'It's all over, no more nasty examinations. It's all right'.

But the girls, even at their young age, could tell from the manner in which the doctor placed the implement down on a chair, from the concentration that was momentarily too prolonged, and from the way his posture stiffened as he rose and turned to face Ivy, that there was no reassurance to come.

'I'm afraid,' he began in a lowered voice as Ivy raised both hands to her face.

'Oh no, oh my dear God, no,' she cried. Lily stepped to her sister's side, automatically seeking to embrace her while defiantly studying the doctor's face for any minor movement about his eyes and mouth that, however improbably, might reveal some cruel deception. She held Ivy's sagging frame as it folded against her, pulsing now with a deep and hidden sobbing.

'What can we do, doctor, surely there must be something?' asked Lily.

'I'm sorry. I'm very sorry. I'm afraid that at this moment medical science – '

'How shall we even pay you?' blurted Ivy. 'We haven't even – '

'Hush now. There is no need. Your husband and I can take care of all of that'.

'Is there nothing? Nothing that we can do?'

'You can pray. The Lord does listen to our prayers and does sometimes deliver miracles,' said Dr Allingham, touching the back of Lily's hand as she held her shaking sister.

Miracles? Letitia knew of many, the loaves and fishes that answered a multitude's hunger and the waste baskets subsequently filled to overflowing with the uneaten remnants of the feast, the man wearing a sheet who had picked up his bed on a flat sandy rooftop and walked. She jumped to her feet in excitement, brimming with optimism and thus alerting everybody to the presence of the two young girls.

'Maud, Letitia, whatever – '

'Get those children away from here. They mustn't be in the house, let alone up here. Get them downstairs immediately!'

The urgency in Dr Allingham's command focused Ivy as well as Lily on the immediate task.

'Are there any other young people living in this house?' he demanded.

'Only my sister's lad, Sidney, sir,' replied Lily.

'How old, the lad? What age is he?'

'He's twelve, sir, going on thirteen this Whitsun. He'll be joining his father full-time then as his apprentice'.

'Twelve, thirteen, should be fine. But these girls, they must not stay in this house. Not another night. Can you take them?'

'Of course I can. And with pleasure,' said Lily 'Of course I can'.

That night Maud and Letitia slept in a large bed in Aunt Lily's house, the bed with huge pillows of goose feathers that tickled and even pricked their faces if they burrowed into them too enthusiastically. They had stayed here before as a treat on occasional evenings, one of the provisos being that they were to wash and prepare themselves for bed and then settle without undue fuss, if Aunt Lily was to have them stay again in the future. But tonight these rules seemed relaxed, abandoned even. Now, Aunt Lily was sitting with them on the bedside seemingly in no hurry for them to settle to sleep or to return downstairs to the living room herself. They had left their own home so hurriedly that they had been unable to collect together their usual nightwear and were now wearing old and slightly too small garments left behind from when they were a little younger.

'This is too tight,' said Maud pulling at the sleeve of her nightdress.

'And mine's a baby's,' added Letitia, even more constricted, although less demonstrative, than her sister.

'Never mind girls. Tonight is a bit different. We're at sixes and sevens. In the morning I can go and fetch all your things'.

'Can we go and see Bertie and Mama?' asked Maud.

'Will Sidney and father be there?' added Letitia.

'Not you two, no. You're too young. You heard what the doctor said. And I expect that your father and Sidney will have to be at the forge'.

'Will Bertie be all right in the morning?' enquired Letitia and the question hung momentarily in the flickering light from the lamp beside the bed.

Maud made to scold her younger sister for her enquiry but checked herself just as Lily placed a kindly hand on her forearm.

'We must all pray for Bertie tonight. Girls, can you do that? Then we will all be praying'.

When they eventually grew sleepy, Lily granted their request for the lamp to be left burning, saying that she would return a little later and dowse the wick if they were then sleeping. They whispered between themselves for some while, their scattered thoughts slowing, their anxieties settling and their words growing fewer with the advancing night.

Suddenly, Letitia remembered. Miss Raggity!

'We've left Miss Raggity,' she exclaimed, prompting a call from her aunt at the bottom of the stairs.

'Come on girls, it's time to settle. No more talking now please. I don't want to have to say so again'

'We've left her in the house. She should be here with us'.

'Letty, will you please settle,' Maud whispered. 'Miss Raggity's only a doll'.

'I want her,' said Letitia, seeing again Dr Allingham's serious presence in their upstairs room. 'I want these girls, and Miss Raggity, out of here straight away,' she said to herself, trying to make the imaginary voice in her head as deep and authoritative as possible by pulling down the sides of her mouth as she rehearsed these words.

'Why are we too young?' she asked Maud, but her sister's form had fallen limp and silent, seemingly relaxed and absorbed by the dip in the centre of the bed. Letitia lay on her side awake for longer with tear-dampened hair against her cheek until she too eventually slipped into sleep.

By the next day the weather had deteriorated further. As Lily and her two nieces returned for further clothes and belongings, bolts and puffs of wind quickly dampened Letitia's cheeks. The brim of the bonnet hurriedly fixed by Lily flexed against this buffeting. The sky was a uniform shade of dull grey with darker trails of smoky clouds scrolling northwards in a strangely uniform progression as if manipulated by some sure and steady hand. Bare branches in the hedgerow scratched at the sky as if attempting to disrupt a motion too orderly for such a wild and ill-disciplined day.

At the gate to the cottage, Lily turned to the two children.

'You must wait here. You do understand that, don't you girls? I will be as quick as I can with your clothes but I do want to see if your poor mother needs anything'.

Lily left the front door slightly open as she disappeared up the stairs.

'I want Miss Raggity,' said Letitia looking at her disappearing form.

'You mustn't,' said Maud, 'you'll get skinned alive'.

But Letitia was beyond threats; Miss Raggity had been abandoned in the house and treated as an irrelevance.

'Letty, you mustn't,' said Maud again to her determined, younger sister. 'I can't – I won't – I'm not going to look, I'm going to look up here instead'. And she turned to face the path and the culvert.

Letitia found again her inconspicuous space at the head of the stairs, low down outside the partially open door but with a view of most of the interior. Bertram was sleeping, a very slight rise and fall of the bedding across his chest, regular and rhythmical and just discernible. The drawn curtains lent an even greater gloom to the corners of the room than that bequeathed to the sky by the wayward weather outside. An oil lamp was burning on a small round bedside table, illuminating Ivy as she knelt at Bertram's side. She was wearing the same long black skirt and apron as when the girls had left the afternoon before, only now these looked too big for her, as if her body had somehow become shrunken by the slow passage of the long night she had surely spent at Bertram's bedside. Lily was standing back from the bed, a sprig of dried shrubs hanging from the ceiling rafters above her and casting a flickering forest of shadows on the wall behind her. Next to her mother though, also with hands clasped in prayer and at the very foot of the bed, knelt Father Reeves.

Father Reeves in his black robes. Not in full voice in his church pulpit, but in their house. Not besides mourners in his graveyard, his the one steadying presence among the tableau of grief beside the excavated plot, but in their house upstairs. Not hurrying across the perfect lawn between his church and the vicarage, struggling with some sermon, high-minded and removed from the blunt concerns of his parishioners, but in their house, upstairs, in the private cloisters of their bedroom. Not striking out against sin, not receiving the tiny children of the May, but knelt in silent prayer beside their mother in their house, upstairs, in their bedroom.

3. ANYTHING SEEMED POSSIBLE

'Apparently, even something as simple as a door knob or a tin opener has a designer working on it beforehand,' explained Les.

On every visit back home to Weymouth, it was the same, Sue and her father ending up in a pirouette around help and resentment, advice and confusion.

'Dad, I'm doing Fine Art. It's nothing like that,' snapped Sue, immediately recognising his good intentions and regretting her hasty response. She knew that her father struggled to understand exactly what she might be qualified for when her course finished.

As did she.

Her sister, Janet, had set the pace in respect of careers by leaving school at sixteen, getting well established as a local junior librarian and marrying before the age of twenty. Sue, by contrast, was horrified at the prospect of regular employment, could think of nothing worse than a settled nine-to-five routine while she waited for the appearance of 'Mr Right', or 'Mr Just-About-Bloody-Bearable' as she had once sarcastically remarked in front of her family. Again, she had alarmed herself with her lack of restraint and been desperate to gather her words up, unheard, and seal them away back behind her teeth.

On one occasion Les raised 'fashion', while joking that he was the least suitable person to be giving advice in that respect.

'Or, there's technical drawing,' he also suggested. 'It's a plum job at our place, the drawing office'.

He frowned.

'Mind you, it's a man's work really. They don't have any women in there'.

The 1960s were drawing to an end and Sue's course was in its final months. To relieve the constant pressure from her family, she found a post as a care auxiliary in an old peoples home in Lewisham, near the college. There would not be a problem if she wanted to continue to use the studios occasionally after she had left, her tutor assured her. So, with a bit of a struggle, she could support herself while continuing to develop her canvases, free at last from what she felt to be the stultifying pressures of course requirements and end-of-year exhibitions.

She told her parents that the job would not be forever but that it would tide her over until she either made a success of being an artist or found what it was that she really wanted to do in life. Surprisingly, her father seemed to approve.

'I had to earn my keep right from the word go,' he said.

Sue had heard a variation on this theme many times as she grew up.

'You have to sort out what's what if you're responsible for your own upkeep,' he added.

'It won't do her any harm having to get herself up of a morning. All that lying around being a student won't have helped,' he advised Avril, when her mother had somehow got it into her head that Sue was committing herself to a lifetime of skivvying in a care home in South London and, even more absurdly, that for some reason they might never see her again.

To Sue, as the autumn days began to shorten and the three-weekly cycle of shifts often forced thoughts of sleep to the top of her priorities, it did feel as if harm was being perpetrated. Harm of a sort, anyway.

Her canvases were barely touched. If she had any energy for her art, it was often at ridiculous times of day or night when the college studio would be shut. True, the women she was now working with at the care home, one or two from old South London families but mostly immigrants from the West Indies and Pakistan, were providing her with a whole new education. But after all the lifting, carrying, feeding, wiping and cleaning, she had little energy left for creative activities. With her previous college friends now dispersed around the country and large chunks of every twenty-four hours spent in physical toil or resting from such exertions, Sue was, by late November, beginning to construe her future as a set of train tracks narrowing to a single point some way ahead in an already visible future.

She had been looking for a new horizon and suddenly there it was. An advert in Time Out. She didn't know the first thing about sailing. In fact, she had been proud, back in the sixth form in Weymouth, to have had not the slightest acquaintance with the snobby social set the pastime seemed to attract.

But cruising the Med, even if it entailed being chief cook and bottle washer, had to be a more promising prospect for the Spring than an unending sequence of staff rotas pinned to a scruffy noticeboard in the rest room. And brushing with the relics of a classical age, the high splendour of Renaissance culture and the string of watering holes favoured by those on the Grand Tour, might be exactly what she needed to kick-start back to life her own rapidly fading artistic ambitions.

The year would turn. She would escape the narrowing confines of winter in the city.

She would sail out into an unimaginable panorama.

Seventeen months later and halfway up a sheer cliff face in Snowdonia – still a hundred and fifty feet from the top – Sue desperately needed the toilet.

From their occasional meetings at college in the autumn term, Sue knew the man she was climbing with to be an assertive and self-confident character. But out on this rock face Giles was at his most self-assured. He would have a solution tucked away up his anorak sleeve. With the narrow platform tapering further in the few inches before the cliff edge and the void, she could get no more than an arm's length from him at best. The wind was picking away at the one dogged clump of heather still clinging to the rock, a tiny, withered bush that offered no shelter or privacy.

When Sue thought about it in her tent that evening after the pub, it was his matter-of-fact, problem solving approach that had impressed her. And his understated consideration. Giles had climbed above to secure her with ropes. He danced on tiptoes along the ledge to check there were no other climbers about to emerge and found items in the emergency first aid kit in his rucksack that would at least afford her a little comfort in that vertical wilderness.

The silly girl, Mary, with whom Sue was sharing the tent was totally untrustworthy as a confidante, so Sue lay awake in silence remembering the speed and agility with which Giles had moved on the rock once she was safely anchored. His polite enquiries from behind his turned back had been without a hint of mockery or teasing.

The second night, when they unzipped his sleeping bag and used it as a cover, he told her that he had never met a girl who could take so much in her stride and laugh about the situation on the ledge. During the day, on the long walk across the snowy plateau with all the members of the mountaineering club, she had been unsure whether he had any interest in her at all, so absorbed was he with route finding and the morale of the weakest and dizziest of the walkers. She was certainly alert to him though, to his thoughtful silences when absorbed with setting his compass, to the way he took in the horizon of bluffs and broken ridges in the moments when the mist briefly parted.

But around the fire after the pub that night, presumably relieved of his responsibilities, he seemed to seek her out across the jubilant flames. His posture was more relaxed, his eyes kindlier. If needs be later, she hoped Mary would be able to work it out for herself and not come looking for her in the night or rousing the whole encampment in a panic.

He described her as an adventurer and not like the girls he had met from the boarding school that had been partnered with his own. She was more irreverent, he said, more fun and less circumspect and restrained. And no mean climber either for a beginner. Her West Country accent amused him and, for once, the impersonations did not rankle with her. Mainly because this was an endeavour at which he was so clearly inept. Squeezed into his one-man tent there was little room for manoeuvre and despite the care they took, any stray soul still abroad on the frozen ground at that hour would not have been able to ignore the occasional buckling and subsiding of the canvass sides.

Over the years she would often re-live their first night together and it was their lightness of being on ground hardened by winter and the warm, sweaty layer of contact between them that she remembered. The whispers, giggles and the huge sense of outrageous secrecy that they had to

42

suppress by deep kisses. Their sleepless energy had threatened to let loose an explosive mischief all around the silent field.

*

From the start they both knew, Sue more strongly than Giles, that their different upbringings and experiences could be a barrier to their relationship.

'He's a public schoolboy, after all,' she had announced as she attempted to give a thumbnail sketch of his character and background to her sister.

'They'll have a few bob then, his family,' was Janet's only comment during this first discussion.

Perhaps, Sue mused, the social divide between her and Giles was now no greater than she experienced with many others in her life.

The grammar school had been the start of it, when Sue passed the eleven plus examination whilst, three years later, Janet's disappointing result secured her a place only at the local secondary modern. From then onwards Sue's friends were all drawn from the school, a few of them youngsters from the estate who had made the transition with her. But she also met others from the further sides of the town, the 'more upmarket areas' as her dad called them. Even when she started going to dances in the town, it was with her friends from school and she exchanged at best only a quick nod of the head with those who lived on the Shorehaven estate but had been routed at eleven towards the single sex secondary moderns.

Art School had, from her mid-teens, come to be her obvious destination. She stayed on into the sixth form more and more irritated by what she saw as the narrowing horizons of her friends. She saw them as carrying their small-town mentalities into the libraries and laboratories of university cities instead of rushing arms-wide into an opening world of experience.

'You'd have called me a right drip if you'd known me in those days,' she told Giles. 'But anything seemed possible. It was 1966 when I first went. I was hungry for everything.'

'Everything?' he teased.

Sue slapped his shoulder.

'Trust you,' she said, widening her striking blue eyes in mock disapproval and then turning her head and staring directly at him. 'But, yes, everything. And I was certainly ready for Rod when I met him at Art School'.

Giles often wanted to talk about Rod for longer than she did when his name cropped up. So, she tried to steer conversations in other directions if she sensed him looming ahead in her stories. He had been her first lover, they had danced right up close to many of the big groups before he decided that dancing was somehow uncool. One of the Moody Blues had even been in the year above them before their first record took off.

Rod was long in the past now, but he had introduced her to dope, Herman Hesse and herpes. His tiny cardboard sculptures, the folded and flapping cuboid shapes which he claimed forced attention onto the bleak and soulless nature of modern urban environments, had come to bore her. She still longed for sweep in her creations, the huge, passionate sprawl of a Turner somehow combined with the existential nihilism of the emerging New York movement.

'I think I would have found you very sexy if you really did have hair all the way down to the small of your back in those days,' seemed sometimes to be Giles' main comment on that era of her life.

He, on the other hand, had spent these self-same years a long way from the fleshpots. Sue admired the fact that he had not slavishly followed the easy path that led to a university course but had instead obtained a VSO post and taken himself off to India at the tender age of eighteen. She could imagine him digging wells by day and studying Hindu scriptures by candlelight at night in his one-bed cell.

'Didn't you miss company during those eighteen months?' she asked him. 'Girls and things?'

'Of course I did,' he replied. 'But I just tried to apply myself more to my textbooks. I was being monastic, delving into eastern mysticism. And teaching myself fluid dynamics as best I could'.

'Oh, we were all doing that,' she said. 'Not the fluid dynamics bit though. Some of them were half way out of their heads a lot of the time too.'

In their early days together, Sue sometimes wondered whether they should pin up a chart in his flat like the ones parents used for their children's heights as they grew. This might help her remember the key points of synchrony and difference in their two timelines before they converged at the point where, as mature students, they met in the college mountaineering club. But she also knew that checking and repeating these chronologies was a ritual that drew them closer together beneath the blankets.

'So, you were sinking into your blue period in a care home in Lewisham while I was settling into studying here,' said Giles one Sunday morning as they sat up in bed. They were eating a birthday breakfast he had made for her.

'Yes, and you were all trussed up in a suit with your short back and sides,' she said. 'Learning how to be a financial whizz kid while I was setting off for my sailing nightmare!'

'The sixties were over by then really,' he said, taking hold of her wrist as if she was a naughty child. 'We were all getting a bit more realistic. And, anyway, I was never going to be your standard money-grubbing businessman'.

Sue could not resist toying with this sensitivity of his. It worked every time. Did he really think she would have fallen for a 'straight' like that? One of capitalism's countless, faceless lackeys?

'I'd seen what could be done in third world countries. With a new attitude to technology,' he added. 'Local, transportable, keeping things on a small scale. I didn't think I had the maths for that sort of engineering, or I'd have gone down that route. I wanted to be part of a new approach for Africa and India. It was still going to need an understanding of commerce, of how to get things done through business channels'.

Sue believed it when Giles told her he had not found himself with like-minded souls in Year One Accountancy and Basic Company Law. And she found it greatly to his credit that he persevered with his vision where others would have lost heart. It was partly due to that time on his own in an alien culture while still in his teens, she thought, and the fact that even then he had what it took to organise a small Himalayan mountaineering expedition with old school friends while he was out there. Or maybe it was just that infamous public school stoicism, those cold showers and the thin sliver of matron's attention that had to serve as his only share of surrogate mothering.

The nightmare in the Med! What she had not bargained for was the effect of all that ozone and sunshine, of being the only female cooped up for days and nights with four increasingly lusty male shipmates. She regretted her naivety many times as they journeyed southwards hugging the Italian shoreline before striking off across the Adriatic towards the Yugoslavian coast. In retrospect, her practised expressions of polite disinterest, first cultivated with the occasional fumbling, tipsy boy at school parties and then, a little less rigorously applied, at druggy all-nighters at Art School, had served her to no advantage out on those crystal waters. There was nowhere to escape to. She could carry her refusals, her tired, sweet smiles and head shakes, only from bow to stern, all of twenty feet or so. Nestling at night in small ports formed from red marble and granite breakwaters, edging beneath soaring crags and capturing warm, driving winds within bulging sails – all had been images which sustained her through the cold winter rain and slush on London pavements. Now, in amongst it all, her thoughts were elsewhere, anywhere away from the unrelenting, unvoiced expectations, the never resting subplot of flight and pursuit.

'Did anyone actually try it on? Get really heavy?' asked Giles when Sue first talked him through this episode.

'Not in so many words,' she replied. 'Nothing, you know, physical – coercive'.

'So you weren't in immediate – '

'It was there all the time. Jokes. Half-finished sentences. Even the most innocent things'. Her gaze fell away from him and towards the floor. 'Nothing felt innocent – everything felt loaded. Day after day. It was like I was going crazy'.

Giles was certain that he would have done the same as Sue in the circumstances. In fact, he would probably have jumped ship long before Athens. She judged she could make do without the month's wages she was owed and use the little money she did still have to hide out in the female only dormitory of the international youth hostel until she could think through her plan for getting home. She sent her parents a telegram from the city's huge, echoing main post office, mainly to assure them that she was well, that there had been a slight change of plan and she would be seeing them within a month or so.

Life in Athens, however, quickly grew to suit her. A Swedish girl from the hostel, Ingrid, found casual work for them both in a hotel kitchen and Sue came to value simple routines and the opportunity to wander alone where she pleased through the city streets. The occasional cat calls and whistles from men were easily shrugged off. Corners could be turned, cafés and small shops entered, and steps, as many as she wished to make, could carry her right away. Through Ingrid she met a young American, Brett, a tall, thin, bearded boy whose loose clothes and beaded necklace almost fell from his limbs and shoulders as if redundant in the increasing heat of the early summer days.

'So, you had a bit of thing about hippies in those days, did you?' asked Giles. 'This guy, Brett. What was he all about?'

'Brett was nice. There was nothing going on. I'd certainly had enough of that sort of thing to last me a while,' explained Sue with a little impatience. 'The three of us just used to hang around. Like a sort of Peter, Paul and Mary. But in reverse'.

When they could no longer stay at the hostel, it was Ingrid who was the keenest to keep travelling eastwards. Sue knew that crossing the Bosporus marked some form of commitment. It was much more than a ferry ride, it was the boundary between who she was, who they all were, and the people they might potentially become. Unfamiliar and unrecognisable even to themselves. There would be no communications, no reassuring cultural landmarks and no turning back.

The final section of Sue's story stimulated Giles' interest the most though, as they both shared their experiences of the huge Asian landmass, frequently seeking common impressions and reactions. Long, unforgettable bus rides through barren, deserted landscapes, the most basic rooms that they came to view as commodious, even homely and welcoming. The wariness of strangers that often eased, if there was time, into generosity and kindness. The German couple who offered them lodgings when they finally arrived in Kabul. Shade from almond trees in the inner courtyard. Simple meals together of spiced lentils and rice. Books they passed around, lengthy explorations of meditation, yoga and tantric chanting. And the occasional, often more than occasional, joint of an evening.

Sue knew that her letters to her parents would take weeks to arrive, probably even months. Nevertheless, she continued to write every few days, partly because she knew how easily they could inculcate in each other an escalating stream of anxiety and distress which could then curdle into disapproval. And also because she had long tracts of time with little else to do. But mainly because she wanted so much to tell whoever might be willing to listen, of the sense of utter contentment she was feeling so frequently under these foreign constellations by night and a blowtorch sun by day.

Her letters would have taken all that time and told all those tales. But that little shit who arrived one day with his fake camaraderie and invented traveller's tales, with his notebook, pencil and camera! At first he was just another member of their transient community. He asked about her home town. He was curious, as they all were, about each other's stories. But he had double-checked the spelling of her name and misunderstood her qualifications. It was too late by the time he had selected her least flattering photograph, the one where she had been caught unawares and appeared drugged and semi-conscious. A double-page newspaper spread would be on her parent's sideboard and those of all their neighbours within days.

She knew then that she must return home. She would apply for a post-graduate teaching certificate and relieve her parents of their worries about her. Her future would be mapped out. The series of trails that had once seemed as if they might wander haphazardly and forever towards horizons in every direction, had in fact all been one glorious illusion now obliterated totally as if in some ferocious and unanticipated overnight sandstorm.

*

As Sue and Giles subsequently found out more about each other in their early months together, she often brought her mother's characters to life for him – old blind Salisbury Granny, Bug Watford with his cane terrorising seven-year-olds on their first day at junior school, her great-uncle still battle-shocked from the Boer War marching up and down in front of all the holiday-makers on the promenade.

Her mother's 'maddening crowd,' Giles once called them.

'It's madding,' she corrected him.

'I'll bet it is,' he replied. 'Bloody infuriating'.

'No, Far From The *Madding* Crowd, was Hardy's book title'.

From the first, Giles had been very keen to meet Les and Avril. In fact, they had even entertained the idea on their first night together in his tent in Snowdonia. He also badgered her several times in their first weeks, wanting to know when she would take him down to what he called 'deepest Darset'.

And for the first time, Sue felt some anxiety on her parents' behalf, some concern about showing Giles their old council house in Weymouth. She had thought that the sixties had put paid to any of that stigma. She had worn her upbringing as a badge of honour at Art School. And anyway, she felt that all that class stuff had never really impinged on her, even during her growing up, in the way that the sociologists were now claiming it must do.

All her friends at school and her previous boyfriends had found Les and Avril fun. More welcoming and less stuffy, less uptight, than their own parents. She had often felt fortunate in this respect and had even once written them a letter to this effect from Art School after an agonisingly embarrassing visit to the Godalming home of a fellow student. This letter was never mentioned again and Sue felt that a deep understanding between her parents and herself rendered any further comment unnecessary.

She need not have harboured reservations about Giles and her home. She had already been impressed by the way he could fit smoothly into a wide range of company, from refined, old academics through to serving ladies in transport cafés on a motorway. But by the time they did make the trip to her parents, she was still not sure whether this was not some carefully cultivated public school charm turned on and off at will or a genuine warmth and ease.

As she had predicted, her mother had been immediately impressed by him. 'He's very well-mannered,' she had whispered to Sue at their first moment alone together. And as she also guessed he would be, her father seemed more cautious in coming to any early judgement. Non-committal perhaps but happily drawn into conversation, first about his chrysanthemums and dahlias and then around Giles' enthusiastic sampling of his home-made beer.

What pleased Sue the most though was Giles' observations about them. Her father he saw as plain speaking, positive and welcoming without making an overly effusive display. Giles had spotted, within one first, short meeting, all these qualities that Sue herself admired the most. As far as her mother was concerned, Giles declared himself bowled over by the high drama and narrative sweep of her stories.

But he did seem to enjoy just a little bit too much teasing Sue about being a 'reformed urchin'. The Shorehaven Estate was hardly a den of iniquity. Their neighbours had in the main been solid and upstanding citizens. True, her Dad was a bit obsessed by the house at the end of their road with the overgrown laurel hedge that the council used to accommodate what Les and Avril called 'problem families'. But they experienced no trouble from these people who seemed to come and then be gone in no time. In the main, their neighbours were older people, especially widows, or families with kids who posed little threat apart from the occasional, and by London standards, very light vandalism.

Sue's parents had approved of Giles from the word go while also being unsure of how to converse with him. The first time she had taken him home to meet them, her father made much of Giles' business studies course.

'It's the way things are going,' said Les. 'Same as where I work. They're all being sent off, the youngsters anyway, on sandwich courses or to night school at least. I'm just in the clerical office, of course.'

Sue was gratified that they had made him welcome, but it irked her that they treated business studies, which to her was basically a training in commercial management, as far superior to her fine art degree and her teaching certificate. They never showed much interest in these, her father never asking any questions about it at any rate.

Her mother was much less confident talking about educational matters – that had always been her husband's department she used to say – and instead asked Giles about his home and family.

'Hertfordshire, Susan says. It's not somewhere I've ever been. Is it nice?'

And this was where Giles showed once again his easy confidence.

'Well, Mrs Roberts,' he said, 'it has its hidden charms but really you are so very fortunate to live here right by the sea. I can see why you wouldn't need to venture very far from home. I wouldn't either if I were you.'

Sue understood the reasons for her parents' uncertainty with Giles. Of course she did. But she would have had far more sympathy if she hadn't been subjected throughout her teenage years to their claims of being no better and no worse than anybody else. All that apparent disdain for people who put on airs and graces, all those assertions about needing to be accepted for what they were or not at all!

'But you didn't go to school there, did you?' her mother continued. 'Susan said you went away to boarding school. I can't imagine that'.

'Oh, I was only just across the border. Nice and easy to pop back for a bit of home cooking whenever I felt the need'.

Avril beamed as she stacked their best table mats between her hands.

Exactly what she expects me to be doing for him, no doubt, thought Sue. *Home cooking!*

'Mum, stop grilling poor Giles,' she said. 'Ask us about our climbing plans or something'.

His parents could not have been more different. They had listened with a genuine interest to Sue's stories about her time in Afghanistan. They even kept the conversation going by asking intelligent, informed questions. Jerry had been stationed further east during the war, in India, and welcomed the rare opportunity to revisit, if only in conversation, the world beyond Europe's borders. Sue found Miriam comical but also admirable, the only person in their village, if not the whole of Hertfordshire, with a postal subscription to Pravda. She could speak at length about the strategic importance of Afghanistan through history with an especially vitriolic take on Britain's past colonial depredations. They were not just showing a polite interest, Sue could tell. 'Not just the discrete charm of the blah di blah di blah' was how she put it to Giles later.

All Sue's own mother could talk about as far as her travels went, when she could bear to talk about them at all, was that blasted newspaper article. She'd been mortified, she later told Sue. Had been unable to show her face at Fellowship meetings for weeks afterwards, she said. Her own daughter splashed across the middle pages of The Sketch. 'British Teacher in Hippy Hell of Kabul!'

Giles, somewhat frustratingly, did not share Sue's anger and impatience with her mother over this matter.

'She was concerned about you,' he said, when they first discussed it. 'Her daughter all that way away, out of contact, among a bunch of wily foreigners'.

'She was concerned about respectability, about what the neighbours would think,' Sue snapped back. 'And they weren't 'wily'. They were the warmest, most accepting people I've ever met'.

'You know what I mean,' he said.

And she did, deep down.

Towards his own mother, however, Giles was more disparaging.

'She sits in that house shunning people and becoming more and more indignant about the world around her,' he said.

'I think she's right though,' argued Sue. 'She doesn't merely accept opinions which have been regurgitated for her second hand. She thinks for herself. I don't blame her for not wanting to spend her time hobnobbing with the rest of the bourgeoisie around there.'

Somehow, in seeing the strengths in each other's mothers, in bringing their redeeming features back into view, Giles and Sue also consolidated the bond between themselves. After making love at night or as a prelude to doing so on lazy weekend mornings, these conversations exercised a strong erotic pull. As they explored their shifting perceptions of who viewed which parent in what light, Giles often saw again the feisty but reflective girl with the windswept straw blonde hair and shirt hanging out from the back of her jeans, who had smiled at him across the campfire. Revealing gradually a little more each day about their experiences of growing up, Sue was reminded of his quiet strength and reserve. She valued again his good manners and rebuked herself for sometimes assuming them to be strategic and calculated.

Independent-minded, confident and at home in his own skin. A leader.

Considerably more, Sue decided, than 'Just-About-Bloody-Bearable'.

4. ONE, TWO, THREE, FOUR

'One, two, three, four
We don't want a nuclear war
Five, six, seven, eight,
We don't want to radiate!'

Sue's friend Jenny had three daughters and they were all in the procession coming down the road and chanting away. In fact, the three McGowan kids were out at the front, their eldest nearly in her teens now and with a CND symbol painted on her face. An obvious ringleader.

Grace was enraptured by it all and wanted to join in but Sue judged her, at five, to be too young. Callum's mood was more one of intrigue mingled with an equal amount of embarrassment.

'What are they shouting, Mummy?' Grace asked.

Sue could hear her own parents in her head as if they were right there beside her.

'I don't mind what they get up to on their own account,' Les would have said. 'It's when they go dragging the kids into it that I object'.

Indeed, he had often said words to that effect when the Jehovah's Witnesses had come knocking on their front door back during Sue's childhood.

'Poor little mites don't have any say in the matter,' Avril might well have added. 'All dressed up in their Sunday best. Getting doors slammed in their faces all the time'.

Their door too, as often as not, Sue reminded herself.

Many of the marchers waved to Sue and her children as they passed. First the kids out in front who had fallen temporarily silent, then young mums with tiny ones in buggies, a few older people soberly dressed and the local

Methodist minister. Among the others, an elderly gentleman in a blue blazer with a row of medals pinned to his chest, hobbling with the aid of a stick. And finally, a few drunks spoiling the decorum that Sue and the other organisers had worked so hard to create. She had done her bit. She had made the posters and put them up all around the town. And if Giles had not been away she would certainly have been striding out proudly among the little crowd.

She had decided that she would join in with Grace and Callum behind the procession to the market square and see how long they would tolerate the speeches before they became too restless. As the head of the march turned into Grassington Road, the drunks peeled off towards The Swan, still yelling incoherently. When they subsided, the chant started up again:

'One, two, three, four
We don't want a nuclear war'

*

Sue felt immensely proud of the achievements of her little group. They had brought a hundred or so local people out onto the streets of the town. And this had been achieved in the two years or so of their campaigning group's life.

She reflected that their move from London when Callum was just a toddler and Grace was on the way had proved the right thing for all of them. The gamble they had taken with Giles' new job was paying off and in the five years since arriving in Yorkshire in 1978, his position had become more secure with the steady growth of interest in alternative technology. Sue had decided that, while the children were still so young, she would put her career on hold. Teaching in London in a unit for what were termed 'maladjusted children' had frequently drained her of energy and she could not contemplate returning to such work until Callum and Grace were considerably older.

She never regretted leaving London even though settling into a new community had proved slower than both she and Giles had anticipated.

'They don't exactly go out of their way to make you feel welcome around here', she had remarked to Giles some months after their arrival.

'They probably think we're stuck up, middle class Southerners,' Giles replied.

'But that's one thing I'm not. Middle class!' said Sue. 'We're completely stretched with our mortgage and we don't have the money to spare that some of them have'.

'We probably are in their eyes,' said Giles. 'You were a teacher. That's still considered posh round here. And I've got a job nobody understands. It'll just take time. We didn't know many people in London, why should it be any different here?'

'I don't know. Perhaps I had an idealistic view of the North,' she said. 'I suppose I'd been blown away by *Kes* when I saw it at the pictures.'

Giles had settled with ease, seeking out and joining the local climbing club within weeks of being in their new, three-bedroomed terraced house, one street back from the main road to Bradford. For Sue, the acclimatisation was more gradual, only really developing when Callum began to attend the local playgroup for two mornings a week. There she met Jenny who had also worked as a teacher and with whom, in late 1981, she attended her first meeting of the local Campaign for Nuclear Disarmament group.

'We've got to do something,' Jenny had said. 'This Reagan character scares me stiff. All that jokey, down home stuff and he's saying he's actually prepared to press the button'.

'Mad! We're ruled by mad men,' said Sue. 'And a mad woman in our case. Did you hear about that government leaflet, 'Protect and Survive'?'

'I've seen it,' said Jenny. 'We're supposed to take doors off and prop them against a wall.   Or shelter under the table. I go from finding it all ridiculous – laughable – to getting really angry and then to thinking about – '

Jenny looked quickly at Sue then down to the floor. She opened her mouth as if to speak then shook her head in one swift movement and said nothing.

'I know. It's the kids, isn't it?' said Sue. 'I'm the same. When I heard about that door and table business I just thought – what if – I mean, what if I couldn't – '

*

Sue's alarm had first been triggered by a lecture on the television that she had watched with Giles, in which a psychologist had explained that human beings could sometimes be unable, when faced with enormous threat, to see what was right in front of them. He had quoted South Sea Islanders seeing Captain Cook's huge ships for the first time off their shores and then continuing unperturbed because vessels of that size were beyond their comprehension.

'I'd like to see the exact evidence,' Giles had said.

'That's a precise example of what he was saying, Giles,' Sue had replied, angry at his reaction. 'Part of this whole denial thing'.

'I'm not denying anything,' he said. 'It was very powerful, but I don't really find it credible. I'd like to know whether there are any established facts behind it. That's all'.

And Sue silently acknowledged that she had perhaps too readily accepted the assertions made in the television lecture, that she had not weighed the rigour of the arguments critically enough. As often before, in matters that she initially felt passionate about, she found herself deferring to Giles' cooler, more analytical approach.

On this occasion, however, and with Jenny's insistence and encouragement, Sue decided that she could not, and would not, sit back and do nothing.

The two friends threw themselves into campaigning – public meetings, leafletting and door-to-door canvassing of their neighbours. Before each new venture, and after the heady enthusiasm of local campaigning committee meetings, Sue felt almost paralysed with apprehension. But she somehow found her voice each time a speaker asked for questions from the audience, she approached people in the street and thrust flyers into their hands and she swallowed hard, cleared her throat, and managed to knock on doors rather than hurry away in a panic.

The biggest event, in late 1983, was the visit to Greenham Common on a coach filled completely by women from the town. She and Jenny had played a large part in filling those forty seats. They had been out of their houses that morning while Giles and the children were still sleeping. The streets of the town had been dark and deserted, their buildings appearing temporary and insubstantial set against the energy rippling up and down the aisle of the coach. A bullet of light, excited exchanges and an atmosphere of determination.

Giles had sat with the children watching the hourly news bulletins on the television that day to see whether and to what degree their actions were receiving coverage. He later said how proud of her he had felt as he watched the footage of the huge crowds. Even sitting on the settee in their living room he had himself felt that strong sense of community and was aware that Sue would be experiencing something similar but one hundred times stronger, surrounded as she was by the linked hands of women extending miles in either direction.

'What are those ladies doing?' asked Grace when she saw the line of women pulling at the fence, creating a steady pulse along the miles of wire mesh. A huge, unruly regiment. The strength of common purpose. An intimacy of strangers. The razor wire against the winter sky.

'It's a demo,' said Callum. 'About bombs and missiles and things.'

Callum sometimes spoke with a sense of authority about such matters ever since all four of them had taken part in a gathering a year or so earlier at an American air base just outside of Manchester. While they had joined Jenny and her children and other families at the perimeter fence, somebody further along the line had managed to cut through and strike out running towards the air strip. Callum had laughed as this trespasser was pursued by three policemen, the chase having the quality of a cartoon film or a knockabout comedy. But when the policemen brought the man to the ground and clasped his hands behind his back with too sure an efficiency, Callum's mood had become more sombre. He knew that his parents, especially his mother, were locked in some unending battle with Mrs Thatcher but being in opposition to the police was a new and worrying consideration. With the smile drained from his face, he looked first to his father and then his mother.

'Is the Queen in CND?' he had finally asked with apprehension in his voice.

Sue knew that these activities were taking their toll on her children and becoming a potential source of tension between her and Giles. When Jenny had been at her house recently preparing posters to advertise the march, Grace and Callum had quickly deteriorated into squabbling, fighting and crying. Both children came to look at the developing posters – the mushroom cloud, the vast devastated city landscape – and Sue was unsettled by seeing Callum's lips silently moving as he attempted to read the text. Neither asked any questions. An unspoken, almost sinister, brake seemed to curb their curiosity.

A television film, one to which she and Jenny had contributed as extras, provided a culmination to all this activity in the autumn of 1984. Sue watched it with Giles, unable to form any words through her mounting fear and anxiety. Giles did not seem aware of the intensity of her mood – she felt aghast that he could not recognise how she was feeling – and when he later said he was ready for bed, she mumbled that she had a few things to tidy in the kitchen.

But, when she had the room to herself, she made herself a mug of coffee and found their pad of writing paper before settling at the dining table. An angle-poise lamp cast down an elongated ellipse of yellow light right in front of her but otherwise the room lay heavy in sleepy shadow.

She began to write:

23rd *Sept 1984*

Dear Sir,
We are writing to you about the programme,
Threads, that has been shown on BBC2 tonight and

*which showed what would happen if a nuclear
bomb was dropped on a British city, namely
Sheffield.*

She had started by automatically including Giles in the
authorship without asking his permission. It seemed
important for them to present a united front in any letter to
the local paper. It made the writing somehow easier. She
decided that she would speak as 'we' while she composed
the letter and then ask later if he wished to be included
before sending it off.

*It need not have been Sheffield, it could have been
Leeds or even Bradford and the consequences for
us would be horrific. This is now all the more likely
because of the changes in nuclear weapons and
how the idea of deterrence is becoming out of date
with politicians talking about the possibility of
waging a small-scale nuclear war.*

Sue was pleased that she had remembered many of the
key facts from all the leaflets she had been reading.

*As a parent, I cannot carry on working, planning
and building for the future if –*

She paused. She had slipped into speaking just for
herself and, as neatly as she could, crossed through the 'I'
and wrote 'we' above. Then she deleted 'a' and added an 's'
to 'parent'. It looked a mess but would suffice as a first
draft.

*As parents, we cannot carry on working, planning
and building for our future if we are also aware
that our own children will not have the chance to
reach adulthood.*

Dragging Giles into it was one thing. He would certainly
tell her if he disapproved. But did she dare refer to the

children, to hint at in writing what she was barely able to contemplate?

She heard a muted thump above her. Callum or Grace must have turned in their sleep, dislodging a book onto their bedroom floor. Otherwise the house was silent, the shadows beyond the pool of lamp light pressing in but unable to still her racing thoughts.

She scratched out the last sentence with her pen then felt the silence in the room castigating her and urging her onwards despite her sudden tiredness.

And they could say what they liked at Grace's nursery or Callum's school if this letter made it into the newspaper.

> *We first became aware of this threat to us all after a lecture that was shown on the television a few years ago now. In case some of your readers did not see it, it was by Dr Nicholas Humphrey who has a PhD in psychology. It was a frightening description about how sometimes people cannot see terrifying things even when they are right on front of them.*

One day she would explain to her children why she had felt compelled to express such terrifying thoughts.

> *We, understandably, prefer to remain optimistic and attempt to deny the dark alternative access to our minds, which is what Dr Humphreys was saying. Some people may be in genuine ignorance of the immense threat –*

Sue could not help but feel angry as she wrote these last words, angry and slightly ashamed. They reminded her that she had shared her worries with her parents a couple of years ago. They were, after all, Grace and Callum's grandparents. And she hoped they would confirm for her the rightness of her actions, guide her back into a world of commitment when her resolve faltered.

But when she raised the issue with her mother for the first time, she was surprised and disappointed not to find an easily shared and unspoken bond, a common pulse along the bloodline.

'Well, I don't know what to think,' Avril had said. 'I'm sure it's not as bad as you're making out'.

> *Some people may be in genuine ignorance of the immense threat. However, we must all have moments when we feel the need to do something about these fears, but this is then pushed to the back of our minds.*

Sue's attempts to give her mother facts and figures in graphic form on leaflets and in pamphlets had proved frustrating.

'What's changed Mum is this development in technology, what they call first strike capability. It means that the old strategy of mutually assured – '.

'Well I don't understand it, it's all too complicated for me,' said Avril. 'You seem to be getting very het up about it? Are you sure you – ?'

'Mum, I'm looking for some support. I'm not doing this for my own sake. I'm – you care what happens to Grace and Callum, don't you?'

'Whatever do you mean?' Avril replied, her voice raised and hurried. 'Of course I do. And so does your father. However could you say such a thing?'

> *We have always considered writing letters to newspapers and MPs on these sort of subjects as a rather self-indulgent activity which cannot have much effect on government policies.*

Sue re-read this last sentence. Its self-effacing tone reassured her. She knew that her mother became uncertain and anxious around conversations that she felt showed up her lack of education. She had often asked Sue to explain things to her and had then looked at her like a reprimanded schoolgirl as Sue employed all her skills as a teacher to package up the requested information, to take it step by step.

And yet, although Sue had been highly regarded by her previous colleagues and head teacher, so many of these attempts to engage with her mother ended the same way. Sue knew that Avril could display great powers of empathy and sensitivity to others, especially towards children. But in conversations that began with Avril requesting some explanation from Sue, she would always eventually claim to be bewildered and anxious to change the subject. And, most frustratingly of all for Sue, she would always close the conversation down on a similar theme.

'I'm not clever like your Dad. Go and talk to him about it.'

> *However, the programme tonight convinced us that we must all try to do something and therefore we are writing to you. MPs need to be aware of the great concern that there is in the country. If they appear genuine in their pursuit of world peace then they will need great support from us. Kissing babies will not be enough!*

That last sentence had its origin somewhere in the unanchored time that follows midnight. Sue had not written it intentionally, it was in the voice of somebody else. She was unsure whether she was being clever and assertive or sarcastic and bumptious.

A siren from a police car or an ambulance out on the Bradford Road reminded her that others were also awake. That other emergencies existed. Ones that might be resolved by quick, decisive action, by clever, sharp technology, or by acts of brave determination.

Talking to her father about anything she felt passionately was invariably frustrating. They had been disagreeing about political matters since she was a teenager, with the Vietnam War being the big one. Her father had remained wedded to something called the 'domino theory', fearing an unstoppable spread of communism if that country, as he put it, 'fell'. What had distressed Sue the most, had caused her anger, concern and confusion in equal measure, was the knowledge that her father was a decent man, a committed provider for his family and a believer in his daughters' wellbeing and advancement. And yet he seemed to show no compassion for the downtrodden and dispossessed or, at least, their plight caused him no discomfort. She was convinced that the blame lay with the daily newspaper that he collected every morning whatever the weather on his way to the bus stop.

'Can't you see,' she had once said to him during one of their disagreements 'that they just pump out propaganda? How can anybody get at the truth? They have an agenda, you know, they're not some well-intentioned, neutral commentator.'

As soon as she had said it, she knew that she had gone too far. She could see her father's posture stiffen. And, although most observers would have noticed no change at all, Sue was familiar with that minimal squaring of his shoulders and the hardening of his gaze as if he was searching down inside himself for some emotionally stabilising mechanism.

She had even heard it coming before he said anything.

'Well, if you think it is all so fine and dandy, perhaps you should try going and living in Russia yourself!'

If our elected representatives fail us, we must choose their successors with far more care next time.

These phrases were alien to her, their tone grandiose. It was as if somebody was sitting beside her, dictating. Somebody who cared less about causing offence, who was well schooled in channelling anger and contempt into agile and fancy wordplay. But it was an entertaining thought, an illicit one almost, this scathing dismissal of authority figures such as members of parliament. This sense of a righteous superiority.

Sue realised that she was smiling to herself, sitting back in her chair pleased with her audacity. She could now make a decent copy and sign the letter but wondered whether she could possibly do this on Giles' behalf without seeking his agreement. And just as she tried to imagine the conversation that might follow from such an act, she heard a creak from the loose landing floorboard above her and then a soft but heavy footfall as Giles descended the stairs.

'I'm just coming,' Sue blurted out as Giles appeared at the doorway in his dressing gown.

'What are you doing?' he asked, rubbing his eyes. 'Whatever time is it? Are you okay?'

'Yes, I'm fine. I was just – I'm trying to – ' Sue replied, pulling at a twist of her hair and inserting it into the side of her mouth. 'Giles, I don't know what – I've been so – so worried,' she said and began to sob.

It was some while before she could speak coherently. When Giles attempted to embrace her, she stiffened at first but then relented and allowed herself to rest her head upon his shoulder. Her body went limp and shuddered with each of her remaining, elongated sobs.

'What is it?' asked Giles, holding her tightly. 'What's the matter? What's that you're writing?'

'I've been trying to write to the local paper', said Sue, wiping her nose noisily with the back of her hand and a little of his dressing gown collar. 'I want to wake people up'.

'Whatever it is it's far too late at night,' he said, rubbing her back with large sweeps of his flattened palm. 'Would you like some drinking chocolate?'

'I'd rather have some wine,' she snuffled.

'We've only got that bottle of your dad's elderflower that's been hanging around since Christmas,' he said. 'And whatever it is, it can't be bad enough to warrant that'.

As she began to chuckle in amongst her crying, Giles manoeuvred her towards the settee.

Although it was almost one o'clock and Giles would have to be at work, Callum at school and Grace at nursery in the morning, they settled in the shadows as if intending to spend much, or all, of the night there. Sue had obscured her letter when Giles had entered the room and when her crying finally subsided, he asked again what she had been writing. With some hesitation, she handed him the writing pad.

'It's only rough and doesn't have to be from us both,' she said, pulling at the fingers of one of her hands with the other. 'I would have asked you. I mean I wouldn't have just – '

But her words bounced off the air of concentration surrounding Giles like hailstones from a car windscreen as he angled the letter towards the lamplight.

'This is very good,' he said.

'Would you have said something different?'

'Perhaps – I don't know. Perhaps, I would have said more about – '

'More about what?' she asked.

'Well, more factual stuff, I suppose. About first strike capabilities and – '

'So, it's no good then?'

'Of course it's good. It's just if it was me, I'd put a different emphasis on it'.

'What does that mean?' she answered, moving herself forward on the settee and raising herself from her slump. 'You think I'm being hysterical, don't you? Just like a woman, spilling out all over the place. Making an exhibition of myself.'

'Hey. That's not what I meant at all,' he fired back. 'Nothing of the sort.'

'You watched that programme,' she said. 'And yet you just went off to bed and fell asleep as if nothing has changed. I can't do that. Carry on as usual. Stick my head in the sand. I've got to do something'.

'I'm not sticking my head in the sand,' he replied. 'And I think it's great that you're doing something'.

'Then how can you just go off to bed like that?' she said, pulling away from his arm that was still placed around her shoulders.

'Susie, I went off to bed because I have to get up in the morning,' he said, his resentment now rising on the eddies of her indignation. 'And so have you. And the kids. Come on now, give it a rest for tonight.'

She turned towards him, suddenly straight-backed and fixing his gaze with red-rimmed but widened eyes.

'Don't drag the kids into this. I won't – '

'I'm not dragging anybody into this. I'm just saying – '

'I'm only doing this *for* the kids,' she answered, failing to control the rising pitch of her voice. 'Do you think I want to be dragging myself to meetings, thinking about all this stuff, worrying about what will – don't you think I'd rather just be toddling along as if everything's all right with the world?'

Sitting with Giles like this, exhausted and almost resigned to spending the night there on the settee, Sue felt ready to share with him the terrifying thoughts that she had been carrying alone for some time. But her attention was instead drawn to the slowly opening door to the staircase. Grace shuffled into the room wearing a long blue nightdress patterned with sailing boats, buckets and spades and clutching to her side a toy rabbit with long, straggly ears.

Giles turned to follow Sue's gaze.

'You never came to tuck me in,' said the little girl, shuffling towards her parents with unsteady steps as if treading between small dream clouds.

'Come here, sleepy head,' said Giles extending both his arms towards his daughter.

Sue had read the report about the likely consequences of a missile attack on various of the country's major cities and what might happen in more suburban areas like their own.

'Nobody came to see me', said Grace, almost in a trance and rubbing her nose and lips with her rabbit's silky scarf.

They would have to shelter in the cellar that should have been stocked with provisions beforehand.

'Come here, you, little one,' said Giles, as Grace almost floated up onto his lap.

The blast or the aftershocks might bring their whole house down into a huge mound of dust and rubble. Giles might be trapped down there with them or she might be on her own with the children. How could she possibly clear a way back out from beneath a whole collapsed house? And back into what?

Grace rested her head against her father's chest, placed her thumb in her mouth and stared into the empty stillness of the room with huge nocturnal eyes.

She might have to barricade the cellar door and the steps against marauding bands of shocked and sickened survivors, ragged wanderers hungry and inhuman, driven onwards into depravity. Could she possibly construct a barrier that would withstand a battering by a frenzied mob with nowhere left to go? With nothing left to eat?

'Here, let's get this sleepy head back into her bed where she belongs,' said Sue, consciously attempting to distract herself from her nightmares by reaching out to Grace.

She would have to protect Grace and Callum. Above all else. They might already – what if she was the first – what if they outlived her, if she ended up abandoning them –?

'No, I want Daddy to take me,' said Grace, whimpering and clinging onto Giles more tightly.

'Come on, I've got you,' said Giles, holding Grace tightly to his chest in order not to let her slip as he raised himself from the settee.

The last time she had been down in the cellar Sue had taken stock of the bottles on the shelf. She had to force herself to make plans. *White spirit, paint stripper, bicycle oil.*

Could any of these – ? Could she ever – ?

There was also a rusty fret saw and a chisel with a chipped edge. A pair of old garden shears, some pliers.

Grace flopped over Giles's shoulder and looked back at Sue, her eyes still open but her whole limp body lost to sleep.

Hunger and no more food. Ever. Thirst. Dry, skin-cracking thirst. Sickness and crazy fevers.

'Night, night Mummy,' said Giles softly as he opened the door to the staircase.

A six-pound hammer.

Grace's eyes closed and her head fell further. Her hair trailed down her father's back.

The rabbit slipped from her hand and slumped to the floor, a silent puddle with neither structure nor substance.

5. THE PATIENCE OF A SAINT

'I won't tell you what Dad said'.

Sue was talking on the telephone to her sister.

'I wasn't to tell you', Janet confessed. 'Dad said 'don't go telling our Susan, we don't want her down here poking her nose in''.

Sue had rung Janet when she sensed that there had been something odd about her earlier conversation with their father.

''Poking her nose in!' He actually used those words? Is that what trying to help each other in this family amounts to? They make me so – so angry, the pair of them, sometimes'.

When Sue had talked to her father on the phone, they had chatted easily enough about the children, the garden, the weather 'up here' and the weather 'down here'. But the very fact that the two of them were in conversation like this for so long was, in itself, strange. The usual routine – Sue ringing, Les answering and acknowledging her before calling straight away for Avril – had not been triggered.

Her mother had a bad neck, he had said, and could not come to the phone. It was only after Sue had concluded that telephone conversation – their longest ever – that she began to wonder how a bad neck could prevent her garrulous mother from grabbing the phone from him. Remembering then that Avril had been unable to speak on the previous occasion because of a heavy cold or flu or something, Sue decided to contact Janet to see whether she could quell her unease. And that was when her sister confessed that she had been enlisted to keep secret, should Sue contact her, the details of their mother's 'breakdown'.

More secrets! Sue thought. *And how come Janet is allowed to know this and I am not?*

Perhaps she had been just too preoccupied in recent years to see signs of the build-up. Perhaps, because Janet lived closer, still in Weymouth and just along the coast, her sister had been able to visit more frequently and spot what was going on. Or, perhaps Sue had been carrying an image of her parents as a settled and stable couple for so long, each extremely committed to the other and easily able to weather the everyday challenges of life. She had failed to register signs that something might be amiss.

Janet had been unable to provide much by way of further information and Sue experienced a strong desire to see for herself what was happening with her parents. Did she not have a right to know if her mother or father were ill? Was she for some reason being denied the opportunity to be of help? Janet's relayed comment about her poking her nose in, if an accurate account, certainly implied this. Or were her parents just stoically attempting to manage their own affairs and being sensitive to Sue's already busy schedule?

Within two days of the telephone conversations with her father and sister, Sue had briefed Giles on the children's school routines for the rest of that week. He had at first seemed resentful and commented on the awkwardness of being away from work at some crucial stage or other in a project's development. But she reminded him, despite feeling she should not need to, about the extra unpaid hours he often put into his job and the time off in lieu that must surely be owed to him.

She set off very early in their car to make the journey all the way to Portsmouth in one day and as her distance from Yorkshire increased, so too did her desire to know whether

Giles had remembered Callum's school trip money and his PE kit, whether Grace would be delivered to her friend's birthday party after school on time, whether Callum's ear drops would be administered. She had never been so far from Callum and Grace. She wondered what each of them was eating for lunch, even seemed to taste in turn traces of their imagined meals on her own tongue. These worries and daydreams grew as the receding miles jostled in the empty space behind her speeding vehicle.

She had been uncomfortable with her arrival coming as a surprise and when she finally reached their bungalow, her father was just inside the back door at the cooker in the kitchen.

'Hello Susan,' he said. 'What are you doing here? We weren't expecting you'.

'I had some time off and thought I'd come and see you. Look, Dad, I know Mum's not well. That's why I'm here'.

'She'll be all right. I think she's on the mend now'.

'What's been wrong with her? Where is she?'

'She's in bed, I was just getting her some tea. It's only egg and bacon, we can rustle up another plate for you'.

They had slipped so easily into this domestic routine. A sense of the ordinary had already taken over. The tension in her shoulders and back caused by the long drive was being pushed from her awareness and replaced by the smell of frying bacon.

Why had her father shown so little surprise at her arrival? And how had she become so immediately drawn into this old routine around food?

'Who's that out there?' Avril's voice echoed down the gloomy corridor of their bungalow.

'It's me Mum, Susan'.

'Is that Susan? Whatever are you doing here?'

'I've come down to see you, both of you. I'm okay thanks Dad, I stopped on the way for something to eat because I knew you wouldn't be expecting me'.

'What's our Susan doing here?'

Avril was in her bed, the covers to her chin as if she were a sick child, her eyes darker than the already darkened room. Her hair lay straight but disorganised on her pillow. Sue had never seen her without bounce and curls, and she had turned grey in the few months since they had last met. On the bedside table was a half empty glass of water, on the floor a few women's magazines fanned out in a slipshod muddle. A bowl of tired potpourri on the dressing table failed to replace an air of mustiness and lethargy.

'What are you doing here, Susan? You don't want to go looking at me. Our Dad is just dishing up some tea, I think. I don't know whether he's got enough for you. I expect he can find something'.

'It's okay, I've eaten. What's wrong with you then? You're not looking your usual self. It's not like you to be ill in bed and in the daytime'.

'I've not been at all well, Susan, I've been really bad. Your Dad's been wonderful. He's looked after me day after day. He's strong your Dad. I'm not, I'm really silly at times, but he's been wonderful'.

'What's been the matter? How long have you been like this? What started it?'

'Tea's up!' Les called from the kitchen. 'Are you having yours in there or coming to sit up with us?'

'Oh, I don't feel up to sitting at the table. Tell him I'll have mine in here, if that's all right. Just leave me in here, please'.

Sue and her father sat at the table, his tea and her glass of water.

'We've had a right game here, and no mistake,' said Les. 'She hasn't got up, except to go the loo, for the best part of six weeks but I think she's slowly on the mend. She's eating more now and not awake half the night going on and on'.

'What's been wrong? When did all this start?'

'What are you two talking about out there?'

'Nothing, we're just catching up,' called Sue.

'Never mind about us, just get on with your tea!' added Les.

'How long has she been like this? What does the doctor say?'

'All of six weeks now. She had to go into hospital and after she came out she seemed all right for a couple of days and then all this started. She hasn't got up, she doesn't sleep and she just wants to keep going over and over the same things for hours on end. I don't mind telling you, there have been some days when I've had a right basinful of it'.

'What kinds of things?'

'How do you mean?'

'What kind of things has she been going over and over?'

'Oh, you name it, daft stuff, most of it didn't make any sense'.

'Daft stuff like what?'

'Oh everything, when we lived in Weymouth, when you two were little, her history class, French, family. No rhyme or reason to any of it as far as I can see. And she wants me to talk about it all the time with her. Round and round we seem to go, there's no end to it'.

'Why was she in hospital? I didn't know about this'.

'It was women's things. I won't go boring you with all the gory details'.

'You wouldn't be boring me, Dad'.

'I can hear you two talking out there. What are you saying?'

That evening, as Les and Sue settled to watch the television in the front room, there were footsteps in the hallway. The door sighed on its hinges, and Avril appeared barefooted, her hair still lank, and in an old blue dressing gown.

'I'll just sit myself down over here,' she whispered to herself, detached and looking around the floor by the empty armchair. 'You just – just don't mind me,' she mumbled.

Les' gaze remained on the unnamed documentary and Sue felt pulled towards it too, away from either of their faces.

'Is anybody watching this?' said Les. The programme was about the behaviour of desert rodents in the American west. 'Shall I see if there's anything else on?' he added, when neither Sue nor Avril answered.

'No, no, whatever you like,' Sue said, Avril still silent in her corner chair.

They found and stayed with *The Two Ronnies* and then returned to the final five minutes of the programme about the gophers. As it concluded, Les, slightly sunken in his armchair, flattened his hands out along its arms like an ailing monarch and arranged his feet at ten to two.

'Well, if it's all right with everybody else, I'm ready for bed. Anybody else turning in, or are you sitting up a bit longer? Mum, what about you? Susan, are you all right?'

'You go on, I'll stay here a bit longer and talk to our Susan,' said Avril.

When they then heard Les click the bolt on the bathroom door, Avril looked directly at Sue.

'Well, what do you think of me then, like this? I expect you're surprised aren't you?'

'What's going on Mum, what's all this about?'

'I've been so unwell but your dad kept saying you *will* get better, you *will* pull through. I don't know how he kept going with me the way I was. He's got the patience of a saint'.

'Did this start with you being in hospital? What was that about, why were you in hospital?'

'Didn't Dad tell you? Well no, he wouldn't I suppose. They said I had to have a hystory – a hystic – I can't say it, what is it you have – what women have?'

'A hysterectomy?'

'Yes, one of those'.

'That's not nice, it does upset a lot of women. Couldn't the doctor help in any way?'

'They said when I was in there that I'd got an infection or something, that I could give it to everybody else, so they put me in this room on my own and it had this tent sort of thing, made of plastic, and Dad when he visited he had to speak through a microphone to me and I hated it. The doctor, he was a coloured man, a Pakistani, he said to our Dad, if you can look after her at home, if you are sure that you are all right with that, she can go home. He said I was probably better off there being looked after than in hospital. I was proper glad to get to out of there, I can tell you'.

'So, what went wrong, how did all this start?'

'I don't know, I just went like this, I don't know why. I've been keeping your Dad up at nights and not letting him get any sleep. He always said that I would get better no matter how hard it got. I didn't think I would, I was really bad, but he always kept saying that he knew I would'.

'Why ever didn't you let me know about this?'

'Oh, I wouldn't go worrying you with it!'

'I would want to know. It wouldn't be worrying me'.

'Oh no, I daren't'.

'What do you mean you daren't, I would want to help'.

'There was nothing you could do. I would just be worrying you, getting *you* into a state'.

'You would not be worrying me, okay? It helps to have somebody else to talk to – '

'I daren't! Your Dad wouldn't let me anyway, he doesn't approve of that sort of thing, telling everybody your business. I don't want you worrying'.

'Oh for God's sake! How many times do I have to say I am not worrying. Will you stop saying that. Anyway, I'm not 'everybody'.

'Well, you sound like you're worrying to me. You're getting all het up'.

They heard the toilet flush from the bathroom down the end of the passage and drew shallower breaths until Les' footsteps ceased with the closing of the bedroom door.

'Look, I'm not worrying or getting het up or whatever you call it because you've been ill, I just get exasperated when you won't talk to me. That's what families are supposed to be for. It's no good bolting the doors and battening down the hatches. That *is* the way to – '

'You think I'm mad, don't you?'

'No – I think you've been through something really awful, you're probably not out the other side of it yet, not completely, but I don't think you're mad. You've always been very sensitive, and you feel things deeply sometimes'.

82

'Dad says it's because I've got an artistic temperament'.

'What's been the matter then, what have you been wanting to talk about?'

'Oh, just silly stuff, all of it that was going through my mind. It can't have made much sense. I can be a bit silly. It's because I was spoilt, allowed to have my own way as a child. It's not good for a child. My Dad thought the world of me and because he was away at sea for so long when he came home I could have anything I wanted. He used to ride around on his bike with me up in the basket in front of his handlebars.'

'You're quite hard on yourself, you know. And that's a lovely image anyway, you up on those handlebars. Everybody has times when they feel a bit down'.

'Oh I wasn't *down*, Susan. I just couldn't get out of bed, I couldn't do anything. Dad had to keep listening to my nonsense, it must have driven him mad'.

'Well, sometimes we need to talk, we need to just get it all out of our system and to know that somebody has listened to us. We all need that sometimes'.

'You haven't been bad like I have, have you? You're strong you are like our Dad, aren't you? You went off gallivanting round the world, with all those Arabs and everything, when you were only twenty something.'

'I don't know if I am strong like Dad or not but I have felt down at times, fed up with things. It's natural. We all feel that sometimes'.

'Normally, I'm lively, that's what Dad says. He likes me because I've got a bit of get up and go he says. Not like a lot of poor souls you meet going about all day with a long face. It's no good walking around like that all the time'.

'You should talk about things if they are getting you down. We aren't the sort of family that does that, but we should. You can always talk to me'.

'Oh, I'm not one for moaning and groaning all the time. You just got to get on with it in life sometimes, haven't you?'

'Yes, but sometimes you've got to talk too. You've been talking haven't you? To Dad. You've just said that you wanted to talk and talk'.

'That's me being silly'.

'Mum, if you felt that bad, that's not being silly'.

'Well what is it then, what is it if it isn't being silly?'

'It's something like water pressure building up. If you don't let the pressure off, it just keeps on building and building and eventually something gives'.

'You're clever, aren't you? I'm not. Well I'm not stupid, not by a long chalk. I could have gone to the grammar like my sister, like you, but I was wilful and when I did that eleven plus I just sat there. Didn't want to do it so I just sat there and didn't write anything. Stubborn, see. That's because I was spoilt. Just decided I'd break my pencil that day and that was that. Our Mum was very strict but our Dad was soft. I could twist him round my little finger'.

'Tell me about your Mum, I don't really know anything about her'.

'She was strict with me. Gave me a right telling off once. She found this note, it was nothing really, just something some boy had scribbled saying he wanted to meet me on the corner of our street that evening. I'd put it in my gym slip, it used to have a pocket up here on the shoulder where you could tuck things and I'd put it in there and forgotten to take it out. Well, she found it and she was shaking me, told me not to be so silly and what was I thinking of, hanging around with boys on the street corner? She was really cross with me'.

'She must have been for you to remember it all these years. How old were you?'

'Oh, I don't know, thirteen or fourteen, I suppose'.

'And isn't that what thirteen- and fourteen-year olds do? It's what I did.'

'Did you? I never knew that. Our Mum was really cross with me. I was a show-off, see, but it made me a bit funny about boys after that'.

'I'm not surprised. But you weren't doing anything wrong. Lads and girls do these sorts of things all the time, it's not wrong. Sounds to me like your mum was over-reacting'.

'You don't usually hold my hand, Susan'.

'No, I don't, do I? But it seems like the right thing to do while we are sitting here like this talking'.

'So, you don't think I'm silly then?'

'No, I don't. I think you've been very depressed and it's been very difficult to get out of it. Women do often have these sorts of problems after a hysterectomy. You and Dad must have had a hell of a time of it by the sounds of it. It's a pity you didn't talk to people, I could have perhaps helped'.

'Our Dad wouldn't let anybody in that door. Dilys from across the road came over and said she hadn't seen me for a while and was asking if I was all right. Our Dad sent her away, didn't want her in here poking about. I didn't either, I was in a right state'.

'But you could tell me. It's like that water, just letting the pressure off. We should talk more, Mum. We've been talking this evening and that's been all right, hasn't it?'

'Yes, that's been all right. You're clever, aren't you? I don't know why I get like this'.

'Have you been like this before then?'

'Oh, I've always been a bit excitable. And I just get like this at times. Your Dad is very good with me'.

'It's a pity you can't spot when it's coming on and then maybe you could do something about it before it gets too bad'.

'How would I do that? I don't know when it's 'coming on', as you call it. And I don't know what I would do if I did'.

'Well, that's when you could talk to somebody. Me. I'd like to talk to you then. It might help. Would you ring me up? Talking like this is good, isn't it? It hasn't done us any harm this evening has it?'

'No, it's not done us any harm'.

'So, shall we try to talk a bit more, woman to woman? About important things, if we feel the need to'.

'All right Susan, let's try to do that'.

The next morning Avril dressed herself, the first time in weeks, brushed her hair and put on make-up. Les called them to lunch in the spare room, the drop leaf table having been erected and laid out with table mats with views of London, the best cutlery, salt, pepper and the gravy boat.

'It's only simple fare, but it's decent and honest,' he said, bringing in the shepherd's pie and setting it down next to the dishes of carrots and broccoli. They talked about the children, Sue's and Janet's, their garden and how tasty the food was, the three of them lightly conversational.

'But what about God, Susan?' Avril suddenly enquired.

'Stop that!' Les commanded.

Sue hadn't been able to answer quickly enough.

'But what do you think about God then?'

'Stop that right now!'

'I think Mum ought to be allowed – '

'We don't want any more of that. We've had quite enough, thank you very much. Just get on with your lunch'.

Sue wondered whether she was included in the injunction. Her mother's head was now bowed over her plate, her father had taken a mouthful that was too hot and was trying to cool it by making rhythmic, worried-sounding exhalations.

A conversation forbidden.

An anxiety corralled.

A calm restored.

A few minutes later Avril left the table muttering something Sue could not hear. When she didn't return, Sue followed her out into the hallway where a strong odour of bleach exuded from the half-closed bathroom door. Inside, Avril was bent over scrubbing the toilet bowl.

'Mum what are you doing that for right now? Come back and eat your lunch'.

'I've got to. I just keep doing it, I don't know why'.

*

'Hello, is that Dr Weston? My name is Sue Mortimer and I'm ringing about my mother, Avril, who is a patient of yours'.

Sue had telephoned as soon as she was able after arriving back home.

'Ah yes, hello. What can I do for you?'

'I'm afraid that I don't know the protocols here,' Sue said. 'But I am very worried about my mum and wondered if I could outline my concerns to you. I'm wondering whether somebody could perhaps visit her'.

'That's not something I can just agree to over the phone, you know'. He sounded like a reasonable man but there was wariness in his tone. 'Your mother is my patient and it would be up to her whether somebody visits her or not'.

'No, I realise that, but can I perhaps explain? I've just come back from a visit to my parents and my mum has not been very well at all. She has apparently been in bed for the past six weeks or so, ever since she had an operation'.

'That's right. She's been convalescing'.

'No it's not just that. She's been acting strangely, going over and over things according to my Dad, seeming very upset. Yesterday she went out in the middle of lunch and began frantically scrubbing the toilet with bleach'.

'Well, that's not – '

'It's more than that though – sorry – I'm sorry. I shouldn't have interrupted you'.

When Sue had been rehearsing beforehand what she intended to say, she had told herself that she must not gabble, that she must give a measured account. And yet straight away she was trying to describe everything in a matter of seconds.

'Mum says she has had these spells before but I hadn't known. They tell me stories though, lies really, so I don't know what's going on a lot of the time. It's not for me to say but it seems to be a psychiatric sort of thing with her'.

'I can't discuss your mother's health record with you, I'm afraid. She's my patient and her medical history has to remain confidential'.

'Yes, I appreciate that. I'm sorry. I was just wondering whether anybody could visit to make a more objective assessment or something?'

'I have visited your mother, about a week after she came out of hospital, and she told me she was recovering slowly but was definitely moving in the right direction. Your dad was doing a grand job looking after her, making the meals and everything, and in the circumstances, I thought they were coping admirably'.

'Yes, but – '

'Your mum was bright and conversational with me and was quite clear that she didn't want any additional help. She just needs rest and they do both know that they can phone here at any time if they need to. But I will ask a nurse to call in if you like, just to make sure she keeps up that progress'.

Sue put the phone down at the end of this conversation seething with frustration. Every conversation she tried to have about her family seemed blocked or diverted. Dr Weston had treated her like a child and patronised her as if she were a betrayer of confidences. Her attempt to help had been thrown back at her as if it were an ill-intentioned interference. Her parents had suppressed news of Avril's illness for more than six weeks. Her father had maintained a cheerful, chatty veneer on the telephone as if warding off some distrusted, nosey neighbour. Janet had been a ready accomplice in the deception, her reserve and reluctance to spill the beans perhaps demonstrating disapproval or wariness of her sister. Perhaps even dislike.

Somebody's got to burst this bubble. Speak the bloody truth.

She wasn't 'poking her nose in'. She could help make their lives more comfortable sometimes, if only they would allow it.

Or is it me? Am I the awkward one? Secretly enjoying the melodrama? Unable to leave sleeping dogs alone?

No. Her motives were sincere.

All those hours in buses through eastern Turkey and beyond, the weeks out of contact without any hint of home. The lonely ledges halfway up cliffs dispensing a rope to Giles high above her and out of earshot.

There had been time to think, to gain some sense of the things that motivated her.

The troubled young people with whom she had worked, who had trashed her helping overtures with sneers and suspicion. The night cries of her hungry babies.

Like some wind-scoured sandstone pinnacle on a desert plain, she was the unique sum of all the forces that had shaped her and made their mark upon her life. She made mistakes, got things wrong. But in all of it she must have learned some patience. Some tolerance.

Love, even.

She would persist, attempt to help her family, be a good daughter and sister. But she would, whatever they all said, also commit herself to hauling back from obscurity that poor woman who had been denied any connection with her descendants – that unnamed grandmother in the sea.

6. GIVING UP THE GHOST

'What do you mean Dad can't drink? Is he – ?'

'Chewing gum, everything, they were trying. Water, they all had these bottles, trying to get him to have a sip'.

Sue could hear her mother inhaling deeply down the telephone.

'Hang on, hang on. Who had these bottles?' said Sue, aware that she was as much trying to her quell her own mounting panic as slow her mother's erratic account.

'The other people on the coach. You can imagine your Dad with all that fuss going on. He hated it. Said there was nothing wrong with him, he just wanted to get back to his own chair in his own home. They said 'if you have this chewing gum it'll make your saliva start working again'.

'When was this, I thought you were still in France?'

'Yesterday, we got back. He just wanted them to leave him alone, said all he wanted was to get back to his chair'.

In the three years since Avril's breakdown – or 'funny turn' as Sue's parents called it, if they referred to the period at all – in that time their lives had seemed to settle back into to a comfortable pattern. Avril and Les once again became enthusiastic about dinner-dances, adult education classes in French and history, and regular holidays abroad.

Until this coach trip through northern France.

'Mum, what was wrong with him?'

'Well, we didn't know, that's the thing. His mouth seemed to dry up, he couldn't swallow. They were all at it, fussing around him, 'try this, try that'. He couldn't even drink water, let alone eat anything'.

'What does the doctor say?'

'Oh, our Dad was adamant, he wasn't going to have no Froggie doctor messing about with him. He just wanted to get back to his chair. I didn't think he was going to make it at times on that journey back. They dropped us off in London, Victoria Station, and we had to wait for this other bus and then I had to almost drag him onto that. People were looking, wondering whatever was the matter with him'.

Images of great impersonal city centre transport hubs came to Sue, her parents struggling like tiny ants over huge obstacles, determined against the odds.

'This sounds like a nightmare. Why didn't you ring me? You should have called an ambulance'.

'Can you imagine your dad in an ambulance? He wouldn't have let me do anything like that'.

'Mum, it's not about what he wants, not when – '

'He would never allow it! Your dad wouldn't be seen dead in an amb – '

'Stop, stop! Has he seen the doctor now?'

'It had been a lovely holiday up until then, we don't usually go on a coach tour but we saw it in the window at the last minute and we just said to each other – '

'Mother! Is he drinking now?'

'Only sips. I have to give it to him but most of it dribbles back out again. He's normally such a jolly man and he was just sat there on the coach in his seat, propped up in a corner'.

'Look, he has to see a doctor – and fast! You can't mess around if somebody isn't taking in fluids. I'll do it if you want. You'll have to remind me who your doctor is though'.

'Oh, he'd be ever so cross if he knew I was going behind his back. What am I going to do, Susan? What am I going to do? He's just sat in his chair. I've put the television on but he doesn't seem very interested, not even in the football'.

'Bloody hell, mother, he needs a doctor right away, a home visit. If he's going to get better he has to see a doctor'.

'Oh don't talk like that. Of course he's going to get better. Don't tell me off. You're being so serious. I can't help it. I'm doing my best'.

Their conversation continued with both becoming increasingly fraught, but Sue did manage to obtain from her the number of their general practitioner and telephoned the practice the following morning.

'Diabetes, that's what Dr Weston says he's got. Who would have thought it in our Dad?' Avril said when Sue called the next evening to learn the outcome from the doctor's emergency visit.

'Well, it's not uncommon in – what are the implications, does he have – ?'

'He might have to have a stick for walking. He says he's not going to go out and be seen like that if he does. Dr Weston says he might have to have injections, might have to have them for the rest of his life. But they're going to try a special diet first. They can have that special chocolate, diabetics. My old aunt used to have it but I never liked the taste, she used to let me have a bit when I was little although she wasn't supposed to. It didn't taste like proper chocolate to me'.

'What else does this diet involve, apart from chocolate?'

'Well, he can't have his beer, that's the main thing, and he likes his beer. He can have two half pints I think it is every day, so he could have one at lunchtime and then another in the evening. Or, he can have sherry, or wine, or spirits, but he doesn't like spirits so that's not a lot of use'.

Once again, Sue's mother seemed to have a reasonable grip on details while at the same time being tantalisingly detached from a sense of their underlying rationale. The alcoholic drinks were being cited as if they were a prescription.

'That doesn't sound too bad, he's just going to have to adjust to – '

'And fresh vegetables and fruit but that's all right because we always have vegetables with our dinner. And he's always had brown bread for as long as I can remember. They're going to monitor him, that's what they call it, keep their eyes on him and see how he gets on with that. But I don't fancy injections, I don't fancy them at all. Dr Weston says he thinks I might be able to do them because our Dad certainly won't want to be doing them himself. But I don't know. We've just got to hope that it doesn't come to that'.

'And it's important to keep on with as many normal things as possible, for him to carry on doing the things he enjoys. For both of you to'.

'He doesn't want to go out because he doesn't want anybody to see him. I go up to do the shopping, he doesn't mind if I leave him'.

'What about his bridge group, he's not giving that up is he?'

'Oh, he won't see them. They came to the door, that young woman, the teacher, who used to give him a lift. But he wouldn't see her. She came again with a card they'd all signed and a present, said that they all wanted to come down and see him, but he wouldn't have it. They all like him, see, he's popular, but he won't have anything to do with them'.

'That's a real pity. Why won't he even see them?'

'Oh, that's the way he is, our Dad. He liked that bridge group, used to look forward to it, saying 'My little girlie will be here in a minute to pick me up'. He's got a good mind, you see, he needs that sort of stimulation, I can't give him that'.

*

From subsequent telephone conversations and on visits, Sue formed an impression of her parents' narrowing down their social activities but also settling into a new pattern of life that seemed reasonably adjusted to the new strictures and routines arising from Les' diabetes.

Sue was aware that Giles tried to be sensitive to the additional pressures on her occasioned by her father's illness and that he did try to contribute to the balancing act that was their family's life at that time. She was also greatly relieved that his parents had not repeated the clumsy intervention that had caused such trouble at the time when Callum was approaching secondary school age.

They had made a suggestion, an offer, that alarmed Sue and led to a chafing of the relationship between her and Giles deeper than any marital friction they had previously experienced.

On a weekend visit to Ilkley, as they all walked up onto the moors towards the Cow and Calf on a blustery early spring day, Giles had apparently been taken aside by his father and the idea of Callum attending a boarding school had been mooted.

'It was well meant,' whispered Giles when he relayed the gist of this conversation to Sue in their bedroom that night.

'Well meant!' she hissed. 'How bloody dare they! And how bloody dare they sneak about behind my back suggesting these things. Even if the money didn't make it impossible, there's still no way I'd let him – let either of them – go away and – I want us to be a proper family not one that – '

'Well, finances wouldn't be an issue,' said Giles keeping his voice lowered and level. 'They are offering to put up the money. It's an incredible – '

'They are what! How dare they! And don't shush me – I hope they do hear,' said Sue with all the menace of a rising mass of agitated water about to contest its banks.

'Sue, nobody's sneaking about. And it was well intentioned,' repeated Giles, still moderate and conciliatory in his tone. 'It was only a suggestion, as much to take the pressure off you – off us – as about Callum.'

'I don't want any pressure taking off me,' she growled. 'Don't they know anything about me? Don't you? When I first met your mother, she used to sit there reading from Pravda, for God's sake!'

'That doesn't necessarily – '

'It does! It's sheer bloody hypocrisy, Giles. Grrr …!'

And she pounded her pillows with a stifled anger before gathering the duvet tightly around her, sealing in every inch of indignation, grabbing handfuls more to reinforce her feathered citadel of rage.

'And you don't even see what's wrong with it. Privilege. You're steeped in it too, just like them. There is no way that Callum is getting sucked into all that!'

She wished them all out of her house. Out of her sight. How dare they? Out on the blasted heath. In their pyjamas.

How *dare* they? A cold wind howling all around their stuck-up, bourgeois insensitivities!

For many hours afterwards, Giles found himself balancing precariously along the narrow edge of mattress left available to him, uncovered and wondering how long it had been since the central heating had switched itself off for the night.

*

'He's at eight and a half!'

Avril was shouting down the phone.

'How do you mean, he's at eight and a half?' asked Sue.

'His reading, it's at eight and a half. It shouldn't be that'.

'What should it be?'

'Not that, not *eight and a half*. What shall I do, I don't want him to go all funny on me'.

As the alarm in Avril's voice rose even further Sue was aware that her efforts to resist joining in the panic must appear as cold and indifferent.

'Okay, so what have you been told to do? Is there a level that triggers something, something you have to do or somebody you have to contact? I'm sorry I don't understand the system Is eight and a half too high or too low?'

'Of course it's too high, Susan, it shouldn't be up there at all!'

'Okay, where should it be, what reading would be all right for him?'

'I've got to stop him having a hypo!'

Sue realised that she needed far more information.

'What's a hypo?'

'He goes all funny, talking all sorts of nonsense. It frightened me to death when it happened before, I didn't know what was going on'.

'You should phone the doctor, Mum, if you're worried. They will know what to do. Nobody's expecting you to look after Dad all on your own. That's what they're there for'.

The idea of a doctor seemed to make no impression on Avril, carried along as she seemed to be by a tide of anxiety.

'Really angry with me he was. But that's what they're like, diabetics. He doesn't mean anything by it, he doesn't know what he's saying half the time when he's in that state. Having a hypo'.

'Mum, I can't suggest anything because I don't know what these readings mean. I'm assuming there's a figure that's acceptable or average. Or maybe there's a range. What are his readings normally when the doctor says he's doing all right?'

'Oh he's doing all right. Apart from that hypo. Dr Weston is pleased with our Dad. When we went up to the surgery he came out on the top of the stairs, ever so nice, and he said 'Don't you go coming up these stairs, Mr Roberts, I'll come down there and join you'. Very nice to me he is as well'.

'Okay, that *is* nice, isn't it? So what are his readings usually when he's just going along normally, when Dr Weston's pleased with him?'

'I don't think I could be a doctor, all those miserable people every day with something wrong with them. And having to be touching people all over the place all the time. I don't know how they do it, it wouldn't suit me at all'.

A savagely sarcastic remark sprang into Sue's mind and she supressed it.

'He likes our Dad because our Dad makes him laugh. He thinks up a little joke before he goes in because it must be *horrible* having to see all those mis – '

'Does Dad tell him what's wrong with him? Do you tell him when you're worried? He can't do anything if he doesn't know what's really happening!'

'Oh, he *knows* what's happening all right. He looks at me with his eyes, sort of looks straight at me like he can see what I'm thinking. He reminds me of your Giles a bit. He's got these photographs of these two children on his desk, a boy and a girl. About the same age as yours too, well the same age as they used to be. He's divorced but you certainly wouldn't think it when you meet him, he's ever such a nice man'.

'Do you tell him you're worried, that you don't know what to do sometimes? You've got to let him know what's going on, what Dad's symptoms are. Otherwise, how can he possibly help you?'

'Oh, we don't go loading him up with all our worries. He's got enough of that with those poor souls and all their aches and pains cluttering up his waiting room. Our Dad likes to have a *laugh* with him. Not sitting there moaning and groaning like some of them. Proper miseries they are. Dad likes to cheer him up a bit. That's how he is, your Dad'.

*

Sue's exasperation with her mother, with both her parents, for huddling together and hiding from the world as if in the depths of their own dark, fairy-tale forest, demanded a listening ear into which she could pour her raging frustration. Giles was sympathetic to a degree. He had, after all, known Les and Avril for almost twenty years and had always appreciated their zest and lack of inhibition. But he was stumped when it came to practical suggestions about ways in which they might actively intervene and reduce the stresses for his now ageing and ailing in-laws.

So, Sue decided that it was necessary to try with her sister to re-establish a more open and honest relationship. There were times when she had bitterly regretted the lack of a closer bond between them. If she could make rewarding and trusting friendships with people like Jenny and others through her life, then why was it so difficult with her own sister?

All along their differences had seemingly been apparent to observers, or at least that was the account their parents had frequently presented.

'Our Janet's like your Dad,' her mother would say. 'Steady, takes her time and works things out'.

'You're more like Mum,' Les had ventured. 'Impatient, always want to get things done and over with. Temperamental'.

'*Biographical imposition*,' one of the lecturers on a training course had once called those repeatedly asserted characterisations and cameo roles.

But Sue could see the truth in some of her parents' contrasting descriptions. Or perhaps, she sometimes wondered, had she and her sister grown into the people they were like vines tied and trained into certain configurations, permitted only one course of development?

Other, more tangible differences were certainly indisputable. Sue was wiry and agile, taller than her sister and had always worn her blonde, now silvering, hair long. Janet, on the other hand, was of a shorter and stouter build with bobbed and regularly-tinted auburn hair. She dressed more in the style of their parents' generation and, unlike Sue, had certainly never been seen in denim jeans or whimsical and flowing floral skirts. Although their differences in personality had, by all accounts, been noticeable from a very early age, their styles diverged even more after the eleven plus exam which propelled Sue towards the grammar school and Janet, with most of the others from their estate, to the secondary modern.

'We have to keep more in touch,' Sue said to her sister on the telephone. 'They are going through a very difficult time and I don't trust either of them to tell me what's really going on'.

Janet agreed but made no suggestions about how they might achieve this. '*Blood out of a stone*' was Sue's shorthand summation. And it had always felt the same for as long as she could remember. The great school schism at eleven may have been the start of it, although Sue's sense was that this was even older. Janet's job in the children's library from sixteen while Sue fell headlong into life in London, into art school, widened the deep rift valley between them further, seemingly permanently. Sue had made the effort on visits home to talk about new library acquisitions. She enquired about changes in borrowing quotas and the construction of Dewey's classification system. But there was never an opportunity to even allude to Warhol, Hockney or the Velvet Underground.

*

'What's the food like, Dad?'

Les was sitting up in new pyjamas and Sue was surprised by how much younger he looked, freshly shaven, hair combed and seemingly happy propped up in his bed in the corner of the ward watching the comings and goings of the staff.

'Uh, they bring it round, you know, on a trolley, want you to fill in a card saying whether you want this or that, like it's a hotel or something'.

'But what's it like?'

'It's all this vegetarian stuff, not what I call proper food'.

'That may be no bad thing, Dad, with all this about B.S.E. in the news at the moment. You know, all this worry about beef and maybe other animals as well'.

'They mix it all up, you can't see what's in it, could be putting anything in it for all I know'.

'Well, I've been vegetarian for a couple of years now, you know I have. And it's done me no harm. Sounds to me like they're looking after you. Have they told you when you can go home?'

Sue's plans with Janet had brought little resolution to her concerns. Six months or so after Les' diagnosis, after her attempts to forge a common purpose and strategy with her sister, she had had to drag from her mother, during a regular telephone call, the information that Les had been rushed into hospital by ambulance after experiencing another 'hypo'.

'They come round asking me how I'm feeling. They all want to know that. 'How are you today, Les?' If I've told one of them, I must have told a hundred'.

In the opposite corner of the room a nurse had drawn a curtain around a bed and her brisk, cheerful tone suggested that she was administering some medication that required a certain discretion. A television set above an adjacent bed provided a muted commentary to a football match that nobody was watching.

'They're looking after you. That's what you need. It'll give Mum a break too'.

'Oh she comes up every day. Likes to have her lunch in the canteen. They've got this canteen down on the ground floor. She seems to have got to know all the staff down there. Course, she'll talk to anyone, your Mum, talk the hind leg off a donkey. I tell her she doesn't need to keep visiting me but I think she comes up as much for a gossip and her dinner. She says they've started keeping a pudding for her if she's late any day'.

'Good, it sounds like you're both getting a bit of looking after. It won't do either of you any harm. It's funny seeing you sat in your pyjamas in a strange bed like this'.

'They say they're going to move me to Stretley, to a gerry – a getri – a different kind of hospital'.

'Geriatric?'

'Yes, I think that's it. They said it'll be nearer for me. I said 'nearer to where – Heaven?' They all laughed at that'.

*

Sue was in a meeting at work. The whole staff were, it had been a three-line whip. A visit from the Director of Education to inform them all in advance about the implications of a forthcoming major reorganisation of schooling in their locality. When the door at the back of the room opened only a quarter of an hour after the start and the head's secretary glided in and began to search the rows of attentive figures, everybody feared they might be the chosen one. She walked to the end of Sue's row, stared hard to gain her attention and gave one distinct and insistent nod.

'Your sister's on the phone, she insists it's an emergency,' she whispered after she had closed the door behind them without the slightest sound.

'Dad says he wants to die. He told Dr Weston that. Says he doesn't want to go into hospital again. Said he's been rushed in three times these past couple of years and he just wants to die. Asked how he could do it. Apparently, Dr Weston told him that if he stopped taking his insulin he'd be dead within forty eight hours'.

*

'Who's that? Oh, it's our Susan'.

'Yes it's me, Dad, I've come down to see how you're getting on'.

'Oh, you know, not so good really'.

'No, okay, I'll just stay in here with you. Go back to sleep if you want to. Do you need anything? Shall we try to get these sheets straightened up a bit?'

*

'No, no, don't, I'm going to be sick!'

'Okay, okay. Sorry. I'll just rub your back like this a bit. I won't pat it, I'll just rub it. Is this better?'

'Your Mum's not well'.

'I know. Don't worry, we'll look after her. Go back to sleep if you want to, I'll lie here with you'.

*

'Dad, you and me we've never really – '

'Uhh – '

'Sorry, you sleep. I'm sorry'.

*

'Oh, oh, oh – '

'It's okay Dad. It's all right'

'Umm – no – it's all very well with this decimalisation but the columns are all over the place now'.

'You're dreaming Dad, it's all right'.

'They don't think about that bit'.

'It's a bugger, isn't it?'

*

'It's all over the place. Milk. All over the place'.
'We'll clear it up, don't worry'.

*

'Dad...?'

*

'What are you going phoning people up for, Susan, telling everybody?'

'They've got to know Mum, you go on into the kitchen with Janet and have a cup of tea while I do this'.

Avril had remained dignified and quietly spoken as Dr Weston and then the men from the funeral parlour, with their discretely folded large, black, zippered bag had arrived. She had appeared attentive and responsive to the young man in the suit from the funeral directors who worked his way through the questions on the sheet fixed to his clip board.

'I wonder if you have given any thought yet to arrangements in terms of burial or cremation?' he asked. 'We can provide – '

He's not much more than Callum's age, this boy, all trussed up in his collar and tie on such a blisteringly hot summer morning, thought Sue. *And how many times has he already tip-toed through this word-perfect script? Would Callum have the first idea how to conduct himself in such a situation? Would he and his sixth-form mates even know how to begin?*

Avril answered every question in the same way.

'Oh, I don't know,' she said and then turned to Sue and Janet, gripping the latter's hand tightly. 'What do you two think?'

Avril had remained composed when Dr Weston had asked her how she was bearing up and had then stared out the window as the doctor took Sue aside and walked with her out to the bungalow's tiny front garden.

'A remarkable man, your father,' he said when he was sure they were out of earshot of the others.

'I've never known anybody be so matter-of-fact, so calm about dying. He'd had enough, he told me, and just wanted to die. And that's what he did. He must have been suffering terribly with his diabetes at times but every time they turned up at the surgery he was putting a best face on it. They kept struggling on, wouldn't have a home visit, not even at the end'.

Sue thanked him for all that he had done, pleased that they could talk more freely about her father than had once seemed the case. She felt strangely unsettled but energised by this brief conversation.

Was she enjoying being treated to the doctor's confidence in this way? Was this some awful tickling of her vanity? Today of all days!

No. It wasn't. It was being able to be an adult. And be treated as one.

An adult in her parents' house!

'I'll just wait until the undertakers have all finished up inside,' Dr Weston said. 'They're usually pretty speedy'.

'I was glad to have known your dad,' he added, looking down at the ragged patch of grass and clover.

Avril had been unable to remain in the kitchen once the professionals left, once Les remained only as a floating but forceful presence in the house. She lingered just inside the frosted glass door to the living room, immune to Janet's attempts to lure her back to the kitchen.

'I want to hear what you're telling them. Why have they all got to know?'

'Mum, it's what you do, I'm only phoning close relatives, they might want to come to the funeral'.

'Funeral? I'm not having any funeral!'

'Mum, go and have that cup of tea with Janet. Come on, let's take you into the kitchen. I'll do this in a minute'.

'What's going to happen to me? What am I going to do? I never thought he was going to die'.

'You're going to be all right, Mum. It'll take a bit of time. You're bound to be shocked at the moment'.

'What am I going to do? You know about these sorts of things, Susan, what's going to happen to me?'

'Nothing's going to happen to you, you'll be fine. Everything feels awful right now and it will do for quite a while. But it will get better, in time'.

'I don't want a funeral. Your Dad would hate it'.

'Well, he's hardly going to – Mum, we can't have an argument about this, he's got to have a funeral. It's what you do. In fact, it's probably against the law not – '

'Don't talk so silly! What's going to happen to me? Tell me!'

'Well, you're going to feel all at sixes and sevens for days but don't worry. We're all going to look after you. You've got Dilys across the road and Pat next door – '

'I don't want them in here!'

'Well, they will want to help. It's better when people support each other'.

'But what am I going to do, what's going to happen to me?'

'Mum, I don't really know what you're – '

'Tell me, tell me what's going to happen!'

'Well, we're all going to look after you. After the – when – when you feel you want to you can go back to the church meetings up the road. Is it the Fellowship you call it? Do you still go there? Then there's your history classes and French, you've always enjoyed them. There's lots of things going on and there's lots of people who like you and want to do things with you'.

'Yes, but what am I going to do? Tell me what I'm going to do!'

'You're going to be all right, Mum. I don't know what else I can say at the moment except what I've said'.

'What have you said? Tell me again'.

'Okay, well there's your friends and neighbours – '

'Who?'

'Dilys, there's Dilys and there's Pat next door, you know lots of other – '

'I don't want them in here. What am I going to do?'

'Mum, you're just very distressed at the moment. Are you able to stop your elbows and knees moving like that? It's very – this isn't the best time really. It's only a couple of hours – let's talk about it at some other time'.

'No, tell me what's going to happen. Tell me what you said again'.

'Well, there's your history class and French. There's all those other clubs up at the centre, they do holidays and everything. There's something called Cruise counselling, somebody at my work does it, it's for people who've lost someone and just want somebody to listen to them, to have a chat with'.

'I don't want you to go telling people. And I don't want a funeral. And that's that!'

7. IN THE TURNING

Brilliant winter days accompanied Bertram's illness. Maud and Letitia were vibrant in their schemes and machinations, often including Bertram as an imaginary presence, asking and then answering their own questions to him. On such days, Ivy built up the fire in the bedroom with a sense of determination, hopeful of hurrying the return of Bertram to health. Mostly though, dim and overcast skies leaked out from the last reaches of the night to languish through the merest of zeniths. At these times, the children's games descended more rapidly into irritable squabbling, a lassitude replaced their sprightly imaginings, and the tiredness that was held heavily in Ivy's being became more apparent to her family.

But spring would eventually replace this worn out winter. Dr Allingwood, when he had called again very early in the New Year, had invited Ivy to maintain her prayers and in turn Maud and Letitia had become more aware of the flickers of liveliness reappearing within their mother's overall weariness. Dr Allingwood had allowed them to return from their stay at Aunt Lily's house after a fortnight on the understanding that they refrain completely from attempting to play with, or even to nurse, their younger brother. He had also impressed upon them that they must seek to aid and assist their mother in every request she might make of them. Bertram had been moved to the girls' bedroom because it faced skies that would soon be lightening daily, the direction from which the Spring and then the Summer would make their return.

Letitia knew that she should not resent having to share with Maud the darker, smaller room normally occupied by

Bertram and Sidney. Her older brother, after all, had agreed ungrudgingly to sleep behind a curtain in the downstairs living room. But she noticed that her mother replenished the piggy in Bertram's bed with hot water from the kettle on a regular basis whilst hers was allowed to cool and become a cold stony presence to be avoided by her feet at the bottom of her bed. She also knew that resentment on her part, even any silent manifestation of it, was somehow unhelpful to her mother, as unhelpful as leaving her doll and bricks where someone might trip on them, or complaining about having to reach inside the hen coup to the furthest nesting box for any additional egg laid by one of the hens during the night.

The girls returned to Miss Coker's class in the village school after the Christmas holiday, both eager to be back among the spelling and the reckoning, Letitia especially enjoying the occasions when she was included by Maud in her games with the older girls. Sidney too was required to resume his attendance for the remaining months before his twelfth birthday. Letitia, when she glimpsed him through the high windows, found him comical, oversized and squashed into the creaking, wooden furniture of the older children's classroom. The occasional, holiday-time tasks that he performed for his father at the forge, cleaning the stall and replenishing the hay ready for each new customer's horse or keeping up a steady heat with his increasingly skilled application of the old wheezing bellows, could then be included in his full-time employment as an apprentice.

His father sometimes grumbled during particularly busy periods when Sidney's labour would have been most useful to him.

'Can't see how his staying on for another year's going to make any difference to him now'.

'He may not be a scholar but learning's never wasted, George,' replied Ivy. 'Just look at our Maud. And our Letty'.

'What is a scholar?' asked Letty.

'Somebody with their nose in a book all the time when they could be doing a day's work'.

'George, you'll have him soon enough. Don't tell Letty such nonsense. A scholar, Letty, is a very clever person who studies very hard and makes a living with his brain'.

Letitia was confused about the seemingly magical properties of brains. Among the offal from the Triscott farm she had seen one or two from sheep and cattle, grey, sloppy and inert. She was unable to make the link with worthy pursuits and achievements and screwed up her mouth and nose trying to feel the presence of her own brain and its workings.

'You've got the makings of a little scholar. And your sister,' said her mother. 'You take what's offered you and make the most of it'.

Bertram remained weak and in bed for the first few months of the year, his recovery slow despite the passing of the fever. His breathing became more regular again and a more typical, sickly pallor replaced the ashen greyness. Father Reeves had visited a number of times during the height of the illness but as warmer weather unfurled the lambs tails on the hazel trees and the daffodils clustered in full flower, he ceased to call at the cottage. The vigour and colour of occasional early Spring days became more commonplace and Ivy decided that Bertram, suitably wrapped in winter clothes and a blanket, could be seated outside the scullery door to be nourished by the sun's newly confident, noonday strength. And when the summer extended fully into the days, bright and ready before the children's waking, humid and unhurried into their nights, Maud and Letitia began to forget the unspoken concerns that had penned them inside the house during the bleakest weeks of the winter.

Sidney finally left school at the beginning of the long holiday. Maud became eager to return to occupy his, or an adjacent, chair in the top classroom. Letitia wondered whether she would acquire new responsibilities when the time came for Bertram to begin his own journey into the world of formal instruction. For now though, Bertram was still protected from the hurly burly of the games played by his sisters and the village children, as he still lacked the will to be up and among them as an often bewildered but cosseted figure.

One day in early August, Ivy heard the raised voices of her two daughters whom she had left with Bertram playing in the vegetable garden outside the scullery door.

'What's all this ruckus about out here?' she said, appearing at the door in a faded, plain linen apron with her paring knife and a half-peeled potato in her hand. 'Bertie doesn't like all the fuss, girls, he gets easily upset if he hears you two arguing. It's still going to be a while yet before he's his old self again'.

'Letty's silly Mama, she thinks rhubarb can think,' said Maud.

'I'm not silly, Mama, Maud's being horrid,' objected Letitia.

Bertram, whose contribution to any argument between them would once have been to run excitedly between the two, barging into them, now sat in a disconsolate fashion turning his head towards each speaker in turn. Maud's scorn raised a faintly complicit smile from him, Letitia's protestations a more tearful apprehension.

'Letty asked me why you put this old bucket and sacking over the rhubarb and – '

'I said – '

'Now now, one of you at once,' said Ivy 'what is it you want to know Letty?'

'She – '

'Let her answer, Maud. Look how your carrying on is upsetting Bertie. You're supposed to be helping me and looking after him'.

'I said why do you cover up the rhubarb like that?' said Letitia in a quiet voice, looking down at her feet.

'And I said it's because when the rhubarb comes up out of the ground and it's all dark it thinks it must still be under the ground and it keeps on growing'.

'That's right. Now why is there all this arguing?'

''Cause then she said 'can rhubarb think then?' and that's silly. Rhubarb can't think. It's only rhubarb'.

'Now come along,' said Ivy attempting to pull them both in to towards her in an embrace. 'Don't be so strict, Maud. That's a very good question, Letty. She isn't being silly'.

Bertram looked less apprehensive and more reassured as his mother resolved the squabbling between his sisters.

'Our Letty's a proper little thinker, she really is,' said Ivy, giving her back an extra little rub. 'You all are. What clever children I've got'.

At harvest time, when his family lent their labour to Farmer Triscott in the fields, Bertram was allowed to watch but not participate. The huge blades of the reaping machine

113

clattered up towards the sky before swooping downwards to perform a level sweep across the base of the stalks of ripened wheat. The two horses were lost to their task and the lad with his swish stick redundant as the rickety contraption seemed to progress on some set course of its own towards the far end of the field. There, a line of elms, tall and independent, picked at the sky with their sticky web of twigs and upper branches. In the nearby corner, George and Sidney rolled their arms and shoulders with the flow of their scythes, tightly-bunched clusters of wheat falling under the rhythmic slicing like squads of executed soldiers. When one or the other straightened to whisk a sharpening stone across his blade, he shouted across to Bertram, attempting to cheer him. Ivy and the two girls gathered armfuls of stalks felled by the machine and by the men, as if combing and collecting debris after some hurricane. Heaped upright and taller than the children, the bound stooks stood about like onlookers, their nobbled heads heavy with grain and bending with a melancholy air.

Slumped beneath one of these constructions, as if held in its embrace, Bertram was miserable and inactive too, his jacket buttoned tight to his neck and his cap falling across his brow. He breathed in the dust, dry and stale from the thunder haze being raised as the wheat was severed, raked and bundled. As the first darkening of dusk began to feed into the heavy air, Ivy informed the children that they would need to be soon home and in their beds.

'Are Sidney and Papa coming too?' asked Maud.

Behind and above them, rooks were raising a racket and making slow, springy steps from the topmost reaches of the elms into the sky and then back down again.

'The men will have to work on as long as they can. In case that's rain in the air,' explained Ivy. 'They'll have earned their day of Farmer Triscott's ale by the time this lot's in'.

By harvest thanksgiving, when an autumnal freshness followed parishioners in through the arched doorway of the church and nipped at their measured steps up the central aisle, Bertram was sat upright and attentive among his family on their regular pew, listening to Father Reeves' celebration of their efforts. More imposing than their parson on this occasion though was the huge display spread across the chancel steps. On the tiled floor, beets, turnips and potatoes, bullets and bombs, from the earth. Peas in their green stringy casings, beans padded and swollen, carrots with their feathered tops, onions twisted into strings long enough to tether a goat. To the side, baskets of fruit. Among the apples, pears and berries, Letitia's favourites, the plums. So many, purple and fleshy, a lifetime's supply, juicy indulgences worth the threat of later stomach aches. Sheaves of wheat, tidy and symmetrical, not the hastily bundled stalks from their late summer evenings in the fields. Next to them, huge sculptures of bread, woven into harvest shapes, the dough baked particularly brown and polished on the curves and contours. Nature's abundance had been gathered in and stored and a modest satisfaction with their shared accomplishment rippled around the congregation.

As Father Reeves climbed into the pulpit by the few stone steps at the rear he seemed to be concentrating on some internal conversation, as if wondering whether he was at liberty to share it with his congregation. Letitia, she knew, was one of his flock, Bertram a lamb. Especially when Bertram had been so ill on that very first day, Letitia had known Father Reeves to be a shepherd, their good shepherd.

Father Reeves now stood above and before them, arms wide apart and gripping the sides of the pulpit, inhaling deeply and seeming to steady himself. They were all his flock, thought Letitia, Mrs Triscott, her burly farm hands and even Mrs Wakeham with her huge hips and bosom. All to be tended and protected equally. But it was Bertram who had been personally carried back into the fold from the desolation, a limp and silent figure. Now from the prominence of the pulpit, Father Reeves addressed them, every one, with a clear authority, his attention ranging across the rows of figures and never lingering in any one place. But Letitia knew, felt deeply reassured by the shared secret, that a miracle had taken place and that she had been its chosen witness.

It was not until Christmas time, however, a whole year after Bertram's disastrous decline into fever and lifelessness, that the never-mentioned fear haunting the family finally dissipated. It then became possible to think again about future events, the familiar pageants of the church calendar, the scattered chimes of birthdays, and the stubborn pulse of seed and crop. And it was not until the year had finally turned that their sorrow at the tragedies of the Cotton boy and, soon after him, two other children in neighbouring villages, could find a safe containment.

Soon it became difficult for Letitia to retain a memory of Sidney as a pupil at the local school. At the smithy he was becoming an artisan so much in the image of their father, his physique expanding as he daily pounded lengths and rings of molten iron, lifted white hot and tensile from the fire, against the anvil's steady bulk. Maud became a serious pupil, conscientious and anxious to avoid any displeasure on the part of her teacher, Miss Daniels. Letitia, on the other hand, took a far more impulsive approach towards her studies and, although she sometimes earned rebukes from Miss Coker for her inattention and restless manner, these were gentle in nature and she managed to acquire the basic building blocks of early scholarship with a far greater ease than her older brother and sister at that age. And as Maud approached the set date when her education would be completed and Letitia would at last become the most senior family member at the school, Bertram too entered the door to that establishment for the first time.

At around this time, Letitia took to walking to church on Sunday mornings with Sidney and ahead of the rest of her family. On the first occasion, they gathered Spring flowers for Letitia, Sidney at seventeen now a man in the eyes of the villagers, Letitia a child grown tall for her age and elegant of step at his side. Despite this distraction, they still arrived at the church entrance almost the first of the parishioners, Sidney seeming especially keen that it was so. Then they stood inside the sandstone arch of the porch and watched the people from their village and the outlying farms as they made their entrance. Father Reeves stood there too, welcoming people with a few pleasantries and Letitia wondered how he could think of so many different things to say to each of them.

'Can't we go in now?' she asked.

'In a minute, just wait one more minute or two,' Sidney replied.

But they remained in the porch far longer than that. Mr and Mrs Wakeman greeted them and asked whether they were waiting for the rest of their family.

'They hadn't set off when we left,' she added. 'They were stood at your door, I don't think your Bertram was quite ready. Letitia, those are lovely flowers, you look quite the young lady'.

But Letitia had become more conscious of her posy, as if she were engaged in some ceremony and uncertain of the part required from her.

'Good morning Mrs Wakeman, Mr Wakeman,' said Father Reeves. 'You bring the fine weather with you. That's always very welcome'.

'Shall we go and wait for the others in there?' Letitia asked.

'Yes, you youngsters. Why don't you go and get yourself settled,' added Father Reeves.

'Just a few moments more,' said Sidney, attempting to look around the trunk of the huge yew tree beside the churchyard gate and down the lane beyond.

As the volume of worshippers increased, Father Reeves told them that he must go inside and prepare for the service.

'Perhaps, I ought to leave the welcomes in your safe hands,' he said and Letitia savoured the sense of trust she felt to be wrapped within the jest.

The porch became more crowded and Letitia held her flowers behind her back, less for their protection amidst the bustle and more because she was aware of the attention they were attracting. Among the crowd, children she knew from her school pushed past her with their parents and then quite suddenly Sidney said.

'Come on Letty, we have to go in. Come on, quickly now. Give me those flowers straight away if I tell you to'.

'Why?'

'Letty, don't be awkward'.

'But why do I have to give them to you? Why do you want them?'

'I can't tell you. It's like a secret, something private'.

He pushed her ahead of him, his hands on her shoulders, into the densest portion of the crowd so that she was almost pressing into the back of Amelia Critchley's elder sister, Sidney still moving her forward by means of tiny marching steps as if keeping time with some rhythm only he could measure.

The pew that her family usually occupied, three rows back on the left hand side, close to and almost beneath the pulpit, had not been claimed during their delay so Letitia and Sidney assumed their normal places. Letitia looked back towards the doorway and soon her parents appeared with Maud and Bertram, her little brother acknowledging her with a brief and unostentatious wave. She still clasped the flowers that had come to seem more important to Sidney than to her while he now seemed more interested in the front rows across the aisle where the Critchleys were seated.

The following Sunday, Sidney again suggested to Letitia that they might walk early to church. She agreed; there was adventure in being among village society without her parents and in the company of her handsome, older brother. But she declined his offer to pick for her another bunch of celandines and violets, a refusal that provoked an unexpected insistence that she reconsider and change her mind. Again Sidney wanted to linger outside the doorway and again, but without flowers this time, Letitia complied. This week, however, Sidney decided that they should make their entrance after only a short delay and once more there was insistence in his tone as he steered Letitia into the church. Inside, however, he was eager that they took completely different seats despite the fact that their usual pew was currently empty.

Sidney moved Letitia along the wooden bench and gestured for her stop at around the half-way point. As he joined her, she mimed that she was she unable to see around the person in front of her but he shook his head in an irritated fashion. She continued to stare at him as he took his seat beside her, trying to express her frustration solely by widening her eyes and tightening her lips. In reply he gave her one curt nod and then turned towards the altar and pulpit with a smile suggesting a newly acquired satisfaction. Letitia leaned to one side and then the other in an attempt to see around the head of the person in front of her, a head widened by a wriggling mass of auburn curls, her view further obstructed by the yellow ribbon in the girls' hair, the yellow ribbon in the hair of her classmate Amelia's older sister, Edith Critchley.

As the weeks progressed, Letitia returned to sit with her own family despite Sidney's protestations that they could see better from the new position that he favoured. The secrecy that was somehow bound up in this intrigued her but she struggled with a loyalty to Sidney that, despite his recent strangeness, prevented her from sharing with Maud her sense of disquiet mixed somehow with excitement. One Sunday after the service, as members of the congregation were making their exit down the side and central aisles, Letitia noticed Sidney standing awkwardly in conversation with Edith Critchley. Within a few more weeks, Edith was sitting with a small bunch of flowers in her hand, Sidney right beside her.

Maud and Letitia were now alive to the occasion, hurrying to church each Sunday, impatient not only with

Bertram for his customary tardiness but also with their parents as they stopped on their way to talk with other villagers.

'She'll be wearing her bonnet with them ribbons again'.

'Them yellow ones or different?'

'She's got lots, I'll bet. She can wear different ones any time she likes'.

'Do you think our Sidney – do you think he has affections for her?'

'Ooh Letty, don't say that'.

'Why not, she loves him probably, she's always talking with him after church and Amelia seen him walking up towards their lane one day. Amelia says in school that Edith's always talking about him, that he's nice and he's very handsome'.

'Our Sidney? He's not, he's really bossy sometimes. And I don't think he's handsome. Not very much, anyway'.

Edith began to join Sidney's family on their regular pew much to the delight of the two young girls and with a genuine warmth and acceptance also being offered by their parents. Both Maud and Letitia looked up at Edith, at her bonnet, her beautifully patterned dress, and at her open and modest expression. She was a girl but almost as tall as their mother, a woman but somehow one of their kind too.

'Can Edith sit by me?' said Letitia one day.

'No, by me,' said Maud. 'She sat by you last week'.

'But I knew about her first,' complained Letitia. 'I was the only one who knew about the flowers and all'.

'Everybody knew about Sidney and his flowers,' hissed Maud. 'Don't be such a baby, it wasn't your secret'.

Sidney turned his head away from his sisters, looked at Edith with an air of concern, then to his mother with a sense of mounting frustration.

'She can sit between us, in the middle here,' said Maud. 'Then everybody's happy'.

'But I knew about the miracle, about our Bertram, and you didn't,' muttered Letitia. 'I saw Father Reeves and you didn't,' she added, before taking up the position on the pew allocated to her by Maud and sitting for some time in a stubborn and resentful silence.

Sometimes Sidney, usually with both sisters but never Bertam, joined Edith's family on the opposite side of the aisle. And by the time an additional evening service was called to commemorate the ending of the nineteenth century and the beginning of the twentieth, both families were sitting together, Sidney's parents next to Edith's on the less familiar benches. Candles, many more than usual, were burning, beaming shivery shadows on to the stone walls. They were a little further away from Father Reeves than was usual, but his presence remained imposing. Smoky air lingered under archways as he surveyed the parishioners, nodding emphatically but silently, acknowledging the complex mix of fear, excitement and anticipation that lay in many of their hearts.

'By God's mercy, we live to witness a turn in history and we wonder what this new century will bring. Those older members among you will recall a very different time in which you grew up and you yet to reach a majority will live to see many changes that we, from this standpoint, cannot contemplate'.

Letitia wondered about the changes she would see. Would the dancehall in the nearby town arrange more dances on public holidays? Might she one day accompany Maud and her friends, and some of their parents, to such a dance, to take delight in a level of sophistication not available within the usual village entertainments? Would she one day own a pair of the black patent shoes with large golden buckles that were all the fashion among the smarter young women she saw on her occasional visits to town with her mother? And how would she earn the money for them? What employment would she undertake? And if Sidney was to marry Edith, whoever was there in this village for her? What was to be her destiny?

'Many of us have seen changes that we could never have anticipated. With the intelligence that God has granted them, some men have invented wonderful contraptions capable of enriching all our lives'.

Maud was soon to work in service for the Evershams and had been made aware of the electricity that was illuminating the main rooms of the house. She had told Letitia that all the lamps in a room could be brought to life simultaneously with the turning of just one handle, even lamps as far apart as the lower hall, the main staircase and the first floor gallery. All with one turn, all at the same time. Soon, Maud had been informed, inventors would devise a means whereby this same facility could be extended below stairs so that she and the others might have a range a lamps, rather than just the solitary central one, so that they could attend to their various cleaning, polishing and mending duties more easily.

'Advances in medical science have been nothing less than marvellous. Who knows where, with God's blessing, these developments may lead and what advances we are yet to witness? There are confident reports that these last few years, especially, have brought us far closer to the prospect of a new century free from pain and disease'.

Although Letitia sat as silently as the other members of her family, Father Reeves' words were releasing for her a cavalcade of optimistic images and wonder. She imagined doctors in every village and babies born as pink and plump as month-old piglets. Mothers retaining their first flush of youth and smiling in their sculleries. Children laughing in the gardens, men returning from their labours upright and loose of limb. Sickness lightly borne, illnesses accommodated within light and airy rooms. The scent of meadow flowers all about their dwellings and the sun ripening copious provision in the fields.

'There are some of you here whose families were touched by the former war in Southern Africa. And now again, our men are called to fight in that far off land. As before, our armies will not be found wanting in battle. When barbarous forces rise up against the Christian values by which we here live our lives, values our Empire has so successfully spread across the world, we will resist with all our might. And should it prove necessary, we will again make the ultimate sacrifice for our Queen and country. And we will ensure that civilisation triumphs and brings peace to all in the new century'.

Father had not been a coward, he had not been called. If he had been he would have gone willingly. If those Africans, those Zulus and everything, had come to their village all armed with their spears, black faces painted with hideous stripes, bones through their noses and their cries like nightmare animals in the jungle, then father would have fought as fiercely and as bravely as any other man. Lifting tongs and hammer, or red hissing irons from the fire, he

124

could have quelled the blood thirst of any number of savages at the foundry door, scattering their bodies across the flagstone floor. Uncle Edgar had not been a coward either and he had died on that mysterious continent carrying the love of Jesus into the heart of that empty expanse. He was a hero as were all the other soldiers. But father was not a coward.

'May goodness and mercy follow you all the days of your life'.

All the days. All the years. Fifty nine years of age she would be, an old, old lady, by the exact middle of the next century. One hundred and nine at its closing. Not that people lived that long, only very rare exceptions like Methuselah. Bertram would be a bit younger, only one hundred and six, Sidney older and into the teens, his second teens. And as for mother and father – No! People do not live that long.

'For Thine is the Kingdom, the Power and the Glory, for ever and ever'.

Mother and father, Sidney and Edith, Maud, Letitia and Bertram. A day, a week, a year. The house, Easter and Christmas, the culvert, the lane with the geese, the summer flowers and the bite of late autumn mornings. Miss Coker's classroom and Miss Daniels'. The larks high in the spring sky, the rooks on the harvest stubble.

For ever and ever.

8. THE FISH IN THE SEA

The women in huge leather aprons worked swiftly, their hair tucked tightly inside headscarves. Although red raw, their hands and fingers remained nimble and precise as they slit and scraped at the slippery carcases just recently lifted from the sea. Other women, their clothes shabby but not reeking of fish nor stained blue and grey with offal, queued with baskets to purchase a few of the fillets for the family's dinner. Outside the echoing shed, on the dockside itself, men dressed in battered oilskins guided the winch operator as he manoeuvred a full net of dripping fish up from a moored fishing vessel. The men reached out, uttering brief and guttural instructions, while all around them and almost within touching distance, gulls screamed, bobbing recklessly like huge snowflakes in some wild, demented blizzard.

Above the din of birds, their hysteria drawing in still others from the far side of the harbour as if by some contagion, the instruction to release the bottom of the net was given. The polished cargo spilled out still wriggling and intimate into the waiting bins. The sorters worked among these bins and the various baskets with a fervour that met the agitated commentary still issuing from the gulls. Baskets, when filled, were loaded onto carts stationed alongside, the blinkered dray horses between their shafts content to tread softly against the stone flags of the jetty, moving and yet stationary.

Letitia moved purposefully through the bustle with her tally sheet and order forms clipped to a board, her clothes setting her apart from the others. She checked the composition of each basket on the first cart as well as she was able to by peering through the weave, and marked this load and the others as complete and ready for the short journey to the railway station. She ignored the lazy stares of the men by the quayside who, when she passed, stopped straightening and folding the nets still heavy from the sea. Stepping over coils and the mess of ropes trailing beside the mooring bollards, in black patent shoes rather than the working boots of the others, she picked her way back to the office at the end of the cutting and filleting shed.

Although her main duties were clerical and secretarial and therefore carried out within this small, square-shaped office with its window facing away from the jetty and towards the street that led in to the town centre, there was no avoiding the screech and stink of the arena in which they all made their livelihood. Her clothes may have been purchased at the main department store in town but she still carried with her the trademark smells of her employment. And although her hands had not been split and coarsened by constant exposure to salt, bone and scale, her spirit had been roughened by the fragile economics of the trade, by worries about transport delays resulting in nauseous mounds of rotting fish, by empty catches, storms at sea and worse.

Still, she had been extremely fortunate to gain employment that capitalised on her arithmetical abilities and her general competence and efficiency in matters commercial and clerical. True, she had to share this cramped office with the manager, her boss Mr Rickards, a short and rotund man of middle age given to frequent mumbled resentments about the efficiency of his workers. This did strain her patience at times and occasionally demanded almost more in the way of diplomacy than she was able to muster. But she was always aware of how fortunate she was to be indoors and seated for much of her working day. In addition, she could wear clothes that would not be despoiled by her work and, most of all, she was spared the back-breaking labour that was the lot of the majority of men and women from her background.

She mused sometimes that these events could not have come about had it not been for certain changes in the circumstances of her sister Maud. And then, a further link in the unforeseeable pattern of destiny, Maud's new employment in this harbour town some full day's journey from their home village, had led to Letitia's name being mentioned to the business's owner. A subsequent trial period as a clerical assistant in Mr Rickard's office was successfully completed, securing her a permanent position.

One of the least agreeable of her new duties, checking dockside weighing and dispatch arrangements among the all male workforce on the quay, had in itself leant substance to one of her mother's favourite saws, that every cloud had a silver lining. For it was during such an inspection on one particular sultry summer's day, when full, heavy clouds pressed down on both the water and the land but refused break into a storm and even the fish seemed to fall lethargically and with resignation into the sorting bins, that she first encountered William. He was looking up at her from the deck of a trawler and squinting against the sunless glare from sky.

Maud had first moved to this town after eight years in the employment of the Evershams. She had established herself as a conscientious worker and it was her utter reliability that had commended itself to a friend the Evershams who had stopped there one evening to dine with them. The offer of the post of assistant housekeeper with the family of the wealthy fish merchant was considered by Ivy and by Maud herself to be an honour and, at only twenty years of age, an opportunity not to be declined. The prospect of life by the sea seemed an enviable one too. The family tried to imagine the tenor of ordinary life as it might be lived in a place that they could only envisage as the magical destination of very occasional charabanc outings for country people.

Of course, the prospect of Maud leaving home, indeed of any of her family not living within very easy reach of their village, unsettled Letitia's notions of their future together. She became one moment irritated by conversation about any such prospect and then, the next, excited about the possibilities for adventure, high fashion and, yes, love that might await her sister. And herself too, on the holiday visits she was already contemplating.

Once Maud was gone, Letitia's tapestry of the future seemed a less perfect construction. Pulling at one thread of possibility revealed other loose ends liable, under further scrutiny, to fray further. So it was that her position as assistant in the village general store, a role that had seemed to match her talents so perfectly when she was offered the post upon completing her schooling, came to seem too predictable and no longer satisfying. The Triscott hands seemed clumsy and unsophisticated when they came into the shop in twos and threes to feign an extended indecision about their purchases.

'No, no, go on. As you were. I'll 'ave that'n, that big 'un up there on that top shelf'.

Their snorts and laughter seemed nothing more than the banter of schoolboys, big lumbering lads grunting and as silly sometimes as the beasts they tended.

Her contempt, when raised in this way, could even extend to more kindly figures like Mrs Wakeham.

'Letitia, look at you. Working in the store, running it some days from what I hear. Having you at home is a blessing for your parents, it really is. Especially with that Maud of yours off living the high life with the likes of them seaside gentry'.

Mrs Wakeham heaved her bosom upwards with her crossed forearms and smiled a patronising smile. Or was it? She had been a good neighbour and some vicarious satisfaction at Letitia's accomplishments was surely permissible? But she still seemed to Letitia, on days when this mood of dissatisfaction spread across all that she had once considered homely and reassuring, she still seemed overly predictable like some endlessly fussy surrogate mother.

Miss Daniels had said to Letitia, during her last week at the village school, that she had a particular aptitude for scholastic activities. It was true that Letitia derived great pleasure from, as well as excelled at, penmanship, spelling, recalling stories from the scriptures and, uncommonly for a girl Miss Daniels had added, arithmetical reckoning. Her sister too had been an accomplished scholar but what Maud achieved with diligence and perseverance, Letitia seemed to acquire in an incidental fashion. It was as if her mind was busily engaged elsewhere with its own exaggerated imaginings while Miss Daniels' teachings accommodated themselves of their own accord somehow into Letitia's private store of knowledge and learning.

It had not been so with Sidney nor, as events subsequently transpired, with Bertram. Whilst Sidney's build and temperament had always seemed destined for the adult workplace, her younger brother fitted naturally into neither the routines of the school room nor yet, as far as anybody could imagine, into some obvious form of future employment. His dreamy manner and open, trusting nature made him agreeable company, and each member of his family at varying times found that their mood could be lifted by time spent in his presence.

So, it came as a surprise to Letitia as much as to anyone, when Bertram at twelve years old announced that he wished to work on the railways, that he intended to enquire into how he might become, at first perhaps, a station porter but then ultimately an onboard employee like a ticket inspector. Letitia found it hard to imagine Bertie, braced against the rocking of a railway carriage and leaning hard against a sliding compartment door, consulting some book of timetables. And although she could envisage him somewhat comically trussed up in an inspector's uniform, she found it very hard to believe any passengers would grant him the necessary respect that such a role would demand. So occupied was she after Bertram's announcement with thoughts of steam and soot, and with the huge, airless vacuum of tunnels, that it was a little while before the full implication of what he was saying occurred to her. There was no train station in their village, not even a halt, and the railway network was vast and still expanding across the whole country. Employment was certainly available, but relocation was the very likely price to be paid for it.

Once she had accepted that Bertram too might leave the village, that her sister's departure had not been a freak accident over which time was now manufacturing some healing salve, then Letitia grew ever more impatient with her rootedness in village and home. In her correspondence with Maud, she expressed her envy that her sister could enjoy promenades beside the sea in a fine hat on her afternoon off while she remained joylessly stuck behind a scrubbed wooden counter in a dingy store patiently waiting for her customers to make their slow-witted decisions about subsidiary purchases. Maud, in return, reprimanded her for her ungenerous portrayals of the solid, dependable characters among whom they had grown up.

> *But if you could stand beside me as some invisible presence..*

she wrote to Maud

> *... you too would want to speed them up, their actions, their thoughts even. Some days, sister, I could pack their bags and boxes for them before they had removed just one of their gloves. By the time they were saying 'now, let me see', this is what they say all the time, they really do, I could be presenting them with a fully packed load and inviting them to remove any odd item that on this occasion was extra to their needs. Oh Maud, I long to be away from this place, not from Mamma and Father obviously, but away from the dreary round that greets me every working day and may, I fear, unless I take some action, be my lot through all the days of my life.*

And so, as the correspondence between the two sisters continued, the sense of despondency in Letitia's letters grew. She remained as efficient as ever in her duties at the store and as supportive a daughter at home as she had always been. Her increasing sense of the restrictions hedging in her future she kept inwardly, except for their ready release in her regular letters to her sister.

It was more than just another example of her general helpfulness then, when Maud's employer mused in front of her one day that he seemed unable to recruit clerical staff of the necessary calibre for his office on the dock, that she immediately raised Letitia's name. The idea seemed plausible, Maud's much appreciated qualities serving as a sound testimonial to what her sister might also offer. Mr Rickards had protested with a splutter that dockside duties required a man's temperament and, when overruled on that count, that having a woman working in the office alongside him would lead to a general lessening of efficiency all round. Again, his opinion was discounted, such was the good name automatically attaching to Letitia by virtue of being Maud's sister.

When Letitia finally settled into her new position, suitable lodgings having been found for her on an initial visit made by means of a complicated railway journey with her mother, she soon impressed her new colleagues with the sharpness of her wit and observations. Mr Rickards had insisted that he explain office procedures thoroughly and that glib, initial assumptions about what a task might demand were often the precursor to a disaster. At such times, Letitia suppressed her desire to reveal her grasp too readily and stayed attentive to the laborious steps of the sequence being presented her. Gradually, by such discretion but also as a result of her quickly-growing command of the fish trade and its everyday demands, she earned even Mr Rickards' approval and acceptance.

'You in charge, Miss?' William shouted up from the deck of the small trawler, its nets discharged and slack over the ship's starboard side. 'I've got to get these disload papers signed'.

Letitia looked down at the young man, slight of build, wiry rather than skinny, with a smile on his face. It was an open smile, relaxed in the way that a vast stretch of settled open water against a sunset might be thought relaxed, not contained and calculating like the fixed grins, leers almost, to be experienced more commonly on the cramped and busy dock.

'We can do that for you. Come up,' she shouted back.

The gulls, now that the most recent catch had been sealed ready for dispatch, had settled back into the water, their frenzy past. Bouncing on the ripples created by small passing craft, some flicked a wing or tucked back a feather with an automatic movement, others pecked idly at specks on the surface. It was now much harder to believe that the pulsing agitation that had so recently filled the sky was a mania borne of near starvation and not some grand theatricality performed out of instinct but with regularity and gusto, day in and day out.

The trawler man seemed a little taller when standing beside her tapping a newly-rolled cigarette on his tin. He seemed to be refraining from lighting it in her presence. In his huge oilskin breeches, with the bib like a breastplate covering most of what was left of him, he seemed lost and, like a manikin, not completely in control of his own movements. But, up close, his face provided the animation lacking in the rest of his frame, his eyes bluish grey and looking directly into hers, the weather-scoured lines around his eyes suggesting an ease with play and laughter.

'You're new. Bit of an improvement all round on old Rickards'.

'Shush, don't say such things. Bring that schedule round to the office. Mr Rickards will sign it for you and make sure the ledger is all up to date'.

'Sorry. I thought he must have gone. I thought they'd seen sense, put somebody in charge who'd be good for business. What do they call you?'

'Why should you need to know that? I'm just the clerical support, assistant to Mr Rickards, to make sure the paperwork doesn't run away with him'.

'Well I wouldn't blame the paperwork if it wanted to run away with you,' he said lightly, his look inviting her to laugh with him at the notion. 'Come on, aren't you going to tell me your name? I might need to ask for you in person at some time'.

She knew he wouldn't need to but she told him anyway. And then asked for his.

*

The opportunities for Maud and Letitia to meet, to exchange accounts of their working days and to relay to each other any news from home, proved to be far less frequent than Letitia had initially expected. Back in the village store, she had often imagined herself and Maud in fine new clothes beneath gaily coloured parasols, strolling arm in arm along the esplanade. She had foreseen them affecting a haughty indifference to the attentions of the various young men whose stares they would inevitably attract.

They did meet as often as they could, they even acquired the umbrellas and the dresses, although Letitia felt she could never completely rid herself of the smell of fish that persisted despite the application of any amount of soaps and perfumes. Attending a church near Maud's place of employment meant a walk of more than two miles from her lodgings on Sunday mornings, across the large wooden bridge that spanned the upper reaches of the harbour where it dwindled to a shallow lake, past the railway station, then taking a longer route to avoid the little houses where the poorest people lived cramped into narrow streets. She would continue until she was finally among the elegant detached houses, each growing more splendid the further from the centre and the harbour she walked. In this way, the two sisters were able to spend regular time together, walking along the seafront to the large church that drew its congregation disproportionately from this better end of the town.

When William asked one early autumn day whether he might walk with her when she had finished her work for the afternoon, as his boat was not to be putting to sea again until the following morning, her first thought was less about matters of propriety. She was instead aware of them being well matched in terms of the odours they carried from their particular employment and of therefore being less likely to cause each other offense. And their compatibility, it soon became clear, was more than skin deep. He showed a sympathetic interest in the tales of her family that were relayed alternatively to her and to Maud by Edith, who had become the chronicler of events concerning the family she had married into. Letitia, in her turn, was excited by William's accounts of his seafaring, his having worked on board fishing vessels for almost ten years since the young age of fourteen.

Although she had been able to talk of little else, Letitia was not able to introduce William to Maud for many weeks, his brief and unpredictable periods of shore leave never seeming to coincide with Maud's half days or other occasional release from her duties. She wanted to avoid the formality that would attach itself to any meeting involving church going. When eventually the availability of all three did coincide, they arranged to meet late afternoon one Wednesday in November at tearooms near the junction of the main street and the esplanade.

Maud poured tea for her sister and William, while Letitia sliced and buttered scones for them all, a shiver of excitement passing through her as she attempted to ease the initial stiffness between them with inconsequential chatter. Her heightened feeling had arisen from a flicker of memory of herself and Maud as children arranging tea parties in their living room or garden back at home. This man, William, was as silent and respectful now of the sister's forced remarks as Bertram, as a baby, had been bemused before the two girls' exaggerated ministrations. But, unlike then, this man, once the conversation loosened and then began to flow, was able to entertain the two sisters, not with innocent and comical misunderstandings, but with stories of the heroics and self-sacrificing camaraderie of men tipped this way and that in ships that rolled and coursed towards rocks like teeth rising and falling in the pounding swell of a night time gale.

When alone with her sister on their next Sunday walk to church, Maud was eager to share with Letitia her approval, no, her enthusiasm for William as an appropriate suitor to her younger sister.

'And when might there be a young man that you would be eager to introduce to me?' Letitia enquired, then adding 'And to William too, of course'.

'Well, Letty, it's too early for anything like that but let's just say that there's been a visitor to the house in recent weeks who seems to have taken a fancy to me, if that's the right way of putting it'.

Maud twisted the hem of her jacket sleeve and appeared to chew the inside of her bottom lip. A wind was picking up straight in off the sea, usually a sign of impending rain.

'I can't tell you any more than that but his name is Alastair. He talks really strangely, he's all the way from Scotland, but he is an intelligent man with qualifications, brought in to make some assessment of the state of the roofs and gables, to see whether any major repairs might be necessary'.

Letitia had never seen her sister so bashful, she had given this account while completely avoiding Letitia's gaze and her eager smile.

'Bring him out, let me meet him. Please Maud,' she insisted.

'Letty, it's nothing like that. These things either take their course or they don't. There isn't anything anybody can do to make them happen or hurry them along,' she explained, her caution contrasting, block like, with her sister's arousal and excitement. As so many times before.

But, whether because of Letty's encouragement or not, something happened and within a few weeks she and Maud were engaged in the ever more complicated scheduling required for a meeting between the four of them. By good fortune, the evening when all four were available coincided with an evening of dance arranged at one of the town's grandest restaurants located at the entrance to the harbour-side pier. As it was still winter, there was no opportunity to stroll to the end of the pier and to take in the view of the distant cliffs that rose up out along the coast beyond Maud's, and temporarily, Alastair's place of employment.

Huddled in the warmth inside the dance hall instead, introductions were made across their small corner table. A large space had been cleared in the centre of the dining room with every table around the periphery occupied by noisy young people of a similar age. Letitia, making her first appraisal of this new figure in their lives and energised by the buzz of conversation and laughter from all around her, wondered whether she had ever before felt such a sense of joyful completeness. It was as though she had arrived at some personal destination that only now she could begin to recognise as having been her goal all along.

Alastair took out a case from the inside pocket of his blazer and offered cigarettes first to Maud, then Letitia and finally, William. To Letitia's surprise, Maud confidently slipped one out from the restraining elastic band and put it to her mouth, looking to Alastair to light it for her when the sharing out was completed. Letitia recoiled slightly when presented with the open case and shook her head, rather too vigorously she later felt. And William, whom Letitia had reprimanded on a previous occasion for bringing out his weathered old tobacco tin in front of others in a cafeteria, glanced quickly towards her now before reaching out to accept.

Of the two men, Alastair seemed far the more confident. He spoke firmly, more loudly than was required to be heard above the orchestra that had begun to play. Whereas William, for all his storm-tossed adventures on the neighbouring seas, had only ever ventured a few miles by land from his home, Alastair had, although not yet thirty, already travelled extensively as a junior construction engineer on the continent of Europe and even to Africa. When he took Maud's hand and escorted her onto the dance floor, Letitia was struck by his easy authority, sure enough in himself to guide and reassure her initially hesitant sister.

The brass section of the orchestra sliced into the waltz's sentimental melody and Letitia watched as Alastair steered Maud around the room in time with the other dancers. The music made Letitia restless, shivery almost, and she was uncertain whether she was eager to join the floor or anxious to be away from the crowd altogether. The music ended and the dancers all turned, side by side, to applaud the orchestra. Before Maud and Alastair could decide whether or not to return their seats, the mood switched dramatically with the opening blast of the latest tune from the new ragtime craze.

Many of the couples launched themselves as if unthinkingly into an agitated motion in time with the music that soon filled the hall. Alastair seized Maud who tottered uncertainly for a moment then kicked up her heel and threw her head back to look up at the huge chandelier on the ceiling. Giggling, she fell back against Alastair's shoulder and asked to be led back to her seat. Letitia welcomed her back from the floor, realising that she was seeing an aspect of Maud that she had never before witnessed nor even guessed at.

Letitia began to feel less sophisticated than on previous visits to dances with William, as if the parochial routines of her village upbringing had become embedded more deeply in her character than she had realised. She reassured herself however that she was more than content with this life. Her happy outings with William had in no sense lost any of the sparkle of their first few times together but she also realised that evening that perhaps Maud might be destined for even grander venues and might again disrupt the deep comfort she drew from their sisterly liaisons.

Whether provoked in some way by Alastair's appearance in her sister's, and their own lives, or whether it was just some natural development that happened at this stage with all young couples, Letitia was not completely sure. But she did find the topic of the future, a time beyond the next bank holiday and the reappearance of the warmer weather, one that seemed to occupy more frequently her conversations with William. And it was a subject initiated as much by him as by her. Of course, the news some years earlier of the birth of twins to Sidney and Edith had stirred again in Letitia and, she assumed, in her sister too, questions about the likely course of her own life. But it had taken Alastair's accounts of long journeys across the baked clay of an alien continent, of huge and unobtainable horizons, to provide the jolt of recognition that the future was already upon Letitia and William and had in fact been passing, outside of their awareness, for some time.

They decided one particular, early summer evening, before they were to walk out along the pier with Maud and Alastair, to hold back news of their intention to become engaged until the matter of Bertram, the shock that had been raised in Edith's most recent letter, had been discussed.

'Mother will be so disappointed, she always set such high hopes for all of us,' said Maud.

'Well it's work, there are plenty who would be grateful for the opportunity. And he's got the build for it, by all accounts,' said Alastair.

'But the Triscott's. A farm hand. And right in the village for everybody to see'.

William walked on the outside, nearest the railing and the drop into the milky green water. A man in a sequined jacket was rotating the arm of a barrel organ and tipped his brightly coloured bowler hat, but William was the only one of the party to notice and to return the greeting.

'Tell me again exactly how it happened,' he asked.

'Well, according to Edith, he ended up putting an elderly gentleman on a train and leaving his wife stranded and beside herself on the platform'.

Alastair began to chuckle and Maud reprimanded him.

'At least it wasn't the express, he could have ended up in Timbuctoo'.

Letitia too then began to giggle.

'He lost his job, Letty. It isn't funny. Poor Bertie,' Maud scolded.

'Sounds like he wasn't suited to it anyway,' said Alastair. 'That wasn't the first time, from what you've told me. What about that time when he ended up on the train himself with the luggage and the passenger left behind on the platform?'

The notes from the organ plucked at the surface of the sea and Letitia had to suppress another fit of giggles. And then, suddenly, a most terrible sense of sadness and loss as well.

Lights of all colours appeared back along the esplanade, dipping like flimsy chains between their supporting posts. The air was still warm although the dusk was settling about them. Suddenly, Maud turned to Letitia and her eyes widened like the huge full moon that was dragging itself up from beyond the horizon way out at sea.

'Letty, I've been waiting to tell you. I've been waiting till we could be together, I have such exciting news'.

Letitia smiled back at her sister hoping that she could control the mounting sense of apprehension she was feeling. She feigned surprise and anticipation, but she knew already.

'Alastair and I are to be married. And as soon as possible. You are the first to know'.

Letitia had indeed been the first to know but even she had not been expecting what Maud was to say next.

'And that's not all. We are to live in Canada. Canada, can you believe it?'

'Canada?' said Letitia, a chill from the sea now all around her.

'Canada?' William echoed.

'Yes, it's such an opportunity. Alastair will build us a house, it will be as big and modern as any grand house here. Bigger. And more modern too'.

'You just fell your own timber, the land is so cheap. You can be your own master, make your own way in the world'.

'But what about wild animals, bears and wolves and things?' said Letitia, regretting almost immediately that she had said it. 'And do they have Red Indians still?' she added, caring less now what she was saying.

'No, none of those. We put paid to their warlike ways years ago,' said Alastair in a manner, thought Letitia, suggesting that he had personally carried out some of these actions all by himself. 'The animals aren't a problem, that's what you have rifles for. If you're worried, I'll teach Maud how to shoot as well. I'll bet she'll be a crack shot'.

'Oh Letty, you mustn't say anything in your letters. I'll go home as soon as I can, to tell Mama. And Father too, and to arrange with Father Reeves about the wedding. There's so much to do and we hope to be ready to sail by the autumn'.

When William walked her back to her lodgings on the opposite side of the harbour later that evening, she had about her nothing of her usual buoyancy. Both had known as soon as Maud had made her announcement that their own intentions would remain unvoiced that evening. The bridge across the lake creaked on its joists, as it did in even the slightest of breezes. The smell from the fish jetty seemed unfamiliar tonight, a stench that she wished, at that very moment, to be a hundred miles away from. William tried to console her but his comments seemed weak and ineffectual.

A man leading a shire horse plodded past them on the bridge but only William returned his neighbourly 'Good evening'. Although fully awake, Letitia was experiencing a jumbled dream of sun-baked Arctic wastes with polar bears and then with elephants and lions, of huge deep drifts of powdered snow packed between tree trunks on the edges of the jungles of Africa.

Suddenly, she turned to William, as if angry and about to address a stranger. He looked back at her and she could see that he had no inkling of the terrible panic and geographical nightmare with which she was grappling. She felt her shoulders drop, her knees begin to sag.

'Oh William, you will always love me, won't you?'

'Of course I will, Letty'.

'You will?'

'Yes, of course. Don't be daft. I'll always love you. As long as there are fishes in the sea'.

9. WORLDS APART

Two small children and now a war, chaos ripping across a continent.

Letitia and William stood on the dockside with their young family as the crane lowered the huge, heavy weapon onto the deck of the fishing boat. Letitia held the baby tightly wrapped against the chill March air. The tiny patch of contact between their two faces seemed as cold as the grey gun metal that jerked and revolved this way and that as it was lowered down before them on its rope.

'Hah, wait 'til they get near that thing with their U-boats,' said William, 'Big surprise they'll have then, picking on an innocent fishing boat'.

The young girl, no older than four, watched the manoeuvre without speaking. She gripped Letitia's coat, the thumb of her other hand in her mouth.

'Don't say it like that,' said Letitia. 'As if you're enjoying it'.

'Letty, it's them or us, soft hearts and kind words ain't going to win this war'

'We shouldn't have brought the children, it's not a thing for them to see'.

Mary looked up at her father and then towards her mother.

'Is Daddy going to shoot that gun?'

'Do you see, her imagination is already running riot? I'm going to take them home'.

The long tapering barrel of the gun slid round towards them in its lazy orbit and Mary clung more tightly to the hands of her parents, crouching and turning away as the eye of the barrel settled its regard directly on her. She gave an alarmed cry and pressed her face into her mother's coat.

'Don't worry, Mary, we're going back home. This isn't a nice place to be'.

'I want to stay, I want to watch Daddy,' said Mary.

Letitia looked about her at the dock that had once been her place of employment. The bustle then had often been exhausting, there had been anxiety about meeting train departure times, the threat of delayed and deteriorating cargoes. Even more serious, there had been concern that a fishing crew, William among them, might fail to return to harbour after a night of vicious storms. Or, that no ship's shape would re-emerge from a sea fog persisting through the longest of days across miles of empty, lifeless water. Despite these worries, Letitia had moved swiftly, organising the men at their sorting and loading, circumventing old Rickards with charm when necessary, and creating a surprising sense of confidence among the others by her command of both paperwork and people.

But Kaiser Bill was different. Letitia had stood among the other women on the pier while the first cohorts of volunteers were marched from the railway station and marshalled beside the huge troop ship at anchor there. Between the disciplined ranks on the pier and the black anonymity of the ship's hold, each man was briefly alone for the last time as he stepped across the narrow gangplank. Letitia felt compelled to remember the expression on the face of each individual soldier as he briskly crossed the plank and disappeared through the watertight door that was clamped open to receive them all. Quickly overwhelmed, she could retain no more than the first half dozen before the rest became blurred in the unending parade of figures in regulation brown uniforms, packs and kitbags on their backs, rifles hanging low from their shoulders, some with hands raised to caps caught in the draft ferrying down between the ship and pier. As compassion had broken within her, she turned away, as unable to meet the faces of the other women in the crowd as she was to extract any sense of their individual lives from the procession of soldiers.

'Mary, we are going home. Daddy has to work soon and he'll be out to sea anyway. We won't see anything'.

'Will we see the gun? Will it make a big, big bang?'

'That's only there to frighten them off. Nobody's going to go shooting a gun or anything. William, say something to her'.

But Letitia was unsure that William would be able to provide the reassurance she knew their daughter required. In fact, she feared from their previous conversations that William would not appreciate the need for it, would be keen to furnish just the opposite.

'Mary, we are going home, that's all there is to it. Come on, help me with baby Douglas'.

Of course the war had to be won and of course everybody must be allowed to play their part. She had no doubts about the barbarity of the enemy they faced, none whatsoever. Nobody with a shred of conscience could stand by and let such atrocities go unchallenged. Everybody had heard how the Germans had paraded around some Belgian village with those babies impaled on their bayonets. It was a horror that echoed in her imagination frequently when she was not fully occupied with her children. She held little Douglas even more tightly and shivered, the awful images intensifying rather than dissipating in the caress. The war was going well. The British had soon shown their superiority on those foreign battlefields and were making determined incursions into the fickle lines of their cruel and cowardly enemies. More troops now, more volunteers, would bring a speedy end to all this, she knew.

And yet, increasingly, her conversations with William and with one or two of her friends seemed to pull from her thoughts and opinions she could barely recognise as her own. Her neighbour from three doors down, Flo Merryfield, had two small children with a third on the way and had always seemed a reliable and sympathetic ally. Blunter than Maud definitely, less well-educated really. Maud would never have worn a headscarf outdoors like that for instance. But a partial substitute nonetheless for her sister all that way away.

'Your William still not going then, not off to France with the others?' Flo asked one morning as her son looked at Mary across Letitia's front gate as if wondering which of the two children might be the first to speak and to suggest some game they might both play.

'He's more than ready but it's the fishing, we've got to keep the fishing going or they'll starve us out,' replied Letitia.

'People doing more than starving though, people in Belgium. And the Froggies too,' said Flo, putting a hand on her small son's shoulder. 'Men at our Tom's factory talking about all going out together, one job lot. Work together well so they ought to be able to fight together well. Not just the lads going either. Our Tom and the other men, all of 'em'.

'Perhaps William will go. Especially if they can get somebody else to man the boats but it's not easy to pick it all up. He was years learning it all, there's more to fishing than people think. It isn't any battlefield but it's still dangerous out in some of those seas'.

The children were watching a snail creep up the gatepost, its antennae probing the damp morning. Still not speaking, they looked from the small creature to each other and back again. Their silent smiles brimmed with childish complicity.

'Same as our Tom says, there's plenty ready to let others do the fighting for them. Not saying your William or anything, but there's plenty as could be helping out and ain't'.

Letitia rubbed at the back of one hand with her other.

'Does your Billy want to come in and play with our Mary? It'd be no trouble, they get on ever so well together'.

But Flo shook her head, leading Billy by his shoulder away from the gate. 'No, not today thank you. We've got something to do for our Tom in town. No time for playing right now'.

Letitia, like Flo and everybody else, had seen the posters that had appeared in the town during the first month of the war.

'ANOTHER 100,000 MEN WANTED'.

Lord, that would be the whole town, three or four times the whole town.

> *'In the grave National Emergency that confronts the Empire Lord Kitchener asks with renewed confidence that another 100,000 men will now come forward'.*

William had attended the meeting advertised on the poster. In the market place the crowd was so large that many were left packed into side streets unable to see or even hear the colonel on the platform. The thump and blare of the brass band that played before and after the speech nonetheless carried around the buildings to the furthest away of the assembled people. Strangers had come into town from the surrounding villages, men of all ages, some with their sons. William had been pinned close up in the densest, forward area of the crush, and had been ready after the speeches to join the jostling but good-humoured men and lads queuing to sign up that night. But he had held back remembering his captain's advice, that the Government needed men to maintain the nation's food supplies, that they were working particularly hard at plans that would allow people like him to volunteer as soon as everything was sorted out.

'Reckon we'll still get our chance, if the pen pushers can get a move on and sort it out,' William had told Letitia. 'Captain says they'll still have a need for the likes of us out there'.

'I wish you wouldn't talk like that,' said Letitia. 'You sound as if you want to go, as if you would be quite happy to leave me with the children worrying myself sick about you'.

'Letty, you women have to play your part too. Look at Flo, she's setting to while her husband's off doing his bit. Not sitting complaining'.

The fear that had stilled Letitia's feelings was swept away by a rush of anger and then, as her words and thoughts struggled and failed to converge, her tears broke alongside an unchecked groan.

William hurried to his wife's side, his embrace accepted and then resisted a number of times as he attempted to hold Letitia close to him. She felt the strength in his arms increasing, was seized by memories of him hauling ropes over pulleys on the docks, grim-faced and steady in concentration as huge loads were lifted in dripping nets from his boat. The more she remembered the strength of her early love for him, the angrier she felt about the inescapability of the war.

'Letty, Letty, I'm sorry,' he said. 'What's the matter? I don't want to upset you. I wouldn't upset you for the world'.

Letitia had felt increasingly unsettled in recent days, unsteady in her opinions, as if every perspective was blocked, walled in by sandbags. The night of the meeting, that morning when Flo had raised William's not having signed up, and now here on the dock with this murderous machine pointing straight at Mary. She pushed Douglas in his perambulator along the esplanade, wanting to be home before the wet mist turned to heavier rain in the freshening breeze. But Mary could only walk so fast and today she was even slower, her attention diverted by activity down on the beach. Men had driven stakes into the sand, criss-crossed like wickerwork, and were tentatively unrolling coils of barbed wire and attempting to string it between the posts. Like terrible Christmas decorations, thought Letitia, out of season, on a windy beach, spiked and cruel.

She was reassured, heartened even at times, by the thought of some murderous invader impaled and captured before he could break through with his rifle and bayonet into streets where children played and neighbours went about their business. But she also struggled with sensations that she deemed unworthy, traitorous. There were times when the metal pricked her own flesh, began to tear her if she made the slightest attempt at escape. The hot, deep pain of the enemy, the increasing intensity of the incisions as he became more entangled in his struggling, became her own, as severe and as terrifying as any real wounds. She feared her own screams would no longer be containable, that they would burst from her into the world. It was unforgiveable.

The evening after her visit to the harbour with the children, when Mary was asleep and the baby was lying awake in his cradle making only occasional cooing noises, Letitia settled to write to Maud. William's ship was fishing through the night hoping, given the tides and season, to be fortunate and land a significant catch of mackerel and creel from the shallow channel that ran beneath high cliffs to the east of the town. Although she always cleared away the dishes from the table straight after a meal, this evening she merely pushed them to one side, clearing just enough space on the thick table cloth for her writing pad and envelopes.

There was always so much family information to exchange with Maud. Just as she waited with an increasing longing for Maud's letters from Canada, she knew that Maud too depended on her regular communications for her own happiness in a country so far from her place of birth. As ever, Letitia had news and stories concerning William and her own children, of Sidney and Edith and their growing twins, of Bertram and the excitement of his new employment, and of mother and father who, she knew, despite their stoicism were feeling increasingly isolated now that their own children were fully grown.

But the words failed, the sentences seemed clumsy and overly formal, the story they told was not Letitia's. She wasted two sheets of paper, putting aside this first account and beginning again. Within half a page, she knew that once more she had lost what she wished to convey to Maud. By her side, the baby coughed, such a small but perfect exhalation.

She began for the third time.

Dear Maud

There is so much to tell as there always is. I have news of all the family. Perhaps you have heard from Edith and she has brought you up to date with all of their news? I heard from her a week ago. Their twins are growing, eight years old now they are and full of life I understand.

The biggest surprise we have all had is that our Bertram has been accepted into the constabulary. Can you imagine it? Our Bertram in a policeman's uniform? Since he's been courting seriously, Martha has made him think about whether he wants to be a farm hand all his life or whether he wants to make a bit more of himself. And, of course, he will be doing his duty being a policeman so probably won't be able to go the Front.

Letitia put down her pen and blotted the page as Douglas stirred and gave a small cry. She held her breath and looked at the laundry hanging from the rack below the ceiling, huge vests and bloomers belonging to William and her and, beside them, tiny items belonging to the girls, the contrasts comical and somehow tragic. The baby settled again and Letitia picked up the pen and dipped it into the ink very carefully in an attempt to avoid the slightest clink of contact. With the next drop of ink, black blood on the nib, Letitia turned to the events of the day.

Maud, sometimes I wish so much that we could talk together like we used to when we were young. Sometimes I think such silly things and I dare not let them slip out when everybody seems to be making such sacrifices. But, it is times like today, when I need to buck myself up, that I wish you were here.

Letitia hesitated, ready again to waste another sheet of paper by tearing it from its pad and screwing it into a ball. Although tired, she felt her energies rise and forced the pen back onto the paper, a wave of defiance obliterating the nagging presence of the un-ironed laundry and the un-cleared dishes.

I went along the esplanade at lunchtime today, pushing Douglas in his pram and with Mary walking. You wouldn't believe how it has changed. Do you remember how warm the sun was those mornings when we used to walk to church? And how blue the sea? Now it seems grey and cold all the time. The holiday makers are gone of course with the winter and I don't think they will ever return again.

Do you remember the crowds? All those people enjoying themselves. There is nobody here now except soldiers, hundreds of them sometimes. I know we must all play our part but today I thought of Alastair and William when we first met them, when we all used to go to dances, it was often still warm in the evenings and the sea would be so calm. And the worst thing, I feel so weak and silly saying it, but do you remember those beautiful little carts that children used to ride in, pulled by the goats? All decorated like a royal carriage? They are gone too. And just as I was walking past where they used to be, up opposite the Empire Hotel, I looked at Mary and I thought how much she ...

Letitia sat upright, stiffened her back and took a very deep breath.

... would have ...

Her breath became ragged and unchecked, and she stamped her fist against the table in an attempt to check her tears. Ink from the pen, like the tracks of a tiny creature in snow, fled across the page faster than any eye could follow. She tore the page from the pad and gave out a low, involuntary groan. She startled Douglas who began crying again, not occasional and half-hearted this time, but fully from the start. Letitia wanted no more of letters, she reached into the cradle, lifted her wailing baby and sat rocking with the child to her breast on into the night, long after the small pools of ink had dried.

10. A WARTIME WEDDING

Maud and Letitia did however maintain their correspondence, their memories of times before the war flowering in their exchanges as an inexpressible dread continued to drone beneath the everyday, surface drabness. Bertram's wedding to Martha brought happiness to the whole family and a welcome distraction after more than two whole years of war. Letitia and William travelled by train with their two excited children back to her home village, the shrill whistle of escaping steam, the thrust of the pistons and the huge revolving wheels at first filling the little ones with terror. As they journeyed though the children quickly relaxed and even became comforted by the racket and rickety rush over unfamiliar landscapes, arriving to their grandparents, aunts, uncles and cousins, weary, apprehensive and curious as to whether their dimly-remembered images matched the actual appearances of these relatives.

Letitia was pregnant again and troubled by the uncertain future that awaited her children. She was most intensely worried for the child as-yet unborn, the one who still seemed protected and safe within her own body, the one she would before long deprive of this security and deliver into a threatening and threatened world.

But the wedding, both in prospect and during the companionable bustle of the preparations and the day itself, leant Letitia a comfort deeper than she could have anticipated.

'I had wanted a white dress,' Martha confided in Letitia who had helped her try on her suit the afternoon before the wedding. 'But this war has messed those plans up. I could have made a veil to go with it without too much trouble and all'.

'Martha, you look delightful,' her new sister-in-law-to-be replied. 'Everybody thinks so. And that suit is all the fashion with that skirt there, cut off like that'.

'I took up it up myself,' said Martha, smoothing down the front of her tailored dove grey skirt.

'It's very modern. But dignified too,' said Letitia. 'And stilettoes! You look beautiful'.

Bertram and Martha had been insistent on Father Reeves conducting their ceremony despite accounts of the clergyman's failing mastery over clerical rituals that had once seemed second nature to him. The young server at the altar was clearly very familiar with both Father Reeves' waning powers and the order of the wedding service itself and provided gentle and unobtrusive support. As her younger brother knelt with his bride before this once-familiar officiator, Letitia felt a surge through her body, not the baby kicking this time but a deep power from her earliest memories.

Memories of Father Reeves and Ivy kneeling in the bedroom. Prayers, during those dark winter days, to prevent Bertram's passage from this world into the next. Now the journey was into the blessed state of matrimony. Surrendering to God's mercy, Father Reeves the representative and agent of God's will. The miracle of delivery. A world that might have been, one without Bertram, and the world that had come to pass.

'Our Bertie's gone and managed it then. Poor Martha's been daft enough to take him on,' said Sidney afterwards at the wedding tea in the church hall.

'Shush, Sidney,' Letitia told her older brother, who stood tall and ruddy in his Sunday clothes and a buttoned shirt collar that seemed too tight for his muscular neck. 'What an awful thing to say, even as a joke. Today of all days. Come along, bring Edith and those big sons of yours over here to see their cousins. Come and sit with mother and father. Let's all be together while we can'.

Edith stood by Sidney's side beaming at Letitia.

'Ah, Letty, Letty, my dear, how wonderful to have you here with us again – all of you. Your letters are wonderful but it is so nice to see you in the flesh. And to see you blooming and so well'.

'Oh, Edith, I don't know where I'd be without your letters sometimes,' replied Letitia, remembering her first childhood glimpses of Edith and her complicity in Sidney's courting of her. 'I feel I'm there with you sometimes, with Sidney and your twins. And with Mama and Father. You can't know how much joy your letters give me, the lift to my spirits when I see your handwriting on those envelopes on my door mat'.

George and Ivy had seated themselves at the end of a trestle table covered with a delicately embroidered cloth that had not only served Letitia for her wedding but had been given to Ivy herself when she had married George back in the previous century. Laid out on the table were two huge plates of sandwiches, the first of ham from one of Farmer Triscott's pigs, with pickle made by Ivy. The equally large mound at the other end was of cheese obtained from a dairy in the neighbouring village.

Letitia was aware of her parents having aged noticeably since she had last seen them. Both were clearly enjoying having so many of their family, their grandchildren especially, together in one room. But Letitia noticed that her mother seemed to tire more quickly than she once did and that a slightly bemused look and then a sense of panic sometimes slipped across her father's face during conversations. The daily running of the smithy was now in Sidney's hands although George still apparently rose and took his breakfast at the same time he always had and accompanied his son to work. Letitia knew Sidney well enough to be confident that he could delegate or create tasks for their father that capitalised on his experience at the forge whilst also minimising the risks that might follow from a moment of inattention or failed physical strength in the vicinity of that mighty heat.

'Children, come and sit down, there's elderflower press if you want it, or milk,' said Letitia, attempting with a sideways motion of her head to direct Mary and Douglas into chairs besides George and Ivy. The children though were interested only in the cakes positioned along the table and slightly overwhelmed by having to decide between the lardy, the plum and the apple cake.

'Sit down there besides Grandpa and Grandma. William, can you look after Douglas for me for a minute please?'

She looked around the table at her young children and her parents all dressed in their very best clothes.

'What a pity Maud isn't here. She would love to see everybody, I know'.

'Maud won't be back here in this country,' said George, who had not seemed to be following the conversation. 'At least not until that Alastair of hers has made his fortune. We've seen the last of her if I'm not very much mistaken'.

Guffaws burst from the table next to theirs where Bertram and Martha were talking with some of the Triscott boys. Letitia was very aware of how much these old neighbours of hers had aged and changed, no longer the slow-witted children who had brought about their teachers' exasperation and retribution back in their school days together. A long way too from the lumbering village youths who had teased her and taxed her patience when she worked in the village store. Today, she was warmed by their banter, the predictable silliness and horseplay, and regretted her frequent irritation with them when they were younger. Now, a more sombre air hung about this family, as it did so many others of Letitia's acquaintance. The oldest of the Triscott brothers was away fighting at the Front where he had served unscathed since the very beginning of the war. The brother next in line, however, had enlisted eagerly a few weeks afterwards only to be wiped away with the whole of his platoon, within days of arriving in France, by the huge explosion caused when an enemy shell ignited one of their ammunition dumps. So, Letitia welcomed their high spirits, their contribution to the good cheer that Bertram and Martha deserved and that had been in such short supply for everybody of late. It also helped to drive away her persisting concerns about her husband's place in all of this, her worry that perhaps he should be playing a fuller, more engaged part in the armed hostilities.

Letitia was delighted, along everybody else in her family, at Bertram being accepted into the police force but she noticed that it was his previous workmates, the Triscott lads from the farm, and not his new colleagues who had been invited to the wedding. Perhaps it was the distance, she thought, Bertram having been posted to a town some twenty miles away so that he could develop a new air of authority away from the village people who had known him all his life.

The laughter from the Triscotts centred on a small newspaper cutting that one of them held, a piece of paper that Bertram, partially restrained by Martha, was trying to snatch away.

'It says, what does it say, Ernie? Oh yes, ... *at which* .... What does this say? *Defendant*? All right ... *at which defendant* ... What's that word?'

'Give it to me,' said the youngest of the Triscott brothers, Ernie, resisting Bertram's renewed attempt to get hold of the cutting during its transition from one brother to the other.

'Yes, yes, here we are '... *at which defendant claimed that the police constable had inserted his fingers into his mouth and emitted a most terrifying, shrill whistle. The shock caused by this, defendant claimed, was what led him to press down on the accelerator pedal...*'

'His sergeant gave Bertie a right ticking off,' whispered Sidney, leaning towards Letitia. 'Said he'd got a regulation issue whistle so why didn't he use it? Not a very good start after only a couple of weeks in the job, is it?'

'Poor Bertie,' Letitia replied. 'It sounds as though he was trying to do the right thing. Just doing it with too much gusto. Why do these things always happen to him?'

Letitia's small children were watching their Uncle Bertram tussling playfully with the others over the piece of paper. She was aware that they seemed unsure about the raucous laughter, whether it was something joyful and happy of which they could be a part.

'Don't worry,' she said. 'Those grown-ups are only having a bit of fun, they're not really fighting'.

161

'And then it says,' shouted Ernie above the ruckus '… *defendant's speed must have reached twenty miles an hour*… According to Bertie, anyway'.

'Twenty two or even twenty three I told the court. Not twenty,' protested Bertram.

'Anyway' said Ernie, his voice dropping as he came to the end of the article, 'it says the magistrate told the court there was likely to be an increase in offences of this type if motoring catches on as a pastime among a wider group of people'.

'More work to keep you busy then, Bertie!' shouted another of the brothers.

The melee around the Triscotts subsided and Letitia was pleased to see that there were chuckles and good-natured slaps to the back involving Bertram and his old friends from the village. Martha led him by the arm to join Letitia and Sidney with the others at the family table.

'You stood up to that ribbing very well,' said Sidney to his younger brother.

'They don't mean anything by it,' said Bertram, 'I've known them all my life, after all'.

'I still don't think it's dignified,' said Martha, straightening Bertam's tie that had become twisted during his scuffles. 'People expect a bit more decorum from somebody in your position. And they should show a bit more respect too, while they're at it'.

And then, when the children had taken themselves off to explore the dusty anteroom at the end of the hall and their men were talking among themselves, Martha gestured to her new sisters-in-law, Edith and Letitia, with widened eyes that suggested she had a confidence to impart. Bringing their lowered heads together, Martha whispered.

'Don't tell everybody but Bertie has put in for a transfer and guess where to? To the coast, Letty, right where you live. We'll be your next door neighbours, or as near as, if he gets it'.

'Oh Martha, that would be wonderful. It would be so lovely to have you there closer. But what about poor Mama and Father?'

'That's why it's got to be a secret for now,' added Martha, checking to see that the others at the far end of the table were still in conversation and not eavesdropping on theirs. 'We don't want to alarm them with notions about changes that might not take place. But I just know that Bertie has got to get right away from this place where everybody knows him and have a fresh start'.

'We'll all miss you if you go, Martha,' said Edith. 'But I think everybody will understand. Bertie has a chance to make something of himself and you two must take these opportunities if they crop up. There's one thing though. If you do go, I'll have to double my letter writing. There will be you as well as Letty to keep up to date with, not to mention Maud, of course'.

Later, after the tables in the village hall had been cleared away back into the little anteroom and the dishes washed and dried by the three sisters-in-law and other helpers, Letitia and William left with their children to walk the short distance to her Aunt Lily's house, where they were all to spend the night. The children took a while to settle to sleep after the excitement of the day but eventually Letitia and William were able to retire to the very bed where she and Maud had sometimes stayed overnight all those years ago when they themselves were little girls. She told William about these times, remembering how grown up she had always felt when away from her parents, sleeping with her older sister in the grand bed with the feather mattress.

But what a different world that previous century had seemed.

'We never thought there could be a war like this, that Maud and I would grow up and marry men who might have to go off and fight. We used to lie here and the worst thing to be frightened of was Farmer Triscott's geese'.

William turned onto his back and stared at the ceiling.

'There's always been wars Letty, always will be. Sure as eggs are eggs'.

'When I was little, I always thought that somebody could make it stop though,' she said, turning now to lie in parallel with William and fix her focus too on the sagging ceiling, like two statues laid out in a mausoleum. Not cold as marble though but warm together under the blankets, on top of the feather mattress and pillows.

'Only God can stop a war. Who else did you think could when you were small?' he asked.

'It sounds silly now, but I thought Father Reeves could if he really wanted to. It was wonderful to see him again today. And when I was really little, I suppose I thought Mama and Father could too'.

'Oh Letty. You must have been such a funny little child. I had no sense of what a dreamer you were when I first met you,' he said. 'You were such a confident, young woman'.

Letitia was feeling more and more awake and wondered whether this was the time to talk about what had been on her mind of late. About reconsidering her previous reluctance and encouraging William to think about signing up. To do her bit and be strong so that he could do his, like so many of the others.

But William had turned towards her and brought his knees up, curling into sleep. She wished very much to continue their quiet conversation but he had closed his eyes.

'I sometimes thought that Sidney could too and even Maud,' she whispered.

William mumbled something but it was unintelligible. She was losing him to sleep.

'I used to have a doll called Miss Ragitty,' she added, almost involuntarily after lying in silence for some while but William's now pronounced and regular breathing indicated that he was already asleep, a turnabout from those earlier times when Maud always seemed awake and available to her in moments of night-time anxiety. With the whole household except her seemingly asleep, Letitia lay for an hour or more listening to William's occasional snorts and sighs at her side while a pageant of geese, farmhands, clergymen, newly-weds and their guests, fishermen, sailors and soldiers all paraded through her imagination.

The following morning, Letitia was eager to show William her father's forge and Ivy and Aunt Lily agreed to mind the youngsters while they did so. After their breakfast, they walked down the lane and then along the cobbled pavement to the place of fire and noise that she remembered so well from her childhood, a building that had entranced and frightened her in equal measure.

I used to run along here with lunch for Father and Sidney when I was a young girl,' she told William. 'These stones were really slippery when it rained, especially where it starts to slope a bit, but Mama told me not to dawdle. It seemed really important to get their food to them as soon as possible. And what a long way it was then! It's only a short walk now'.

Letitia was surprised that morning by the force with which these memories still affected her, especially when she saw again at the end of the road the old bench and the tethering post for the horses and the low, wide brick archway smudged with soot that formed the entrance to the darkened interior of the forge. She had been right about William too. He was indeed fascinated by this place of industry, this workplace so different from the nautical expanses that were his lot. Inside, the furnace was fully alight and lines of sweat were already slipping along tracks through the grime on Sidney's and to a lesser extent, her father's face. Much remained just as Letitia remembered it, the rows and rows of horseshoes hanging from nails on the high wooden beams, the long metal poles, the huge, heavy forceps and the other mysterious implements, all arranged despite the heavy dust in a neat and easily accessible fashion.

Immediately, however, she was aware of the reversal of the roles of the two men since she was last in this busy workshop. Sidney was now the striker fully in command of the hammer blows while George seemed content with his task of holding with both hands the red, molten metal of a horseshoe in a pair tongs. The two men worked quickly, as if by instinct, the relentless pounding of the one absorbed by the braced shoulders, back and thighs of the other, the rapidly cooling horseshoe turned or readjusted perfectly after each mighty blow in a practised and easy synchrony.

Later, with Mary and Douglas eager to be back on a train for their return journey, the whole family turned out for their departure. Sidney and George came up from the smithy still in their heavy clothes streaked with soot and scorch marks. Edith held Ivy's arm to steady her while her sons raced each other first to one end of the platform and then the other. Bertram and Martha had come too, standing slightly stiffly and looking a little more like casual acquaintances, Letitia felt, than a couple who had embraced at their wedding only the day before.

When aboard and in their compartment, Mary and Douglas were more interested in establishing, with considerable disagreement between themselves, who was to sit in which actual seat rather than in waving goodbye or having one last exchange with their relatives. William pulled down the window so that he and Letitia could make their parting comments. Letitia noticed how Sidney, taller than all the others, put his arms around the shoulders of both his wife and their mother. As if waiting for his nod of approval or some other gesture, everybody on the platform looked to him and he then swept them forward up to the window of the carriage. Letitia felt that she would retain for a long time the memory of Sidney at the forge that morning, his strong handsome face and torso surrounded by a halo of fire, the echoing cacophony of the hammer against the anvil, and the sparks and specks of ash eddying all about him in the dry heat of the forge.

'Children, come and say goodbye to Grandma and Grandpa and everybody,' Letitia urged her children.

'Goodbye!' shouted Mary from inside the carriage, not turning from her argument with Douglas as they both bounced from one seat to the next as if claiming each place in turn as their own.

'Children, come and say goodbye properly,' added William in a sterner tone of voice.

The twins had finally stopped their energetic antics on the platform and had joined the others at the window, all of them seeming to be held as one by the sense of Sidney's extended embrace. The apprentice at the smithy who had escorted his younger sister to church on Sunday mornings back when they were both learning to assume their places in the adult world had become a man easy with his own strength and purpose. He was now a man who unified and gave a sense of security to their family as it continued to disperse across the country and, in Maud and Alastair's case, across the world. As the train pulled away, the huge motive force feeling as much within her own body as in the furnace and the pressurised steam, Letitia trembled at the sight of her loved ones smiling, waving and growing smaller on the platform.

*

Although the wedding had proved a tiring excursion for Letitia and her young family, the sight of all her relatives and the old familiar landscapes had somehow felt new and enlivening. Returning home was like returning to an older world, a chilly, older world and one that generated new fears.

Only weeks before her baby was due to be born, the disastrous news of the death of her friend Flo's husband was reported. The details were unclear but apparently his platoon had suffered heavy losses after a daring raid on enemy lines which resulted in the decimation of their advancing line through sustained machine gun fire. Letitia felt an overpowering need to assist Flo, to find some way to comfort her or just be of practical help, as if she were a member of her own family. But so great was her friend's distress that Letitia's offers were rebuffed, her friend's grief expressing itself as anger and rejection. If passing in the street, Letitia was at a loss how to help when Flo turned her head away without speaking and even on occasions shepherded her children to the opposite pavement as if deliberately to avoid contact.

Flo's loss and her subsequent manner led Letitia to think again about William's contribution to the war effort.

'Do you ever think you should have gone when you see the sacrifices made by men like Flo's husband?' she asked him one morning before he left for work.

'No, not now I don't,' he replied. 'I wanted to be out there with all the others when it started but now we've seen such loss of life everything looks a bit different'.

'Different? What do you mean? Is it because of the risks?'

'We take risks! Every time we leave harbour we – '

'But not like those men in France, not – '

'Letty, you didn't want me to go. When I was all set on it at the beginning, you were worrying away and seemed relieved that I was in a reserved occupation'.

Mary had come out from the kitchen drawn by the raised voices of her parents in the hallway. She stood in the doorway, her bottom lip protruding and her eyes enlarged and watery.

'Go back into the kitchen, Mary,' said Letitia, managing to control her raised emotions in order to speak quietly to her daughter. 'Make sure that Douglas is all right. Daddy and I are just talking about something'.

The little girl turned back into the room without protest or comment, a sure sign that she appreciated the gravity of the conversation she had been overhearing.

'They lost two men only twenty miles down the coast the other month and there was that trawler out of Lowestoft went down in the North Sea last winter. All hands went down, the whole lot of them'.

'I know. It was terrible. But you're used to it, the sea. It's familiar,' said Letitia, feeling less sure now why she was arguing and creating this unhappiness between William and herself. 'It just seems so different what the soldiers are going through, different from being killed by other men. Deliberately killed, I mean'.

'There's no difference, Letty. When you're dead, you're dead,' said William, an uncharacteristic anger in his steady tone.

'William, please think of the children. Don't shout and say such things'.

'Think of the children! That's exactly what I have been doing. That's what you wanted me to do, isn't it?' he said, snatching his cap and muffler from the hooks inside the front door. 'I'm going to work,' he added not turning to kiss her or even look her in the eye.

After William had left and for much of the day until he returned that evening, Letitia thought about what she had said and the half thoughts that she had been trying to express. She had treated William terribly, she knew that now, but also felt that she had let Flo down, abandoned her somehow. When he did return, his anger seemed to have subsided and Letitia was no clearer about what had driven her to confront him in the way she had. And so, between the two of them, an unspoken rule of matrimony was invoked, the matter being left to dissipate of its own accord.

In the final few days before Letitia's confinement, Bertram's wife Martha made the train journey alone to be with her at the time of the birth. As well as her deep gratitude for the extra help in managing the children, Letitia was overjoyed to hear that Bertram's request for a transfer had been approved and that the young couple would be joining them as near neighbours within the next few months. And, given the general uncertainty of the times and the unease that pervaded what were once everyday events, it was a great relief and a source of further rejoicing when the baby Clarry was born without complications one very early morning while William and his fellow crew members were out at sea fishing.

As soon as it was obvious that Letitia's time had come, Martha had run through the still dark streets to alert Mrs Cooper while Letitia struggled to suppress her occasional groans so as not to wake her sleeping children. Mrs Cooper arrived swiftly with a battered, brown leather bag she must have had prepared beforehand, and Martha was back on hand to take care of the children by the time her unavoidable clattering with kettles at the range and her hurried footfalls up and down the stairs inevitably woke them.

The new baby's birth was the swiftest of all three of Letitia's children and, while this meant that household routines were disrupted for a shorter period, Letitia's cries were more intense and audible from downstairs. Douglas appeared unaffected and played with the blocks of wood that William had fashioned and painted for him, while Mary stayed by her Aunt Martha's side in the kitchen as she prepared breakfast. When Letitia's gasps of pain occurred, Mary clung determinedly to her aunt's skirt and Martha pulled her closer and tousled her hair, saying that her mother was safe and would soon be quiet and happy again. In less than an hour Mrs Cooper appeared in the doorway, smiling and with eyes alive, a cheerful and reassuring presence despite the traces of fresh blood amongst the older ingrained stains on her apron.

Clarry's arrival excited the others and the busy schedule of the baby's feeding and sleeping routines allowed Letitia to step aside for a week or two from the mood of austerity and duty that hung about every place where people gathered, like a persistent, thick, white fog spreading a sense of desolation through a town's empty streets. But her energy returned with remarkable rapidity and Letitia was soon reappraised of the tenor of everyday life. The swift victory promised two and a half years ago was still not manifest. There was the new threat of grey, gaseous monsters floating into their skies, huge combustible bladders drifting on a high, silent course above their lives, the shadow deepening across the prospects of them all.

Mary and Douglas continued to play on the street with other children from the immediate neighbourhood, adhering to Letitia's stipulation that they should not stray further than the general store in one direction and the entrance to the timber yard in the other. One day, Mary returned home with her rusty iron hoop scraping the pavement behind her, the sound of metal grating on stone audible from some distance away. Despite being preoccupied with Clarry's bout of colic, Letitia noticed immediately how despondent Mary was as she entered the front door,.

'What's the matter, Mary? Have you been falling out again, you children?' she asked, while Clarry's tiny, podgy legs pedalled the air as if to somehow add greater volume to his protestations.

'Billy Merryfield's being nasty'.

'What do you mean, he's being nasty? What has he done to you? What – '

'He says – Mama – he says – Mama, why is Daddy a coward?'

'Darling,' said Letitia, leaving Clarry on his blanket with all four limbs now in wild animation, and crossing the room to embrace her daughter. 'Daddy's not a coward. Daddy's very brave. Daddy goes out in those very rough seas to make sure that we all have enough food to eat'.

'But Billy – ' the little girl began, now choking on her sobs.

'Billy's just being very silly. He can't help what he's saying. You're not to take any notice. He's only – '

Letitia looked at her distressed daughter and at Douglas who had come out from the parlour sucking on a damp and slightly grubby crust of bread, to see what was causing his sister's upset.

'Quick children!' said Letitia, driven by some impulse she would have found impossible to name. 'Mary can you carry Clarry? I'll get my cleaning things'.

'Where are we going?' asked Mary, as she attempted to comply by lifting her bulky, younger brother.

'There's something we have to do, it's needed doing for ages,' said Letitia.

And then carrying a scrubbing brush, a block of green soap and pail of hot water from the kettle on the hob, she organised her four children out of the house and along the pavement to Flo's house.

'She hasn't had the time,' said Letitia, sloshing her brush into the water and then scraping at the soap to work up a lather. 'Mary, can you keep Douglas away from the bucket, I don't want him with water all down his front'.

With her hair falling into her face, Letitia knelt at Flo's step and began to scrub in a vigorous sideways motion. 'It's only – Mary, be careful, you're throttling him. Hold him underneath his bottom'.

'Maybe, it will – ' began Letita, just as Clarry slipped through Mary's grasp, only his shawl left in her hands as his face slapped against the suds and water at the edge of the step.

As the baby's howl erupted, Letitia threw down the brush and soap, the latter landing in the pail and splashing both of her other children as well as once again wetting Clarry's rapidly reddening face. The sound of bolts rattling and the front door being tugged open preceded Flo appearing on the threshold and towering above her.

'What the bloody hell – '

'Flo, I just thought it – what with everything – ' spluttered Letitia as she attempted to clasp her wildly thrashing and shrieking baby to her own, by now, soaking breast.

'Go away! What right have you – go away – get back to that – to that piano and those pictures on your wall!'

'Flo, I'm so very sorry. I didn't mean to – I was only trying – ' said Letitia, raising herself up from the step and staring deeply into the fury burning in Flo's eyes.

'I wouldn't for the world have – come on, children,' she said looking at them, rooted to the spot, faces drained with fear. 'Let's just – Flo, I'm so very –'.

But she knew that any further words of hers could only make matters worse.

The postmark on the envelope waiting on her doormat was from home. Once inside the house with her children, and before any further attempts to calm them, she glanced at the postmark and felt a spring of happiness. Here would be confirmation of Bertram's transfer date. Having her brother and new sister-in-law nearby would, thank goodness, bring her more peace and relief than she could at the moment otherwise muster.

But the letter was not from Martha. When she looked more closely, the handwriting was quite clearly in Edith's fuller hand. Sidney had received call-up papers! The supply of younger, single men had all but dried up, Edith said. Further sacrifices and determined effort were now required. They were all in a spin. He was to report to the county barracks within the week and would, in all likelihood, be seeing action in the trenches before the month was up.

CHAPTER 11. THREE PHOTOGRAPHS

'What do you think about this then?' said Avril, tossing a weathered, brown envelope into Sue's lap as they sat out on an early summer's day in Avril's garden.

'What are these?' Sue asked, as she looked inside and found three old photographs.

'It's her'.

'Who?'

'Your dad's mother. It's her'.

It was two and a half years since Les' death and Avril's distressed insistence that there should be no funeral. And now these photographs had appeared.

'These are who?' Sue asked again as she stared at the photographs.

'Your dad's mother!'

The first photograph. A young woman posed anxiously before the camera. Head and shoulders with a slight sepia halo, a hazy background. Her top teeth just visible. Dark hair centrally parted and gathered at the level of her ears. Large eyes staring straight ahead, prominent cheekbones, a heavy pendant on a fine chain around her neck, a white or pale coloured blouse with a soft collar. Sue found it hard to place her age, the formality of the photograph probably adding years. No older than twenty, perhaps as young as seventeen. A beautiful young woman.

That face though. Sue had seen it before. The eyes, the bridge of the nose, the mouth slightly open as if in some unvoiced plea. She knew it so well.

She knew it from the old primary school photograph of herself!

The second. The hair identical in style except that the parting had moved to one side, the same woman some fifteen or so years older. Her shoulders were fuller and rounded, slumped almost. Head inclined this time, the same dark pupils intensely fixed. Her mouth was closed, her lips thinner, in a set expression. She wore a matching jacket and skirt in a heavily floral pattern, with a white shirt beneath and a string of dark beads. On a small table beside her was a cat, squat and thickly furred.

The third. Three children, a small child seated on a simple wooden chair with a girl and boy who seemed closer to each other in age, on either side. There was a strong family resemblance between these older two, the boy in a white smock over a shirt and white tie, time having almost bleached these garments. Short trousers, long white socks and buckled shoes. Clipped dark hair cleanly parted and reflecting bright pools of studio lighting. The girl, the tallest of the three, wore a large, white bow in her hair, a short-sleeved dress with three matching rows of embroidery at the hem and cuffs. Between these two with their intense stares, the smaller child, probably four or five years younger than the girl and around four years of age. Unlike the older two though, this youngster had long blond hair reaching in curls down to his shoulders. Clothed identically to the other boy, his eyes seemed caught by something to the side of the camera. He was rounder in the face, seemingly more amenable to fun and play than the other two.

Since the Boxing Day conversation in 1984, Avril had talked only very infrequently about the woman whose suicide had remained a secret for so long. Sue and her mother had the occasional covert conversation, almost always in a kitchen, both of them listening for Les'

177

approaching footfall in the corridor without ever once acknowledging that this was what they were doing.

Sue held the three photographs. So many questions unable to organise themselves. The young woman was looking out directly at her, looking out down the decades.

'*Do something*!' she was pleading.

A blackbird was nesting among the waxy leaves of a laurel bush and made a blustering exit from the thick foliage as they spoke.

'Who was she? What was her – where did you get these from? She's so young. I've always –'

'Your Uncle Rodney sent them. I don't know why he sent them now of all times'.

'What did he say? And why now? Presumably there was a note or something?'

'He didn't say anything. Just scribbled that I might want them and that he didn't have anything else. Seemed quite definite about that. Perhaps he didn't want them after Aunt Mary, Dad's sister, died.'

The fine-featured young woman had been captured in clean detail. She was not some elderly historical figure, some matriarch. Her youthfulness alone demanded that she be named.

The blackbird landed on the grass to their side, bounced once, braced its legs and then, raising its head, gave out a cry full of early summertime.

Sue turned over the postcard-sized photographs, nothing hand-written on the younger one except the number 2803. In smaller lettering across the side was printed 'The Ideal Studios, 120 Western Rd., Hove, Brighton'. Places, real places. On the reverse of the older woman, no mention of either the Ideal Studios or any other firm. More handwriting though, with some numbers, some swift strokes that might have been the initials 'JG' and then across the top 'Miss Constance, 26 3rd Ave'. *Had she once been called Miss Constance?* A face and then almost straightaway a name, a person struggling back into the present after decades of obscurity. *And Brighton, had she once lived there?*

Identifying the children was straightforward. On the reverse, in ink and with flamboyant capital letters, 'Roberts of Newbiggin Rd, Weymouth, Dorset'. Then, to ensure that no mistakes could possibly occur, a vertical list – 'Mary, Douglas, Clarence.'

Clarence! Her father's name was Clarence Leslie. He had always hated the name and was known as Leslie or, more often, Les. This youngest boy was her father! And the others were her Aunt Mary and Uncle Douglas.

So young, seemingly cheerful and perhaps even mischievous. Sue stared in open wonder at the boy she had never known, the open and accepting face of the boy who would become the father she had always found hard to engage with. She could love this boy though, with a clear and uncomplicated affection. Why had she never seen any images like this before? Only photos of him as a young man in a wartime RAF uniform or, in his later years, arm in arm with Avril on their various holidays?

The blackbird hopped towards Sue's feet, pecked once and then again at the ground beside her deckchair before throwing itself into the air with another elongated shriek of mock alarm.

'Did you once tell me that Dad was nine when she died?'

'Nine or maybe twelve, I'm not really sure. My mother swore she had seen her that day, up at the Nothe, walking about very quickly. Going up to people, saying very strange

179

things. She wasn't at all well. My Mum came home very worried. She just knew something was going to happen'.

'Here we are talking about her again and now that I've got a face I realise that I don't even know her name. What was she called?'

'I don't know. Your Dad would never discuss her'.

'I know you said he didn't like to talk about her but, I mean, when the subject of parents came up, did you ever – '

'He never talked about her!'

'Do you mean he *never* mentioned her? You were married for the best part of fifty years. Sometimes you must have talked about your parents'.

'I did, yes. But he wouldn't ever mention *her*'.

'Not even her name or anything, her existence?'

'He never talked about her!'

'Didn't you ask him?'

'Oh no. He wouldn't have wanted me to do that!'

Sue asked whether she could keep the photographs, anxious that they should not disappear back into the silence.

Avril flicked the back of her hand towards Sue and looked away.

Was this a theatrical indifference? Or was it embarrassment, or even fear, masquerading as irritation?

Sue said that she would make copies, slid them back into their envelope, then folded it between the pages of the book she had been reading.

Driving home that evening through the centre of England, emotions seemed to rock the speeding car. Relief that a face had been found. Pity, more direct and uncontained than she had ever experienced, for a woman wiped away by her own family. By *Sue's* own family. Excitement at a barrier trampled. Anticipation for the first few steps of a track newly discernible. Fear that events so fickle could take it all away again. Guilt at her greedy appropriation.

Sue stopped at the first service station on the M1, with an intense desire to look again at the younger photo. The girl was still staring out, still strongly feminine. Sue thought that a man might see an erotic vulnerability in the set of her shoulders or in the words she seemed on the point of speaking. This woman could have glanced across a future or slipped across the past, at any stage. Sue could imagine her among the crowds on VE day in central London, in the awkward embrace of a faceless sailor while her uninhibited office colleague kissed his friend fully on the mouth for the cameras. Or there in a duffle coat and student scarf standing in the sombre queue on the Embankment waiting to pass by Winston Churchill's coffin. Between the tents on a smoky festival evening, in a long suede skirt, floral blouse and headband with feather. Heavy purple lipstick, leather and pins, all front, in the basement club. With a crowd of school friends synchronised in the now of a huge Mediterranean foam party, reluctant to drop the tab. The hunt saboteur out before dawn, breath on the half-light, crouching with camera in her gloved hand. The careful young researcher in the bright laboratory administering her pipettes, hair net and goggles adding to her straight-backed concentration.

Instead, a blank record. Others taking her place. Generations stepping forward, one wave after another. Futures to be populated, a widening fan of talent and promise. Sue felt so angry that this woman had been removed from history's huge parade, side-lined, left at night at the far end of an alleyway behind the cardboard boxes and debris.

And then she was angry with herself for her lack of sympathy with the family that, in desperation, had taken whatever action they needed to hold themselves together after the horror of the suicide. However did they maintain their waking and sleeping routines and give an appearance of coping? How did they close themselves off from the mutterings and innuendo often savoured by others in such circumstances? This photograph of the children – creased, with a folded corner and a small tear – had been revisited far more often than the two cleanly preserved portraits of their mother. They would have been little older than in this photograph at the time of their mother's death. They had needed to survive.

Do something!

The injunction persisted.

But do what?

Giles was away from home with his work and Grace out with a friend, but as soon as Sue arrived back that evening, before unpacking, she booted up her computer. She laid the first photograph, the younger woman, face down on the heavy glass bed of her computer scanner. Quick flicks across the screen and then the hum of a rolling mechanism, light squeezing from the edge of the contraption, scraping each detail from the surface of the photograph, archiving it securely among thousands of pixels. One other button and she appeared on the screen. Addict-like clicks on the magnifier and her face was almost the same size as Sue's, blurring slightly but staring directly at her, two feet away. Fired up, Sue typed an email to Grace and Callum:

'This is your great-grandmother, my grandmother, my dad's mother. I've told you about her. She was never talked

about. This is the FIRST(!!!) photo I've ever seen of her. There's a couple more to come. Watch your Inbox'.

She pressed 'Send' and the woman was gone, dissolving back into molecules of memory, lost again. But not lost. Now they could sieve the galactic swim, collect and reassemble her in an instant. After three quarters of a century undisturbed in the dwindling recall of fewer and fewer people, if not already gone altogether, it was now possible to intercept her among the friendless Dorset lanes or on a whim and if anyone so wished, project her across the walls of huge city buildings criss-crossed with searchlights.

The email with its celebratory attachment was a defiant slap to the past.

But still she had no name.

*

Sue was the last guest at the breakfast table and, as the owner cleared her remaining plate and utensils, he asked whether she was holidaying in the Abbotsbury area. She told him that she had been born and had grown up nearby – 'locally' seemed the wrong word although Weymouth was probably only twenty minutes away by car. Sue's parents had not owned a car in those days, and reaching Abbotsbury would have involved a long, hard cycling trip over empty hills.

'I'm going to do a bit of family research in Dorchester,' she told him 'I'm trying to track down my grandmother who used to live down this way'.

'You want to be a bit careful with all that. Could turn up some nasty surprises. The wife looked into her family and there was this chap, I don't how many great, great, greats ago he was, but apparently it turns out that he was what

183

you'd call a highwayman. A thief really. Went to jail and everything. Managed to get quite a bit of detail on him in the end'.

Sue could have stayed with Janet and Trev, she knew that, but she preferred her own company and the focus of attention this would permit as she began her investigations. Somehow, the prospect of forced conversation, upright and careful as it would be with them, seemed far more daunting than this irritating banter with a stranger.

'Fascinating,' he continued. 'Put the cat among the pigeons with some of her family though'.

Sue was keen to slip away to pack her things. But she also felt a ridiculous need to help clear the dishes as well as guilt about the cost of her one night's bed and breakfast.

A week's camping fees for the whole family, that used to be.

Her younger self could still admonish her.

You deserve it though.

She could usually manage to reply.

Yes, but even so.

The proprietor was waiting for her when she crept back downstairs and followed her to her car.

'County records are what you want. Births, deaths and marriages and all that. But don't say I didn't warn you,' he chuckled as she again tried to take her leave of him.

The Records Office in Dorchester was housed among other red-bricked municipal buildings and Sue entered with an increasing expectation that her grandmother's name, maybe even skeletal facts, were within. Seated behind a desk, a middle-aged woman was speaking quietly into a telephone, apparently answering a query about a baptism certificate.

Through a glass screen Sue could see into a room lined on three walls with bookcases, rows of box files marked with different coloured highlighter pens, pinks and lime greens flashy against the stuffy sets of old bound volumes with gold-lettered spines. There were rows of sloppy, yellow telephone directories besides a sober set of the full Oxford English Dictionary.

In the centre were two rows of tables and at each workstation a person was seated, squinting upwards at the screen of a viewing machine. Some were moving strips like photographic negatives with one hand whilst attending to their screen, others were ready with pens, notepads or scraps of paper. Sue entered and waited by a woman replacing books on one of the wall shelves.

'Excuse me, I wonder if you can help me?'

'I'll try, what is it you want?'

'Well I'm trying to find out some basic facts about my grandmother and I've never used any of these records before. I was wondering if you could get me started'.

Nobody seemed distracted by their hushed conversation.

'I can give you our leaflet explaining what we hold here and where to contact if you want more specialised information. But did you say it was your grandmother? What are you trying to find out exactly?'

'Well, there was a bit of a tragedy and we don't know very much. I'm after fairly basic things really'.

'If it's your grandmother, you are best off talking to whoever is the oldest member of your family. Is that you or do you have – ?'

'No, my mother is still alive. But it was my dad's mother. Actually, she killed herself and we don't really –'

'Oh dear. What you might want to do is trace her family tree, which you can do here. I don't know when we have a vacant slot, these machines have to be booked in advance. Probably not until tomorrow but I'll find out for you. A good place to start might be with her birth certificate because then you can go on to find out about her parents. Do you have a date of birth for her?

'Oh no, nothing like that. It's all been a bit of a family secret, I think there was a lot of shame and – '

'Okay. All right. Then you'll have to do a search by name which will take a lot longer'.

Sue envied those at the tables with their lines of enquiry, their named and peopled strategies, and wanted very much also to be deep among the microfiches and the reference sources. She imagined them picking their way through much earlier histories, epochs and eras that had bored and escaped her as a schoolgirl.

'I don't have a name either'.

'No name? It's very difficult without a name *or* a date of birth. It's like looking for a needle in a haystack. What do you have? Sometimes people pass down jewellery or family bibles, something with a name or somewhere to get started. Perhaps there's something like that?'

'No, there's nothing. There's nobody left alive now and my dad would never talk about her, not even – ' Sue bit her lip and took a deep and measured breath. 'I'm sorry'.

'Oh dear. You have got a task on. I think I'll get Isabel Hodges to go through a few preliminaries with you. Perhaps we can get you started on something'.

Isabel was a short, stout woman probably stuck somewhere in her mid-fifties. As Sue's situation was explained to her a pensive silence flicked across her demeanour before she clicked back into a professionalised jollity.

'Probably best to start with the microfiches and then just slog through. What was your dad's surname?'

'Roberts,' Sue said.

'Hmm. Very unfortunate. No alternative though, just have to work your way through. Let's get you booked in for a viewer. We've nothing today but there is one at two pm tomorrow, they're half an hour slots, and then another on Friday – '

'I hadn't realised. I didn't know anything about how you go about – I'm not going to be here tomorrow. I have to get back – '

'Oh, they're like gold dust. You're lucky we're not as busy as we can be. People book up months in advance. We have a gentleman down that far row, he's come all the way from Ohio'.

Ohio! Sue's six-hour drive was trivial in comparison and her spur of the moment visit seemed self-indulgent and ill-thought out.

'I may have found you a half hour at lunchtime if one of these ladies doesn't need all her time,' said Isabel, after busying herself along the line of purposeful scholars. 'Have a look at these leaflets while you are waiting, you'll see that one day you will be able to log straight into the 1891 census from home. There are a lot of developments in the pipeline'.

Sue thanked her for taking so much extra trouble and remarked upon the helter-skelter advance of the internet.

'Yes, three main uses for the internet – finance, sex and family research. I don't have much money. Not very interested in sex either. So, it's family research for me'.

The free lunchtime slot did appear and another later that afternoon. Isabel showed Sue how to load a microfiche correctly, manipulating the tight, shiny coils so that the immense record of disconnected facts did not spill streamer-like and crackling from her fingers. Between the spindles, cranking through the months and years, the black plastic ribbon was illuminated on the yellowing screen. Dust specks, minor blotches and traces of fluff and hair distracted her from the columns, huge pillars of names in smudged white print against a black background.

Sue calculated that, if her father had been nine when his mother died, as Avril had suggested, then, given that she knew him to have been born in September 1914, she should begin her search around the year 1923. But her plan soon failed to contain the anarchy of the ages as she was made aware of the enormity of the task. Batches of film were boxed in three-month periods and then, within each roll, the huge phalanxes of names and other details were arranged alphabetically. All those dead people, the huge, silent squadrons, lined up in mute witness to the past, their names sometimes partially obscured where the machine's illumination faded at the edges or by leakage that rendered letters like 'a', 'e' and 'o' as identical white blobs like spermatozoa nested among the departed.

People with the same name as Sue's father, the name she herself grew up with. If she moved the operating lever a little more swiftly either by mistake or for the effect, she could create a snowstorm of Roberts, white blur after white blur, an emulsion wash, all dying within the same three months in faraway 1923. Hull, Dumfries, Richmond, Rochdale, Margate, Kircaldy, Truro – a monstrous population scattered across the whole country, swirling beneath her fingers, all united by the same name, all complete strangers to each other and connected only within this musty collection by the timing of their demise.

There was only one entry for 1923 with West Dorset as her place of death:

Roberts Amelia, Mary 72 Bridport 5a 377

The number after the name was presumably the person's age at her death for the majority in the columns ranged from somewhere between fifty and ninety. The other numbers seemed to be administrative in nature and Sue was unsure whether they would be of help to her or not. But this seventy-two-year-old, her only lead after half an hour of scrabbling through the records, was far too old to be a mother to Les, her nine-year-old father.

During her afternoon session, Sue exerted a tighter discipline and made hurried, tabulated notes against her prepared schedule of the years just beyond 1923. As the minute hand ticked up to the hour with quiz show melodrama, she still had unopened boxes but also a longer list than from her first attempt, eight possibilities in all.

Was her grandmother on this new list, pulled back today from obscurity or still buried somewhere on the shelves in this room? This abandoned, nameless woman was here within Sue's reach, within, she sensed, touching distance yet at the same time beyond many lifetimes of random searching.

Most seemed too old, Emily being a possibility if that was a '50' rather than an '80' beneath the white blob that was now indecipherable. Letitia was the youngest by far and Sue had included her on the list to give herself some encouragement even though she had died twenty-five miles away in Bridport and not in the sea off The Nothe as Avril had recalled. Like a dry-mouthed gambler, Sue urgently needed one more throw, just one more half an hour to complete her sweep of the months immediately prior to 1923. One more reel would do it, she was sure.

She enquired about vacant slots the next day and booked the available two. She then walked into the main street and found a public phone box to reassure herself that Grace was comfortable with her being away from home for an extra night. Next she found a more local bed and breakfast and welcomed the landlady's indifference. No small talk. No obligation to present a coherent account of her day's frantic scurrying through the millions of the missing. Just firm strictures about the cut-off time for breakfast.

As Sue reviewed her notes that evening, she made further calculations – how old might her Uncle Douglas be in the photo of her father and his siblings, and based on that guess, how old might the missing grandmother have been when she gave birth to him? And from that guess, could she have a stab at her grandmother's likely year of birth? *Between 1886 and 1890?* This estimate raised more problems than it solved. Her two half-hour slots the next day would hardly give her time to unpack and set up all the microfiches covering this four or five year span let alone allow her to scroll and squint through the huddled thousands. The enormity of the slog Isabel had referred to was now more apparent after her first mad day of point-to-point racing. Sue also recalled Isabel's comment about the disadvantage of searching for somebody with such a common surname.

And then, the breakthrough. The old photograph with its pencilled message broke the impasse – 'Miss Constance' and the address of the Ideal Studios in Brighton. Here surely was a far more circumscribed focus for her search.

And then another thought came to her, so obvious that she wondered how much else she was missing – her grandmother's maiden name would be on the record of her father's birth. *Fool.* Here among these sleeping armies, would be four people whose birthdates were secured, that she did know – her father's, her mother's, Janet's and her own. Checking that they all existed somewhere in these banks of data would restore her confidence in their accuracy and in her ability to wander with some purpose between classificatory structures and intuition, the rational in uneasy tandem with the whimsical.

And there it was the next morning, so quickly found, the record of her father's birth, a fixed and familiar point in amongst centuries of anonymity. *Fool again.* There was his mother's maiden name – Constance!

'Yes!' she hissed despite herself, immediately feeling ridiculous and clichéd. The woman at the screen next to her bowed her head a little, struggled to control a smile and nodded once. With this signal Sue had been admitted to the camaraderie of the quest.

Miss Constance. A face and now a name, enough to fuel the life force, to make her real and living, a whole person contributing to Sue's biology and donating blood and tissue to the future. *Fool three times.* Sue realised that all her scattered, frantic trawling would have been unnecessary had she had just one glimpse of her father's birth certificate.

But did he have one? Of course, he must have. Until Uncle Rodney had sent the one of the three children, Sue had seen no photographs of her parents as children. It was as if she had been raised blindfolded. Contented, but beneath the everyday jollity some unnameable fear had made certain ordinary matters beyond questioning. Why ever should the idea of seeking out her father's birth certificate bring with it a hint of terror? *Like seeing or even touching some intimate part of him.*

Such things had been unthinkable.

Unthinkable and unthought.

Sue returned buoyantly to the records office the next morning, ready to lead Miss Constance by the hand unscathed up through dark and dangerous decades into the brilliance of the present and the summer. She calculated that Miss Constance must have married her grandfather and become Mrs Roberts somewhere between 1904 to 1909. Unlike the millions of Roberts from the previous day, the Constance women were a rarer presence, a total of twelve married in 1905, 1906, 1909 or 1904, although none in West Dorset. By far the most promising was Katherine Constance, married in somewhere called Ticehurst in 1909.

As she waited for her afternoon session, Sue took down an atlas from the nearby shelf and located Ticehurst on the border between Sussex and Kent – within easy travelling distance of the Ideal Studios, Brighton! Katherine Constance was standing on a threshold, at the point of readmission to Sue's family history and to her own.

As a check, and eating up minutes from her second allocation, Sue reverted to the rolls of Roberts, looking for a matching confirmation of her grandfather's marriage to Katherine.

And it was not there.

Her reasoning had been flawed and had failed. Isabel's needle in a haystack. Her half an hour had expired. These were man-made systems with a margin of error. How much should she allow for in wearied eyesight, transcription inattention, blobs that could transmute between vowels? Ten per cent? Five? Five per cent could wipe out cities, whole counties even. And who would ever know? One lost relation searching hopelessly for another in stagnant banks of sea fret. She could trust neither the ledger nor herself. Had her search strategy been methodical enough? Indeed, was such an approach possible? Or, did eventual, successful plucking of one single, impossible figure from the onward rushing, vortex of undigested facts always require some quirk of luck or coincidence?

Sue was too wearied and demoralised by false tracks and blizzards of people reduced to dots and blobs that she was unable to contemplate either another bed and breakfast or the six-hour drive home.

*

'It's really good of you, Janet,' said Sue. 'And of Trev too, of course,' she added.

'It's all right,' her sister replied without, it seemed to Sue, much conviction.

She's always been undemonstrative, thought Sue. *More compliant. Less excitable.* Sue always felt herself to be the one who fitted least easily into their family although, when viewed in terms of temperament, it was Janet who conformed least to the common pattern.

'Couldn't get a word in edgeways, probably,' Les had once said of his younger daughter, displaying what Sue saw as a succinct and perceptive summary of all their characters.

On impulse Sue had phoned her sister and wheedled from her a bed for the night.

'If it is at all inconvenient you really must say so. I won't be offended'.

'No, it's all right'.

They had eaten dinner together, Sue, Janet and Trev.

'It's nothing special,' said Janet, offering up a steak and kidney pie and frozen vegetables from the supermarket.

'Don't know what you're used to up there, but this sort of thing does for us,' said Trev. 'It's nothing fancy but it fills you up'.

There always seemed to be an edge of antagonism about Trev, Sue thought, but then she wondered whether it might just be an awkwardness in her company. They had talked for a while about their respective children and, here again, Sue sensed challenge – or possibly disapproval.

'So, young Grace has the run of the roost at the moment then, does she?' he asked. 'No telling what she'll be getting up to, eh Sue?'

'Grace. Conscientious, studious and taking herself just a little too seriously at times. Callum – a different kettle of fish but away at university.

'I don't worry about Grace,' said Sue. 'She's got more sense than many twice her age. And she's quite happy to be left for a couple of days. Now she's in the sixth form, she's taking her studies very seriously'.

'When the cat's away, Sue. You don't know the half of it, I'll bet'.

The two sisters washed and dried up and, Sue noticed, had to clear the table and put the dishes away all without assistance from Trev who had slumped into an armchair with the sports pages of the local paper. As they finished, he stretched his arms out and announced that he would be going to the snooker.

'Have to love you and leave you,' he said, and Sue heard muttered words from the kitchen as Janet saw him out the door.

Had Janet been investigating their family history, Sue would have been pummelling her sister with questions by this stage. But she was aware that Janet was listening without interjection and felt cautious about presenting too much information at too great a rate. She tried to reduce the ragged line of her enquiries to the main landmarks, to omit the gaps and red herrings, the names that emerged then faded again. Letitia Roberts and Bessy Roberts as remote contenders but dying in Bridport. Kathleen Constance as the possibility sabotaged by the certified absence of their grandfather as a husband.

Janet's eyes, however, widened as Sue's story began to dim.

'Hang on. I've got certificates, births and things, in the attic. We came across them only the other day when we were up there looking for something'.

Certificates. So available. In their hands within minutes.

'Here's Grandad Roberts'. This one's Dad's brother Douglas, the one who emigrated to Australia. And this is his sister, Mary, who was married to Rodney. I don't know why I have these but not the rest of the family. Mum gave them to me for safe keeping ages ago. Didn't she tell you?'

But Sue was staring at one of the documents, their Aunt Mary's birth certificate.

'This is it! Letitia Constance! Aunt Mary's middle names were Letitia and Constance. Mary Letitia Constance Roberts!'

Their grandmother had been born Letitia Constance. She had sent a clue down the century, one right before their eyes, in a place Sue had never thought to look. Coded in the naming of her only daughter. Living on discretely.

Found.

Found at last. Not missing, not forever beyond them. Coming back now, back into the flow of their lives, their histories and their futures. Sleeping that night in their dreams, waking the next morning permanently returned.

Sue was back to the records for a third morning and the checking was now a streamlined, automatic process. Here she was, and here and here, and then once more again for watertight certainty. Letitia Constance, born March 1890 with the birth registered at Wincanton, dying as Letitia Roberts in September 1927 with the death registered at Bridport. Married in December 1910. In Weymouth! And their grandfather, William, correspondingly married there in the same month.

A person now, not a vague impression haunting hurried whisperings at the darkened ends of corridors. Pods of new questions popping open, pages of scribbled notes made irrelevant and redundant. A young woman walking out of southern Somerset over the landscapes of a neighbouring county, or on a railway station platform with a trunk secured by leather straps, or holding onto a wide-brimmed hat in a horse-drawn cart.

But corporeal and real.

Named and known again.

12. THE CIRCUMSTANCES

It needed a proper discussion, Giles was right about that bit at least.

After his unsettled first term, Callum seemed to have pulled himself together and was talking about sticking it out at university and continuing with computer studies after all. Sue could still sometimes detect a tremble in his voice as their weekly telephone conversations were coming to an end, but this was as nothing compared to his raw pleading in some of their exchanges before the Christmas break. Grace, on the other hand, was controlled and composed, almost frighteningly so. Her record in the sixth form so far had been that of a model student and the waitressing job that now filled her remaining spare moments at weekends and during holidays meant that she was barely around the house to witness the turmoil that had engulfed her parents after her father's first mention of the job opening in Canada with that country's government.

'It's not a done deal,' Giles had said. 'But we ought to talk it through as a couple, as a family, in case'.

'You'd be determined to go anyway. What would be the point of talking? Really?' Sue had fired back, breaching a wall of resentment that had been building block by block through each of Giles' annual trips away to Africa and, latterly, India.

'It's just too much change at the moment,' she said. 'What with Callum and then Grace's 'A'-levels. And something has to happen with Mum. She can't carry on living down there on her own for much longer, however much she insists on it'.

'I'm sorry, yeah. Crap timing,' said Giles. 'Let's find a time to sit down and talk over options. Not on the hoof like we always do, but over a meal or a bottle of something'.

'It's too much, Giles. It really is,' said Sue. 'Now is not the time. I'm sorry'.

It would have been Giles' dream job and they should at least have had some sort of a conversation. Sue realised that soon after the closing date for applications. He had said nothing more at the time and she wondered later whether there had also been a resentment growing in him while she was preoccupied with the steps Callum and Grace were taking – his uneasy, hers purposeful – away from their parents and towards adult independence.

Then there was her mother's enflamed grief and distress after Les' death. Janet had informed her by telephone some three months or so after Les' death that Avril had taken herself along to the church that she used to attend at a time when the building was likely to be deserted and had apparently cried for over an hour until she finally felt she could cry no more.

'Poor Mum,' said Sue. 'Why ever did she feel she had to carry all this on her own? When I've visited she has been most subdued, going through the motions really, and not wanting to say anything more than was necessary. What a shame she couldn't tell anybody how she was feeling'.

She sensed Janet drawing breath or delaying a response. Only by a split second but enough to convey a nervousness or apprehension.

'I don't know whether I should tell you this -'

'Janet, we've been through all this. Years ago. We said we wouldn't have any more secrets about Mum and Dad.

You can tell me whatever it is. You can tell me. And you should tell me'.

'Well, she said that she was trying to be strong. Like Dad was. That he would want her to be. And she felt that she had let him down because she couldn't help herself and had cried and cried for all that time.'

'Oh, poor Mum. Poor woman,' said Sue. 'You are right to tell me, Janet. You are right'.

*

Although Avril now seemed less extreme in her emotional fluctuations, Sue remained alert to signs of deterioration in her condition even now, four years after her father's death. Attempts to forge a more open and trusting relationship with Janet sometimes seemed to be bearing fruit. But then at other times, and for no reasons that were obvious to Sue, these hopes felt as dead as heaps of windblown leaves in mid-winter. Sue relied during this period on her sister, who was able to make far more frequent weekend visits to Portsmouth, to keep her informed by telephone of their mother's state of mind.

'It's important, Janet,' said Sue. 'I wouldn't ask if it wasn't'.

'I don't think Trev's going to be very keen,' her sister replied. 'I know he doesn't want to get mixed – '

Why were telephone conversations with Janet still so difficult? She must be familiar enough with a phone. She must be using one all the time, working at the library.

'All he would have to do is pop into the library at Bridport when he's there and photocopy one page from the local paper. Assuming you've been able to track it down through your work. You said he often does jobs in the town'.

'All right,' Janet finally conceded. 'I'll ask him. But I'm not promising anything.'

'If I was closer, I wouldn't ask. I'd do it myself, obviously'.

The idea of a report of the inquest in a local paper of the time, had come from Giles. Sue could still be infuriated by the breadth of his knowledge.

If only he showed an interest, some enthusiasm, when I need him to. If only this could be some sort of joint project. If only. Instead, he seems immune to all the sadness of Letitia's tale. All right on the 'clever dick' dry facts, always able to show me up or make me feel stupid for not having thought of something he thinks is obvious. But never sympathetic, never feeling the need to help.

To help Letitia.

To help save her.

On top of the minimal interest shown by her sister and her husband, Sue felt frustrated by the lack of time she seemed able to muster to really apply herself to Letitia. Even with Grace now at university studying journalism and Callum working a small IT start-up, Sue seemed to have little spare time to devote solely to her own interests. Her children seemed to need her still, to help them decorate, furnish and generally settle into new accommodation, to be a recipient for their phone calls, especially Callum's, when they unburdened all the pressures and uncertainties they faced, and to mend their clothes that they sent her through the post. Her teaching job left her exhausted at weekends and for the first portion of any holiday. Giles' work trips to Canada and the US had become more frequent and, although these granted her time to herself, she found that her energy and focus seemed to evaporate, and she spent much of this time in a listless, almost depressed, state.

She knew that she needed to do something about the continuing pull on her attention exerted by her grandmother's life. Although she hated to admit it, Giles had been right. It had become an obsession, a slow but steady drain on her energies, an increasing barrier to relaxed and harmonious relations with a range of family members.

If Janet and Trev could only provide her with an inquest report she could, she knew, begin to bring all these ragged threads of loss, fear and alienation back into the comfortable weave of a settled, everyday life.

*

Bridport News 11th June 1927

BODY ON BURTON BEACH

WEYMOUTH WOMAN'S END IN THE SEA

CORONER'S ENQUIRY

"FOUND DROWNED" VERDICT RETURNED

NERVOUS BREAKDOWN: "TOO WICKED TO DIE"

As reported in last week's issue, a fully clothed woman's body was discovered by Swindon youths, Edward Cole and Bert Read, on Thursday (the 7th inst.) morning at the beach at Cleeve End, Burton Bradstock. This was identified the same night by Mr William James Roberts, of Weymouth, as that of his wife, Letitia, who had been missing from home since the previous Monday.

On Friday afternoon, sitting without a jury, Mr S. E. Hartley (Deputy Coroner for West Dorset) conducted an inquiry into the circumstances attending the death at the Old Coastguard Station, Burton Bradstock, to the garage of which the body had been removed after being brought from the water.

The deceased's husband, Mr Roberts, was the first witness called, and he deposed that he lived at 87, Newbiggin Road, Weymouth, and was employed as a greaser on one of the G.W.R. Co's cross-Channel boats. His wife was in her thirty eighth year, and they had a family of three children. On Monday, July 18th, he last saw his wife in the morning at ten minutes to eight. Normally, her state of health was very, very good.

The Coroner: Have you noticed any change lately? – Witness: She had a nervous breakdown last August'

The Coroner: Was there any occasion for that? – Witness: I think it was her age, sir.

IMAGINARY SHORTCOMINGS

The Coroner: Did she complain of anything? - Witness: She had no pain, but she had an idea that she was neglecting her children and her home, and that she had been squandering her money. This was purely imaginary.

The Coroner: As a matter of fact, you always found she looked after things well? – Witness: There has never been a better mother. We have always been happy in our married life; no-one could have been happier.

The Coroner: How long have you been married? – Witness: Seventeen years come the 21st December.

The Coroner: When she had this nervous breakdown did she consult anyone? – Witness: We had Dr Heath. She got over that breakdown all right, but three or four months ago she had another breakdown.

The Coroner: Did she seem depressed? – Witness: Only at times. One day she would talk about neglecting things, but the next she would buck up.

The Coroner: Did she ever talk about taking her life? – Witness: I have never heard her threaten to take her life. She said she was too wicked to die.

The Coroner: On Monday morning did you have breakfast with her? – Witness: On Monday morning she got up early, lit the copper and cooked the breakfast.

The Coroner: Unusually early? – Witness: Earlier than she usually does.

Continuing, witness said he had his breakfast with his wife and children, and just before he went out he went to kiss her goodbye, upon which she said "Do not come near me, let me buck up a bit more." Eventually, she kissed witness, and he went on to work. Witness' boat was laid up at the time, so his work did not take him away from Weymouth, his last trip being made a fortnight previously. When he left his wife she started her washing.

The Coroner: Who would be in the house with her? - Witness: The children until nearly ten to nine, when they go to school. The older boy came a little way with me and then went back again.

The Coroner: Had you been troubled about this? - Witness: I had been worried about it. I wanted her to get on.

Proceeding, witness said that his wife spoke to her next-door neighbour after nine o'clock. She did not seem different that morning than on any other morning. In fact, she was brighter the last time he saw her alive. He did not know she was missing until his boy came down to him at the boat just after twelve, upon hearing which he went straight home.

SEEN AT PRESTON

The Coroner: Do you think anyone saw her that morning? – Witness: One neighbour thought she came out without a hat on; but that could not have been because my wife took her hat. About eleven o'clock on Monday morning someone saw her by Overton Café at Preston. As she was walking he asked if she wanted a lift, to which she replied "No".

In reply to Sgt. G. King, who represented the police, witness said his wife would have to walk rather quickly to walk the two miles to Preston.

Edward Cole, a fitter employed by the G.W.R. works at Swindon, living at 32 Westcote Hill in that town, said he was cycling in West Dorset with a friend, and on Wednesday night they spent the night at Burton. On Thursday morning they went down to the beach to see if it was safe for bathing. However, the sea was too rough. Witness and his friend were walking east along the beach in the direction of Burton Hive. In course of their conversation he said to his friend: "I should not like to see the body of a dead man washed up now". Twenty yards further on they saw the body.

Witness described the position of the body, saying that it was lying face downwards and the waves were not quite reaching it. They went fairly close to it and saw that it was dead, so they went back to some men who were hauling sand on the beach and called them and they returned with them to the body. When they first saw the corpse it was about ten minutes to eleven.

John Welbury, of 28, Intake Lane, Burton, said that he was an ex-chief coastguard officer, and the last witness came to him on Thursday morning and said he had discovered a body on the beach. He, with some others, went along at once, reaching the body about 11.15. The tide at the time was flowing and washing around the corpse. He corroborated Cole's evidence as to the position of the body, adding that after finding artificial respiration was no use the police were summoned.

P.C. Wm. James, of Bridport, said he arrived at the scene at 12 p.m. He examined the corpse and saw it answered to the description of a woman who had been missing from her home at Weymouth since the 4th. A search of the pockets and clothes yielded nothing more than a set of false teeth. There was a cut just above the left eye, and a little blood came from the nose. Upon the body were a number of small bruises, which were about the same size as the pebbles on the beach. After the body had been removed to the Coastguard Station garage, his Superintendent sent for Dr. Armistead.

DOCTOR'S TESTIMONY

Dr Armistead, of Bridport, testified that he was sent for at about 7 p.m. on Thursday. He went to the Coastguard Station with P.C. James, and there examined the body.

The Coroner: Could you with certainty say what was the cause of death? – Witness: It was quite clearly caused by asphyxia from water entering the lungs. She was in the water over 48 hours, but he could not say further than that.

Referring to the constable's statement concerning the bruises, the doctor said the small bruises were more changes of death than actual bruises. The cut over the eye, in all probability, was made after death. With regard to the *blood from the nose, it was quite naturally caused, as the lung tended to force blood up through the nose after death. The blood was a bright red colour, which indicated aerating from the lung. Witness did not find it necessary to hold a post-mortem.*

Summing up, the Coroner said it was very difficult to say exactly what happened in that case. From what Mr Roberts had said, the condition of deceased's mind was such that in a moment of loss of control through that mental breakdown she might have taken her own life. He returned a verdict of "found drowned".

Mr Roberts: I never think she took her own life, sir.

The Coroner repeated that the evidence was not sufficiently definite to say anything else than "found drowned." He expressed his sympathy with Mr. Roberts and his family. Sgt King also expressed his sympathy.

The caretaker of the house, Mr S. Jones, handed his fee over to deceased's husband.

*

From a vague tale almost lost from memory to testimony, witness and detail. A precise location, the granularity of sand, the blood and bruising of soft tissue.

The published account though, let alone Avril's whispered recollections, would not tally. Not long in the water, her shoes still on and only slight bruising or the authoritative assertion by Dr Armistead that she had been in the water for over forty-eight hours? Sue felt compelled to pinpoint Letitia's history to exact times and places, as if somehow to finally secure the lineage.

Although in many ways it was an unattractive proposition, Sue thought that the most productive course of action now might be to take up a suggestion made by her friend Jenny, whose cousin, Maurice, worked at the hospital in Bradford as a pathologist. Jenny offered to take him a copy of the inquest report to see what reaction he might have.

'You've met him at my fiftieth, you know what he's like,' said Jenny. 'Not one to spare people's sensitivities but brilliant at what he does by all accounts. I know he would see this as just the sort of challenge he could get his teeth into. If you can cope with his manner, he will probably be able to tell you as much as anybody can'.

Sue did remember Maurice and it was not a fond recollection. He had been propped against a tall fridge freezer in Jenny's kitchen at the party, his spotted yellow bow tie straightaway a marker, a deliberate distancing act from her colleagues.

'In the end, it's not nurture but nature that wins out. You lot, you don't seem to give any credit to genetics. The Human Genome Project, you've heard of that? Well on its way to isolating the genes responsible for all these mental disorders, anti-social behaviour, all that stuff. Put paid to some of you lot it will, social workers and their ilk, in one foul swoop'.

Some, especially a bearded young man, were affronted, their indignation provoking raised eyebrows from Maurice, as if in mock surprise. Others were less easily goaded. One older woman, her long grey hair tied back with a ragged ribbon, looked at him with measured sadness.

'There seems to be a lot of anger here. It's as if it's being displaced onto those trying to help anybody less fortunate than themselves,' she said.

'Who me? I'm not angry, displaced or what not,' he replied, the kitchen lights reflecting from the thick lenses of his spectacles. 'I'm talking about science, that's all. Logic. Nothing to do with anger or what anybody feels'.

He stood more erect, his hair stretching further into the air like foliage from the top of some root vegetable. Sue could not quite shake the thought that, had Giles been with her at that party, he might well have ended up agreeing that Maurice did, in fact and whatever his manner, have a point.

Jenny reported back within a few days of taking the newspaper article.

'Maurice is very keen. He says there are some obvious contradictions, things that don't add up. He's already been onto wherever it is to get copies of the full inquest report but they don't go back that far. If you want to meet him, I'm sure he'll be keen to help you, bearing in mind what I said about his manner'.

Pomposity, aloofness, both tolerable, Sue thought, in the pursuit of essential pieces of the puzzle.

Jenny arranged an evening meeting with Maurice at his house and said she would accompany Sue, that it would give her the opportunity to catch up with her sister and the kids once she had assured herself that Maurice and Sue were hitting it off on the right note. The house was a bay-windowed detached building in one of the wealthier areas of the city and he met them at the front door wearing an old green cardigan that seemed to be falling from his shoulders and baggy, brown, corduroy trousers in even more danger of becoming adrift from their intended position. A honeysuckle bush, arched over the entrance to the porch, obscured much of the illumination from an outside lamp and in this half-light Maurice's ragged appearance gave him a welcoming and an almost affable demeanour.

'Ah, our visitors,' he beamed, haloed with dishevelled hair. 'The seekers after truth. Doreen!' he shouted back into the hallway. 'Come in, come in. Don't stand on ceremony'.

Doreen appeared, a child's cry from further back in the house accompanying her along the passageway.

'Jenny,' she smiled. 'Sorry, we're in hell of a state, but come in. Those two're about to murder each other, if I don't get to them first. Is this your friend?'

After introductions and because the sound of squabbling from behind the frosted kitchen door was escalating, Maurice and Sue were quickly ushered into the large front lounge so that Doreen could lead Jenny back to the kitchen.

'Kids, guess who's here? It's Auntie Jenny'.

Maurice offered Sue a chair after quickly clearing from it a newspaper and piles of giant Lego and Duplo bricks. He was noticeably less assured without the presence of Jenny.

'Excuse the chaos. Perch yourself where you can. Like a ruddy battlefield in here', he muttered, clearing himself a space on the matching dark green leatherette sofa. 'Up to your neck in muck and bullets, most days'.

'Thank you so much for seeing me,' Sue started, although Maurice was still facing away from her. In fact, he seemed to be reading an article on the front page of the local free paper he had been tidying away. 'I'm hoping you might be able to clear up some of these loose ends in this grandmother business for me. It's incredibly good of you'

'You can't trust the newspaper, you know. Print anything. The inquest would just be tidying up matters, leaving things in good order. After they'd made sure nobody'd done her in, that is. Police would have checked family and friends, had a good look at the husband, that sort of thing'.

Grandad!

The shock of the unthinkable, the un-thought, must have been apparent on Sue's face.

'Wouldn't have been the first time! Who was it again, paternal or maternal grandmother?

'My dad's mum. Letitia she was called. She died in 1927. I am really grateful to you for giving up your time like this'.

'Perfectly okay. Tell me what you want to know. How you think I might be able to help you?'

Sue realised, as he did it again, that his deepening frown might reflect shyness or concentration rather than irritation. But she was not completely reassured.

'I'm trying to pin down my grandmother's last movements. It would be really useful if I could be surer about the amount of time she was in the sea. The newspaper reports are a bit contradictory. I'd be really keen to know if, from what you've seen, it's possible to say whether it could have been just hours, minutes even I suppose, or could it have been up to three or four days?'

'Hmm. Well, first thing to decide is how she got in there, was it an accident or could there have been any foul play, anything out of the ordinary? In other words, if it wasn't an accident, did she die by her own hand or that of somebody else? Doesn't sound like an accident, I've been to that bit of the coast, doesn't have cliffs or rocky bits, does it? Hard to fall in accidentally off a gently sloping beach'.

'Yes, although if you do go in somehow, it's not easy to get back out again. The undertow along Chesil Beach is notorious. At least I was brought up to think that'.

'Hardly relevant to the reason why she was in there in the first place though, is it? Wouldn't have been going for an early morning dip draped in all her finery'.

It was annoyance after all and, rather than focusing on Letitia and garnering snippets of information that could anchor or turn her story one way or another, Sue found herself trying to avoid foolish and unconsidered comments.

…one day she would talk about neglecting things

'Seems pretty likely from the social reports that it was suicide'.

… the next she would buck up.

'Why does the length of time matter to you? One way or another, she ended up stone cold dead. And of her own volition almost certainly'.

Too wicked to die

'It would just help me make sense of her and of the ripples that must have gone right through my family afterwards. Perhaps it won't but I feel I've got to try'.

He leaned slightly further to his side, an all-out slump held in check.

'Okay, bodies in water float face down. Head hangs down further. Almost always. So, any abrasions much more likely on prominent points of the face, nose, chin, etcetera. Anterior trunk and extremities as well'.

'There was something about a cut above her eye!'

'Yes, yes,' he straightened up again, his manner more assured as if Sue were his sole student in their own private auditorium. 'Doesn't tell you how long it's been in though, does it? Usually sink, bodies. Air in clothes can keep them up for a while though, specific gravity and all that, pretty similar for bodies and water'.

'So, she hadn't been in for long then, if she was washed up out of the water when they found her?'

The displeasure in his face was surely real this time, questions were clearly for later. The delivery was not to be thrown by interjections, whether pertinent or intemperate.

'Unlikely. Usually sink, I said. Then can drift along the sea bed, bashing into any rocks or obstructions. It's putrefaction, associated gasses, brings them back up eventually. Process slower in water than air and slower again in salt water. Would expect to be seeing a bit of action after a day or two at that time of year though'.

'Why, at that time of year?'

'Temperature. Basic biology. Decay, putrefaction, speed up in summer'.

'Oh yes, of course'.

Sue felt she was wasting his time and that her quest was losing momentum. But he had an expertise she would not easily find elsewhere.

'So, if she was found back up on the beach, it's likely that she had been in the water for a day or two, is it, that she'd risen back up again due to – to gases?'

There was a knock followed by Jenny's head appearing from around the slowly opening the door. When she spoke she whispered with surgery waiting room decorum.

'Just wondering how you're getting on? I won't disturb you if you're deep in conversation'.

'We're doing fine, Maurice is being very – '

'Not telling her what she wants to know though, am I? Can't put her mind at rest definitely one way or the other, you see'.

'Maurice, you've been very helpful and I'm grateful. I think what I'm taking away is that … um … she'd probably been in the water for a day or two. More likely than not'.

'Of course, what might have clinched it was fleas or lice'.

'Fleas or lice! Whatever would – ?

'Steady on, steady on. A good tie-breaker, fleas and lice. Fleas can only survive on a submerged body for twenty-four hours at most, but lice can struggle on, determined little beggars, for another day or so. Just occasionally, that differential proves crucial. Not uncommon either at that time, fleas and lice on people of that social class'.

13. CLEEVE END

'Janet? Whatever are you doing bothering *Janet* with all this?'

'I'm not *bothering* her, Mum. I'm just – she was very interested. Hang on, let me just get parked, then we can go inside and chat properly'.

Sue had decided to visit her mother in Portsmouth on her way to Dorset to seek out Cleeve End, the section of beach where her grandmother had been found. She was exaggerating, lying really, when she described Janet as 'very interested' but her sister had at least agreed to meet her and help locate the exact spot.

'Has Janet said she will put you up?' asked Avril, still blocking Sue's way as she tried to extricate herself from the driver's seat. 'Has Trevor agreed? Whatever makes you think they want to get involved with all this?'

Where had this antagonism sprung so instantaneously from?

'Janet has offered to put me up. And Trevor is fine – Oh, come on mother, let's go inside and – let's just take it easy'.

When they were both seated in Avril's living room, the conversation steered towards safer ground.

'And how are those two children getting on?' asked Avril, seating herself on a settee with a cream coloured cover splattered with huge red roses. 'I say children, but they're not really. They're grown up, aren't they? How are they, anyway?'

Sue looked at her mother from her seat in a matching high-backed chair. She had spent so much time talking with both her parents in this room that her father seemed somehow to hover in the half-light and sweep their conversation on over its awkward cracks and silences.

'They're both doing fine,' said Sue. 'Callum seems settled into his job. He's sharing a flat with some of his mates from university'.

'What does he do about meals?' asked Avril. 'Can he get something at his work mid-days?'

'He's old enough to cook for himself now, Mum,' said Sue. 'I'm not going to fuss around checking up on him.'

'Well, as long as he's getting enough to eat.'

'He must be. He was still alive the last time I looked'.

'Susan! What a terrible thing to say!'

Sue realised that she needed to break out of the cycles of criticism and irritation that she and her mother seemed to fall so easily into.

'Let's think about getting some tea, shall we?' she said. 'I wasn't sure what you would have in, so I grabbed a few things from my fridge before I set off this morning'.

'Oh, I don't keep a lot in these days,' said Avril. 'I just pop round the little supermarket if I need something. That does me'.

Then as Sue wondered once again about her mother's nutritional intake, Avril added

'They're Pakistanis but they're very nice'.

'Mother!'

'What?'

'Oh – oh, come on. Let's get on with something to eat, shall we?'

'Yes, let's have bacon and egg or something,' said Avril. 'I'm only a plain cook. I don't do anything fancy. As long as its tasty. That's the main thing'.

In the kitchen, Sue and Avril fumbled with frying pans, manoeuvring awkwardly around each other in the gloom as the afternoon light outside faded. Neither realised the need to switch on the light until Susan found herself unable to read the 'Use by' date on the egg box.

When they had eaten and returned to the sitting room, Sue suggested that they consulted the Radio Times to find a film or other programme that they could both enjoy. But before this could happen, Avril has returned to their earlier conversation.

'What do you want to go stirring all this up for now anyway?' she asked. 'It was all such a long time ago. You're not going to bring her back, you know'.

And Susan realised there and then that, despite what her mother, sister and husband had all implied at various times, she was not the only family member unable to let this matter drop.

'I'm not trying to stir things up. I know it's really sensitive for people. But they're my relations too, you know. And Janet's. Not as close to me obviously as to you and Dad, but it's still important to know who you're descended from'.

'Why *ever* do you need to know that?' Animation was returning to Avril's voice. 'We just had to get on with it as best we could'.

'Yes I know and it must have been awful. Absolutely awful. I just feel – I mean, we all want to know where we've come from if we possibly can. With kids nowadays, who've been adopted or lost their parents or whatever, they make books with them, anything they can find – photos of their family, their parents, letters, anything from their previous life, so they have a record. It's what people need. We all do'

'Those *poor* little beggars,' she said with her voice stretching and falling around a crescendo in those few short words. 'Do you remember that girl in your class, Linda?' she added, leaning forward and speaking in a tone that suggested irritation.

'They sent her away to Barnardos, that poor little beggar'.

'Yes, I remember her'.

'Do you *remember* her?' she asked again.

'Yes, I do. It's better sometimes to talk about difficult things, however awful they were or are. You certainly like to talk about things sometimes, don't you? You often tell wonderful stories about members of your family and your life when you were younger. I have strong memories – good ones – of all those tales and I know my kids – your grandchildren – they have too. It's important for people.

'You could always talk, Susan. I never had any worries about you. I knew you would always be able to push your barrow'.

'I've probably learned it from you if that's the case. I like being able to talk with people. It's one of life's pleasures'.

'I always knew you'd be all right. When you were a little girl you always had a garden full of kids round, Dad and I counted twenty-one out there one day. You were there telling them all what to do. We even had that Sarah Cheeseman with her little brother trailing up our stairs at Purbeck Road one Sunday morning early when we were all still in bed, calling out 'Susan, Susan!' We never locked our door in those days. Dad used to say that if burglars found anything he'd go halves with them'.

217

In no time, Letitia had become forgotten, an historical irrelevance. Unless Sue held on to her, grabbed at her coat or waded into the surf after her, she and her mother would be submerged again by the swim of stories from their Weymouth home, the cavalcade of neighbours and the ragged tribes of children.

They both sat in silence.

'Life can be bloody tough sometimes, Susan,' Avril said finally, her voice small and fragile.

'I know. It can be terribly tough sometimes. And not fair'.

'You don't know the half of it. I lost my mother too, you know'.

'Oh Mum, Mum. I know you lost your mother. I know that. And I would like to know more. It's very, very difficult and terribly sad, but it must be better to talk about it a bit'.

Letitia, it seemed, was losing, had probably already lost, some competition with Sue's other grandmother.

'What was she called, your Mum?' asked Sue. 'I don't even know that. Dad's Mum was Letitia, that's one thing I have found out about her'.

'Letitia? You don't hear that name very often these days. My mother was Ethel, that's another old name'.

'You all lived up on Fredericks Street, just above the harbour, didn't you? That's where you grew up, isn't it?'

'Yes, yes, but we had to get out of there. In the blitz. I can see it now. We were walking along the harbour side on Westway Road up past the gasometer. Carrying everything we could. I had our canary in a cage and Joyce had the dog, Bruno, on a lead. It was a what-do-you-call-them, a boxer dog, frothing at the mouth, going crazy. Barking. It was pulling our Joyce about, she could hardly hold him'.

218

Sue too had herself walked along that harbour wall many times in her childhood but she had never before heard about this particular night. And just as so often in her childhood, she was pulled into her mother's telling of a story, the setting grittily familiar, the happenings unimaginably fantastical.

'You've never told me this before. I've never heard about any of this. Where were you all going? Did you have somewhere to go or what?'

'Our Aunt Mabel's. She was very good to us, to put us all up when we just arrived there on her doorstep that night, loaded up with everything we could carry and that dog going mad'.

'Had you been bombed out then?'

'Not us. But five doors down were. There was this almighty banging and crashing. We were all in bed, it frightened the life out of me. Crashing and banging. Our Dad went running out to see what the devil was going on and came back in saying we all had to get dressed and grab everything we could. Our Dad was very strict about it. 'Get up, get dressed'. Do you remember him, our Dad?'

'Yes, of course. Did you go back eventually or what? What happened?'

'Not that night. There were fire engines, police, civil defence, everybody trying to put the fires out. It was like the whole road was going up in flames. They'd hit just down the street from us. Trying to get Portland Harbour, see. Joyce and I were looking back at it across the harbour, Weymouth harbour that is, with all those little boats and the Channel Islands paddle steamer. You could see the fire for miles. We thought ours must be done for and our Dad told us to keep walking and not to keep stopping. But that dog

219

was running all over the place, pulling at our Joyce, backwards and forwards. Great big whooshes of red and orange shooting up out of the smoke and yellow flames. And explosions. The gas mains going up, see?'

'Gosh. It must have been absolutely – I can't – was your house destroyed?'

'We got off pretty lightly. They managed to get the fire under control before it got to ours. But the three houses next to ours, they were all gone, burned to the ground. We couldn't go back. Well, we did for a bit afterwards but we had to keep looking at all that rubble every day. Every time we went out the front door. My Mum, it didn't do her any good at all. She had problems with her nerves anyway. That made it a hundred times worse'.

When Sue was a little girl, Avril's vivid accounts had held her in their grip as intensely as any cinema screen. Technicolour panoramas created just for her, living on beyond the telling. Filling the canvas of her imagination.

'Mum, as we're talking about your mother, Ethel, I'm realising that I've never seen a photograph of her? Don't you have any of her?'

'No, your Dad burned the lot. He burned all my photographs'.

'He did *what*? That's -'

'He was trying to help. He was doing what he thought was for the best'.

'What do you mean 'for the best'? When was this? I've never heard of anybody -'

'It was when I wasn't very well. Around the time we were moving here from Weymouth. He did it because he was concerned about me. He was a good man, your dad. He was ever so good to me'.

Sue tried to imagine her father in their Purbeck Road back garden standing beside a fire with shoe boxes or envelopes full of photos and perhaps a spade or fork. Would he have been grimly business-like or cheerful and whistling?

'Yes, he was but nobody has the right to destroy somebody's photographs. You just don't. I can't imagine anybody even considering it'.

'He did it because he thought it would help me pick myself up. I was getting in a bit of a state about things and he was worried about me'.

'But that still doesn't excuse – '

'Don't go on about things, Susan. It's past now'.

'Okay, but – well I just can't imagine how I would feel if I lost my photographs, if somebody destroyed them, whatever the reason. I don't think I could ever forgive somebody for that'.

'You've got to have a bit of give and take in this life, Susan. You can get a bit full of yourself at times'.

'For God's sake. I'm angry on your behalf – because I think it's such a wrong thing to do'.

'I don't need you to be angry on my behalf. Your Dad and me we understood each other. He was very good to me'.

'Okay, okay, I'm sorry. But I just think photographs are so important. It means that I don't have the chance to see her and nor will my kids or any later generations'.

'Well, why ever would *they* want to see them?'

'Oh hell!' Sue felt they were right back where they had started. 'I think we've both probably had enough questions for one day. But have you really not got any photographs at all?'

'Nope, he burned the lot. He was doing it to help me get better, so I didn't just sit there moping and getting in a worse and worse state. Ask me another question, I'll try to answer it for you'.

'Okay. Mum, but let's try not to go getting ourselves worked up about it. Both of us. Shall we?''

'All right, let's do that. Go on, ask away'.

'Okay, well just tell me a bit more about your mother, tell me what she was like'.

'She was a very nervy woman. I knew not to get on the wrong side of her. She was very strict. Not like our Dad, he was soft, especially with me when I was little. I was the first grandchild, see, and proper *spoilt*. If I wanted anything and I couldn't have it, I'd just go on and on about it until I got it'

*

Janet was already waiting in the empty car park the next morning as Sue pulled in beside her, twenty minutes or so late. The adjoining caravan park was now a deserted site, its empty holiday vehicles metallic shells like beetles and grubs sequestered into the damp ground.

'You took your time then,' said Janet by way of greeting.

Sue began to explain that she had left in good time. The drive from their mother's bungalow in Portsmouth had been unexpectedly delayed by road repairs. And then she wondered why she was gabbling, filling their meeting with meaningless details.

'*How about 'Hello' or 'How was the drive?' instead of a complaint,*' she thought.

'Shall we get on with it then?' she said instead, exercising a two-handed grip on the flapping map and peering into the distance. 'It says it's about half a mile along here. There's something about a coastguard station but I think this symbol means it's just a ruin', she added. 'Oh, and before I forget, thank you so much, and Trev as well, for getting that inquest report. It was amazing'.

They were soon coated by a sheen of drizzle as they walked the hundred yards or so over cropped grass to the beach. Sue's anorak, jeans and trainers provided reasonable protection from the deteriorating weather but Janet's camel coat, skirt and sensible shoes seemed to Sue remarkably inappropriate for the conditions.

'And Janet's the one who lives here by the sea,' she thought.

'It's wet,' said Janet, placing each foot carefully onto the loamy, aerated sand.

They plodded southwards, the sea hardened by winter on one side and the weathered grassy bank, too low and wind-battered to rise into a cliff on the other. The continuous line of the shore faded into mist in both directions.

Was this Cleeve End, and no longer marked on maps?

Sue had imagined rocks or some form of indentation, a landmark worthy of naming, some feature that could be deemed to have 'ended'.

Edward Cole and Bert Read would find no shells here. Just rich, wet sand. And why haul sand, whatever that involved, so far from any track?

'This must be about it,' said Sue finally, droplets of spray hanging from her eyebrows and the wisps of hair that had escaped her hood.

Janet had tied a scarf across her head and its loose ends flicked in the little bursts of wind, flapping against her cheeks and chin. Whereas Sue felt invigorated by this elemental buffeting, her younger sister was clearly bedraggled and dejected.

'There's nothing here,' said Sue.

'What were you expecting?' asked Janet, lifting her gaze from the ground and pulling in her coat collar around her neck.

'I don't know. Some feature. A few rocks. An old post or a groyne. Anything. Just something to mark the spot'.

Janet shuddered. She wriggled her upper body, then her legs and finally made little stamping movements with her feet as if the chill had passed all the way down through her body. But she said nothing.

'I would have liked an image to take away in my head,' said Sue. 'To know there was something definite. Something that she would also have seen – '

'Come on. Let's go,' said Janet. 'We can't do anything standing here'.

Sue was barely aware of her sister's discomfort. Her usual curiosity about her family's feelings had somehow been abandoned in the trudge along this monotonous stretch of coast.

Why had her grandmother – their grandmother – walked into the sea here?

Why not some cove, some sharp-edged cliff top, some rocky camouflage?'

She became oblivious to Janet's presence and instead lost to images of a deeply churning sea seizing up a lifeless figure, gliding with it, soaring and tumbling to the sea bottom and way out to beyond the horizon.

To the left or the right, the aspect was the same. Nothing to distinguish the damp and mist in the direction of distant Portland from that blanketing the small port of West Bay.

No detail or distinctive perspective from which to fashion even the slightest abiding commemoration for Letitia.

They drove in convoy back to West Bay and found a small cafe open out of season. The door rattled as it opened, a bell tinkled, and the two sisters stepped into a dimly lit room to find themselves the only customers. They ordered drinks and chose a table furthest from the proprietor. Each scrape of their plastic chairs echoed in the empty room, the slow releases of steam from the coffee-making apparatus finally culminating in a hissing that masked their muttered ruminations.

'Not very salubrious,' mumbled Janet.

'It'll do,' replied Sue. 'What did you make of the beach back there – as a place to – you know?'

'Not much really. It's just what happened a long time ago,' said Janet, stretching and turning her neck a little as if to relieve some slight ache. 'It's over and done with anyway. Nothing we can do about it.'

'But don't you – ' began Sue, rather intensely, just as the café owner stepped towards them with their coffees.

'Take the chill off you a bit, ladies,' he said, placing the two cups onto the table.

If he was hoping that some conversation with these two customers might break the tedium of a slack afternoon, Sue's intense concentration on her teaspoon and her barely audible 'thank you', let alone the nervous squeak in Janet's 'it's lovely thank you', would soon have dispelled any such notion.

'It doesn't make sense when I think about it,' whispered Sue, when the owner had retreated behind his bar. 'I've always thought she threw herself off the Nothe in Weymouth, I remember Mum telling me'.

'She never told me that,' replied Janet. 'Perhaps you've got it wrong'.

'No, she did. To the south of Weymouth you've got Portland blocking the way. Never mind the actual distance involved – what, thirty miles or more – the currents off the east side of Portland are notorious. Dad used to scare me half to death when we were kids, talking about The Race, where seven tides met. It used to feel like certain death, the notion of being anywhere near it. Even just looking in that direction made me feel queasy'.

'I remember going out to Portland with Dad when we were little,' said Janet.

'She must have gone into the sea over this side of Portland. A body couldn't go all that way round,' Sue continued. 'She must have, but how did she get here?' She couldn't have walked all this way from Weymouth. It would take days, where would you sleep at nights?'

Sue paused and realised that she was experiencing – *what? A chill? Or a guilty thrill from the intellectual challenge? Like a crossword with a set of cryptic clues?*

Janet blew the froth across the top of her coffee. Sue became aware for the first time of the tinny sound of the proprietor's radio, its wandering focus as some corny pop song slowly dissolved into a vague, buzzing interference.

I never really knew first-hand what Dad thought. I just assumed that Mum's account was correct. He never mentioned his own mother, but I never had the sense of melancholy haunting him. No wistful lapses as far as I could see.

Sue wondered why she had never sat down quietly with him and found a way to bring the subject up in a confident and calm manner. What had prevented that from happening? Whatever it was, it was strong and had been stripped of any name. He might, she thought, staring intensely now into the catastrophic past, he might have loved the opportunity to spill it all out. If only she could have found a way to start that conversation ten minutes or quarter of an hour into it. With the ice already broken somehow. The permafrost already broken.

'I don't know if it's any use,' said Janet, intruding into Sue's huge, hypnotic absence. 'But Trev did a shower conversion for a chap who used to be the harbour master. Maybe he could tell you all about tides and the weather and that sort of thing'.

The more Sue thought about their father and grandmother, especially here at the actual scene of the tragedy, the less interested she became in the mysterious mechanics and the geography of the drowning. The more instead she wished to give voice to the unspoken, acknowledgement to the anonymous.

But Sue did recognise that Janet's suggestion was the first real sign that she might, after all, be willing to engage with her in this quest.

'Yes, we could follow up records and tides,' she said. 'Look into whether the body could have drifted. Do you remember standing there with Dad at the Portland end of Chesil Beach in winter, watching a battered piece of timber being thrown up onto the pebbles by the sea and then pulled back? Over and over. If you looked away for a while, then looked back, it would have moved further along the beach, on some steady journey to who knows where. Longshore drift they told us it was called in Geography, back at school. But, it makes you wonder, where and why would it finally come to rest. A body, that is'.

Reverie quickly captured Sue again as she spoke. Perhaps Letitia hadn't walked for days through the bird song and nettles of West Dorset lanes. How could she, in her dark check coat, her brown shoes and light stockings, muttering among the cow parsley, unsteady and demented in the rutted byways? Perhaps she had only walked from the Nothe, where their other grandmother had apparently seen her, agitated and pacing, out to the nearest point of access to West Bay? If she had climbed the shingle bank of Chesil and entered the sea there, could she then have bounced and buffeted face down in the foam, all the way, some fifteen miles or more, progressing steadily by night, unobserved during the long, lonely orbit of day, all the way to Cleeve End?

'I don't like to think of a body in the sea there like that,' said Janet, twisting and tearing a sachet of brown sugar so that the contents spilled between her fingers. 'And anyway, Trev says it was a very long time ago and you should – you shouldn't be – '

'Yes, but what do *you* think?' interrupted Sue, dipping her head in an attempt to regain Janet's gaze. 'She was a woman – like us – and she is being written out of history. You can't be – well, *I'm* not happy to let that just happen'.

'It's not going to do Mum any good dredging all this up now. And Dad – well, it can't affect him any more. That's what Trev thinks anyway', replied Janet, lifting her head, momentarily making eye contact and revealing a slight tremor in her lower lip. 'And I do too, really,' she added meekly.

'Everything all right, ladies?' shouted the owner. 'Any top-ups before I start tidying up?'

All is sadly not all right. For a moment it might have been but it's not, thought Sue as Janet hastily shouted back that everything was 'very nice, thank you'.

The afternoon light had failed, their breath and the coffee machine's excess steam had condensed on the inside of the windows. The cold air outside was sliding, curious and wet, across the panes. The owner was straightening already orderly chairs, their springy legs juddering against the floor. Sue and Janet paid for their drinks and left.

*

Setting off that late meant that she would be lucky to arrive home before midnight and that the exhaustion accumulated along the conduit of motorways all the way up through England would still be firmly lodged in her body the following morning. There were strangers all around her also hurtling forwards and she was forced to smooth her way between the lanes and choreograph safe cruising distances. But at the same time, another Sue was swerving out of control across the surface of slippery scenarios, tumbling over topographies and crashing winded and dizzy against the barriers and blockades of dead end speculations and conjectures.

What had Letitia been doing at Preston? Deeply distressed and hurrying off in random directions? Preston was in the opposite direction to the Nothe. If her other grandmother, Avril's mother, had seen her there, she must have criss-crossed the town, a seaside resort in mid-summer, at least once. Hadn't anybody else noticed her agitation, or was one witness account at the inquest sufficient? Perhaps the draw of the sea, of a swallowing and a final expurgation, grew as she passed back and forth, the lure of Chesil Beach beyond Ferrybridge, its unpopulated wastes, sloughing off unsettled onlookers, leaving behind in one huge, dismissible huddle the concerned, the frightened and the disapproving? How would she and her husband have known a car owner? Cars were not plentiful even in Sue's upbringing. Avril and Les had owned one only briefly in the early 1950s.

Taunton. Why did the inquest seem so bothered about whether she had left the house with or without her hat? Was this, in fact, likely confirmation of her intention to be gone for some time or of some disregard for propriety that was also indicative of a troubled state of mind? Perhaps, Sue thought, she needed to know more about the protocols of hat wearing among women, by social class, in the late 1920s? And the demographics of car ownership. Why were her false teeth in her pocket? Would Sue do that, take them out as some form of observation or precaution, if she possessed some and also intended to drown herself? How common was the wearing of false teeth at that time, long before the National Health Service, and by the wife of a greaser on a Channel Islands boat? And what exactly did a greaser do – greasing obviously, but greasing what and was there enough of it to be done and in a skilled enough fashion to warrant it being designated a full-time occupation?

The First Severn Crossing. The M4 intersection. Why had Janet not spared her this drive by offering her a bed for the night? Why had Sue not asked outright. They were sisters after all. Was it Trevor? Did he disapprove of Sue? Or were there just so few touching points between their respective worlds that any conversation felt expeditionary in nature, needing preparation and caution? The long trudge, the threatening environment. The uncertainty of ever reaching the safety of a destination.

Tewkesbury. The M50 slipping in to the side. Kidderminster. Had Letitia been in the sea for days or not? This still seemed to be crucial. One report said she could only have been in the water for a short time because her shoes were still on. Another, a medical opinion – and Sue could not now remember where she had read this one – said a minimum of forty-eight hours. Then there was the report of very minor bruising caused most probably by impact with the beach and a cut above her left eye. All this on a day when Bert Read and Edward Cole judged the sea to be far too rough for swimming.

Solihull. The NEC. Tamworth Services. The coffee was essential. As thick, black and viscous as it could be. Her questions continued to bubble up to the surface, great fountains of ignorance unanswered and instantly dispersing into the air. How much do bodies inflate in water? If it's a noticeable amount, who would be trying mouth-to mouth artificial respiration and not mentioning the puffed-up cheeks, the eyeballs bulging ready to pop, the swelling body straining at tight, restricting clothes? Maurice had not made much of this aspect despite his seeming enthusiasm for all matters biological. Sue reprimanded herself for not remaining more alert with him and becoming too distracted by his harsh and empty jollity. Did she need to find out much more about the decomposition of drowned and waterlogged corpses? Could she possibly face Maurice again?

Sliding onto the M1 just below Derby, pointing due north at last. What did they mean by 'middle class in appearance' – a greaser's wife? Had she worn her best clothes, some ghastly sense of occasion penetrating even the compulsion that drove her one last time from her house? And a coat in

July, was that how women dressed then? Perhaps the weather records, they would surely exist, would give some sense of it – sixty degrees, seventy, seventy-five? And an overcoat?

Not yet at the M62. Past midnight. Three or four days of walking or three or four days in the sea? That was the crunch. Either way the clothes are wrong, blistered feet, brambled stockings and the musty weight of a checked coat. Where would she have slept, obtained food? Witnesses, there would have been farm workers or cottage dwellers, alerted by the stranger, by the sense of disarray. Shoes still on in the sea, the slightest of injuries to her face after striking and scraping along the shingle, three or four days in, out and to the side, foot by foot by yard by mile. In, out and to the side.

Turning at last towards Ilkley. 'Nervous breakdown', when was that phrase first coined, when its common usage? Sue had somehow assumed it entered the collective discourse in the 1950s, imported from the United Sates along with Elvis Presley and I Love Lucy, but it was obviously much earlier. 'There had never been a happier marriage'. Whose voice could possibly contradict or amend the ledger? 'Too wicked to die'. Had this formulation sprung directly from the narrowing tunnel of Letitia's imagination or was it stock fare from the penny dreadfuls of the time? It was new to Sue and some sub editor in 1927 had obviously savoured it too. Why did she feel she had been neglecting her children and squandering William's money? Had anybody given her cause, either maliciously intended or innocently misinterpreted, for such a belief? Was there a deeper shame? Could she possibly have had an affair? A woman with three children in a cramped terraced house, up early to prepare breakfasts, twisted mounds of laundry dragged down the stairs to the scullery, children home for lunch, her husband too? Where in that schedule could there be slits of opportunity, away from the web of neighbourly observations? But if he did exist, could he possibly have been a car owner?

Her street. She needed to check the map again to see what roads and lanes one would actually take from Weymouth to Burton Bradstock ... How busy would the coastline have been at that time? ... Would those two young cyclists have been the first visitors to that beach at nearly eleven o'clock in the morning mid-week in July? ... And just how popular was holiday-making in South Dorset at that time?

Her driveway. Were inquests in those days really motivated to establish painstakingly an incontrovertible truth, or was a plausible narrative, kindly towards the survivors and orderly in its interpretations, the only professional requirement?

Her own front door at last. After Avril's erratic and unreliable recollections, the reports from the Bridport News had seemed like secure accounts, preserved and solid, immune to erosion over the decades ..... And yet, as questions multiplied like spores upon the bodies of other questions, inconsistencies and contradictions had seeped up through the newsprint, staining its accuracy and leeching away its authority ..... If she could bear to do so, how would Sue approach the ex-harbour master? Not straight out with it, obviously ..... Any casual enquiry about floating corpses, longshore drift, tides and tempests, would have to be set in context with reassurances about her motives ..... Where was the précis, the opening gambit, the means of avoiding unravelling the whole set of disconnected threads and loose ends? There was no reason to believe he would be any more relaxed than Maurice, any more sympathetic to the hollowed-out hope suffusing Letitia's last days back in a previous century ..... Sue couldn't contemplate the beginnings of a telephone conversation, nor imagine how she might construct the opening paragraphs of a letter.

In the swirling litter of unanswered questions, the thundering miles still at her back and even now in her exhausted, stationary state somehow seeming to demand extremes of concentration, she closed the front door behind her as quietly as she could.

14. A SEAT UP BY THE DRIVER

'I'm not going there again. It used to be lovely, your Dad and me, we had some *lovely* holidays there. And it was all right for a few times after he died. I went on my own with them and they all made a bit of a fuss of me. I think I was everybody's favourite, cranky grandmother'.

'I can see you in that role'.

'But that last time, it spoilt it all. There were young men out in the corridor clowning about, four o'clock in the morning it was, pulling their trousers down and showing off their backsides. It was drink, you see, they didn't mind that I was there and saw everything that was going on, didn't make any difference at all'.

'Mum, that sounds horrible. There's an awful lot of it goes on these days by all accounts. The British are notorious for it. You ought to think about going on holiday with the Fellowship or something designed specifically for older people. You'd stay in more suitable places'.

'Oh, I wouldn't want to be with a lot of old people, I'm a more lively sort of person. Anyway, if I need anything, I just pretend I'm a bit mad and they all rally round'.

'Hmm. The trouble with going on ordinary trips is you then have to take your chances and this could all happen again'.

'Oh. I don't want any more of that sort of thing'.

'Why don't you want to go on holiday with Dilys?'

'She doesn't want to go on holiday. She's got her daughter over there all the time'.

'Mum, that's not what I've heard, I've heard that she very much wanted to go on holiday with you'.

'No, she doesn't want to. Whoever told you that?'

'Mum, I've heard that you were all set up to go, the two of you, and that you pulled out at the last moment'.

'Where have you got that story from? Who's been telling you all that?'

'Never mind where I've heard it for now, you'd booked Spain I heard and even paid a deposit'.

'Where are you getting all this from? Don't tell me off, Susan. You're like a teacher, I can't help it'.

'Mum, you can't let your friends down like that. You'd paid a deposit and then you let Dilys down. It was even worse than that, I heard'.

'What have you heard?'

'Okay, I heard that you planned to go down the town to pay the deposit and when Dilys came over for you so that you could both catch the bus together you told her that you would meet her down there because you had some other things to do first'.

'Susan, you mustn't go saying these – '

'And then you didn't turn up, you just let her wait there on her own. She must have felt really – she lost her deposit because of that'.

'Stop telling me off, I've been through a lot, you know. I'm doing my best. I lost my deposit too. It's not easy being on your own, you know'.

'Mum, you drive me mad at times. You just won't let anybody help you. Anything I try, well sometimes it feels as if you go out of your way to sabotage it. You're your own worst enemy a lot of the time'.

'Your dad used to say it was because I didn't think logically. He used to say that if I'd learned Latin that would have helped. He had a good brain on him, your Dad, and he always thought that Latin would have helped me'.

'I don't think it's really got anything to do with – '

'People try to take you over, do you find that? They want you to do this and that and before you know it they've taken you over'.

'I don't really find that, no. I think I know what you're getting at but friends are a good thing, they make life worth –'

'Oh, you always had friends, even when you were a little –'

'Mum! Let's finish this conversation about holidays. We're trying to sort out what –'

'Oh, I don't think I shall go on any more holidays for a while. I used to love them but I've gone off them a bit. The last time I went down there to book one I told the girl that I always sat up in the front seat on the coach to the airport, that one on its own up by the driver. She told me it was booked but I could see on that computer of hers that it wasn't. I made a fuss but she was proper obstinate and said I couldn't sit there. So that's that as far as I am concerned. They can like it or lump it'.

*

'I'm glad I've got back into my history classes, I've always liked that but I couldn't go after your dad died. We're doing Napoleon at the moment and I love that. We did the canals before and I didn't find that so interesting'.

'That's really great. Tell me about Napoleon, why do you like that subject so much?'

'Well, it's interesting, that's why. He was a very kind boy, Napoleon, when he was little but he was fiery. So, he

237

was sent away to a school in France when he was nine and he couldn't speak the language'.

'Why, where was he from then?'

'He was from Corsica, of course. Don't you know that? He had to go away to this school where he had to work very hard to try to catch up with all the other children. And he used to wear these really itchy clothes and he had to do all this hard work like scrubbing the floors'.

'I didn't know all this, you have been busy Mum'.

'Oh I like it, I can't stop reading about it sometimes. I go on until three or four in the morning some nights. It's probably why he was like he was, being sent away like that. He was small as well for his age. You knew that, didn't you?'

'Yes, I knew that'.

'With that funny hooked nose. I remember when you were that age. And Callum and Grace. When they were little they used to get up early with me and sit out in the kitchen. I used to feed the birds and they used to come right up to the conservatory window. One day we started playing pubs and then they wanted to do that every morning'.

'I remember the pubs'.

'They used to get the tables moved round to make a counter. Then we had Granddad's barrel of home-made beer and they'd be pouring out little glasses of that. We had all these bottles lined up, I don't know what we didn't have – lemonade, brandy, sherry, tap water. I had to be one of the customers and they used to ask me to pretend to be drunk'.

'I knew you were all having a lot of fun out there'.

'Oh, they didn't want to wake you and Giles up, they wanted it to be just our game. We had a lot of fun with those pubs, we really did'.

'You've always been clever, like Dad. You get it from him'.

'If I am, I get it from you too, Mum'.

'What do you mean, I'm not clever. Too silly, spoilt I was as a little girl, didn't concentrate in school because of it'.

'No, you are clever, in a different way. You know what people need, you can see what's going on. And you can be a lot of fun'.

'But that's not being clever'.

'It is, in a way'.

'Why are you saying these things?'

'Because I want to acknowledge what you've given me, what the nice things are about you'.

'Oh'.

'And to tell you – to let you know – it's those things, you know, well, that's why I love you'.

'Oh'.

'And to say that I wish we could – well, we always seem to be – we don't act as if we do love each other sometimes'.

'Oh, well, what do you suggest?'

'I don't know. We could just listen to each other a bit more. Try to take more care'.

'Do you think that would do it?'

'We could try it. I'd like things to be better between us'.

'Well, let's do that then'.

'Okay, let's do that, listen a bit more and try to keep it like this. Because this feels better, doesn't it?'

'It does, doesn't it? We'll do what you say'.

*

'Mum, can I ask you something about Dad's mum? About her family?'

'Are you still on about that? Sometimes it's best to let sleeping dogs lie, you know'.

'I know. I don't think about it all the time. But I would like to just tidy up one or two things in my mind. Do you remember you told me once, a few years ago, that Dad's mum, Letitia, had brother and sisters? One called Walter and another called Ada?'

'Did I tell you that?'

'You did. I made a note of it in my book'.

'I don't remember saying that'.

'No, but you did. The thing is, I've traced her back in the records and she did have brothers and a sister but I can't find any with those names'.

'Your dad wouldn't ever talk about her'.

'Yes, I know that. But I'm confused about why these things don't all add up'.

'I don't remember saying about any brothers and sisters. There was a Bert, a policeman, he was a brother. But Dad's family didn't have much to do with him.

'Why didn't you tell me about him before?'

'Oh, I don't know. You mustn't take too much notice of me. I'm old, you know. Get things wrong sometimes'.

*

'... I'm sorry I can't take your call at the moment but if you leave your name and number after the – '

'I don't want no number or no ... Whatsit? ... Hello? Susan?'

' – tone, I'll get back to you'.

'Hello? Stop going on about numbers ... I'm not going to ... now what's going on?'

*

'I can't go out into the hallway. Susan, help me. I can't go out of this room'.

'What do you mean Mum, you can't go – '

'I can't. Help me'.

'What do you want me to do, Mum? Can't you call Dilys across the road? Or somebody else nearby. If you give me their numbers, I'll ring for you'.

'Don't go getting them involved. I need somebody to help me. I can't stay in this room all the time. Your Dad used to know how to deal with me, how to control me, when I was like this'.

'Mum, I don't know what I can do, I'm in Ilkley. And I don't want to control you. Why do you think you can't leave the room and go out into the hall?'

'I just can't'.

'Well, perhaps you'll just have to stay where you are until you feel you can'.

'Don't be so silly. This isn't normal, is it?'

'Um, it's not very normal, no. But it will pass. Why don't you just read a magazine or something for a while until you feel okay again'.

'But what if I want a cup of tea or something?'

'Well maybe you'll feel better soon and then you can go and make one'.

'Can't you do something? I need help'.

'Mum, I'm a couple of hundred miles away and I'm helping a friend with a children's birthday party this afternoon. So, we're up to our necks at the moment'.

'What can I do?'

'Look, why don't you stay where you are and don't try to go out of the room and I'll ring you in an hour or so to see how things are then'.

'Do you think that will work and I will be all right?'

'I think it probably will'.

'Okay, if you think that's best, we'll do that. But you will ring won't you?'

'I will'.

*

'I don't know why I get like this. I don't understand it'.

'I think it's just –'.

'Yes, but why do I get like it?'

'I don't really know, maybe it's –'.

'I can't make any sense of it, I wish I could. It's not very nice you know, being like this'.

*

'It's very good of you Margaret. I didn't know who else to contact. I know Mum holds you in very high regard'.

'Well, I went round after your phone call but there was no reply. I'm pretty sure your Mum was in, I could hear her moving around inside and I knocked as loud as I could. I even called out to her through the letterbox'.

'I'm afraid that doesn't surprise me very much. When she's not well she lurches from desperately needing people to repelling all boarders and it's very hard to predict which of those you'll get when'.

'It's very strange because she used to come to the afternoon meetings we used to have at the Fellowship, and she was very popular there, very outgoing and sociable. She even started coming to some of my Sunday services'.

'I wish she would go out to these things. I had hoped that if you called she might stop this silly business of not answering the door'.

'Isn't there anybody who she knows better than me who might persuade her? What if she were to come along with a friend?'

'At times like these, she will only see my sister or me, or maybe her sister, who lives miles away in Kent'.

'Well, I'm very willing to try again, maybe I'll find her in a better frame of mind. But isn't there somebody, her GP or a nurse, who can keep an eye on her?'

'I'm sure there ought to be but it's been extraordinarily hard to make this happen'.

'Well, I'll try again and I'll let you know how I get on'.

*

'Who's that? Is it our Janet?'

'It's me, Mum, you've been sleeping'.

'Who's that? Oh, it's our Susan, I thought it was our Janet'.

'I think you've been dreaming, you were talking about something in your sleep'.

'Was I? What was I saying?'

'Just dreaming, nothing that made much sense really'.

'How did you get here, anyway?'

'I came down when I heard what's been happening, your back door was open and I've been sitting here while you've been sleeping, waiting for you to wake up. You shouldn't leave your door open like that, anybody could walk in'.

'You've been sitting there?'

'Yes, I – '

'They're a devil those kitchen knives. I couldn't get anywhere with the one of them. Blunt as anything'.

'Mum, I don't – '

'Look, just scratches, I couldn't get it to go in'.

'Mum, this is awful, don't talk like that. I don't want to have this conversation'.

'What?'

'I don't want to – I don't like hearing you talk like this. Pull your sleeve down. Who's put that dressing on?'

'I was sawing away'.

'Stop it! Mother, stop it!'

'Why are you saying stop it? You don't know everything, you know'

'Mum, I'm going to call the doctor, you need some help'.

*

'Your mother just needs some company. I've changed her medication, reduced the dosage, which might have been making her a bit distressed. I'll notify her GP after the weekend. But mainly it's company she needs not a doctor. You need to encourage her to get out and about a bit, that's all'

'I know but it's not that easy'.

'Doesn't she have any friends, any groups for older people that she could go to? There are quite few of them about. Can't you sort something out for her?'

'I know but Mum's complicated. And I'm worried about her safety. This morning she was making a cup of tea and she had the kettle full of boiling water in one hand and the teapot in the other, both high up in the air and she was standing on tiptoes for some reason and beginning to sway about as she tried to pour it'.

'I think your mother's very sensible. She mentioned kettles to me, says she knows that she must keep them flat on the kitchen surface. For her age she's remarkably with it.

244

It's company she needs. Surely that's something you can help arrange for her?'

*

'What? What time is it? What are you – '

'I've been worrying about you'.

'What do you mean worrying. Mother, it's five o'clock'.

'I was ever so worried'.

'Mother, go back to bed. There's nothing to worry about'.

'Are you all right?'

'Of course, I'm all right! Apart from you waking me up'.

'I worry about you so much'.

'Stop it! Go back to bed. I was asleep. And you should be too'.

*

'I think I'm the best one there, I'm the teacher's pet'.

'It sounds like you're enjoying it'.

'Oh I am. Well, sort of. I get a taxi comes for me and brings me back. I don't have to pay for it'.

'So, what do you do when you go, what is it, two days a week?'

'Yes, Tuesdays and Thursdays'.

'So, what do you do?'

'Oh, all sorts. You know'.

'Well, I don't, that's why I'm asking'.

'Oh, well, gardening if it's nice. We've got vegetables and a pretty flower garden, I help with that'.

'Sounds good, but you don't do that all day, do you? What if the weather's not so nice?'

'Of course we don't do that all day'.

'So – ? '

245

'Art, we do art. Cooking sometimes. The teacher gets me to help her. Some of the others, they're not quite right, you know, not right in the head'.

'It must be nice for you and for your teacher to –'

'And those poor devils on the top floor, top two floors I think, we don't go up there, the ones with that Altz – I can't say it'.

'Altzheimers. It's a difficult one isn't it?'

'I have to go and talk to the doctor as well, tell her what I'm feeling. She says that I've got to tell her the truth and she knows if I'm making things up. She's very nice though, not very old, not like a proper doctor at all really'.

'Sounds good to me. Having somebody to talk to who knows what they're – '

'I don't think I shall keep going. Can't really see the point'.

'Well, you weren't well, were you – back in the summer? It's obviously helped – '

'Oh, that was back in the summer. No I wasn't well then but I'm fine now'.

'But it might be worth trying to think about whether you can spot when you are not feeling so well, to try to prevent you sliding down into that state again'.

'Oh. I don't want to go thinking about that now. That's all over and done with'.

'But you have had these spells, haven't you, over the years? I just wonder whether you can spot the danger signals so that we can do something about it early if it happens again'.

'Oh, it's not going to happen again. Don't say things like that, I'm absolutely fine. Stop being so serious. You always were serious, right from a little girl'.

'Mother – '

'Get on with you now. Stop acting like a doctor. Do you want a cake? We always have cakes up there of an afternoon. I usually put a few in my bag when nobody's looking. Go on, have a cake'.

15. MUST BUCK UP, GET ON

Buck up. I must buck up. And get on. Along this promenade. Where Maud used to live. This house, lived and worked here she did. A long time ago. Before Alastair led her off to Canada. Before the war took Sidney from us.

Letitia had walked at a furious pace far beyond the line of grand houses on the beach road. Years before she had met her sister here on Sunday mornings. Arm in arm, they had promenaded back into town. Before Alastair and Canada. In their finest clothes they had made their way to church. Before William and the children.

Now she hurried on with no sense of a destination. Movement itself was her purpose. She could as easily turn and retrace her steps as push on beyond the outskirts of town. She talked to herself, repeating snatches of the conversations with Mary that had so distressed her. She added alternative sentences here and there, changed the words. Raising her eyebrows and exaggerating her intonation, she put on such a performance that she could believe that these exchanges had actually taken place.

In the deep pocket of her coat was the prayer book she had been given when she was a child herself. Whenever her fingers traced the pattern across its embossed cover, she was warmed by memories of the wonderful little gatherings that she and the others had shared with Father Reeves. Letitia had felt very privileged to be part of a tiny group of village children sitting in the front pew of an otherwise darkened and empty church. With no other adults present, they had Father Reeves all to themselves. She had loved all the talk about confirming her faith and being old enough to forge her own relationship with the Lord. She had, however, sometimes struggled to accept that Billy Triscott was equally deserving of membership of their group. Not because he was a bit slow on the uptake but because she knew for certain that he did not even try to behave like a committed follower. She shivered with the grandeur and solemnity of it all. And she did not want Billy or anybody else to spoil it.

Letitia had looked forward to sharing this experience with her own children when the time came. She had already told Mary, her eldest, that the treasured prayer book would become hers when she herself completed confirmation classes. Which is why the problems that arose with Mary distressed Letitia all the more.

The parlour had smelled of soap and Mary's freshly washed hair. Douglas and Clarry were watching their older sister with big silent eyes as Mary cried that she did not want to go back to the class for the fourth week. During their conversations in the weeks before commencing these sessions, Mary had been looking forward to them and the prayer book becoming hers. Letitia had, at first, wondered whether the cold might be a problem and had bought her a new, long-sleeved, flannelette vest for the evenings in the church. But her daughter's reactions seemed far in excess of such a simple explanation.

Mary started pulling viciously at her hair. Her face turned red from crying and the muscles in her neck stood out. The other two were silent and uncertain, cowering together in the passageway beneath the hanging overcoats. Mary dug her fingernails into Letitia's hands, clinging to her and screeching, as her mother attempted to comfort her.

Then she pulled herself away suddenly and ran from the room. Before Letitia realised what was happening, the front door had slammed, leaving the curtain rings rattling on the rail like teeth all a-chatter. The boom from the door echoed back along the passage. Letitia hurried to pull it open and saw Mary running up the pavement. Her bonnet had become untied and had fallen into the gutter, where it was left lying as she hurried up towards the main road.

Douglas and Clarry would not be fast enough to give Letitia any chance of catching her daughter. But fortunately, before she reached the far corner, a neighbour stopped her and, after some conversation, led her back. When Letitia and the three children were all back inside the house, Mary fell to the floor wailing. Letitia tried to move the two out of the room, but they seemed rooted to the spot, watching Mary. She was almost retching and, through this heaving and her tears, still refusing to go. Letitia realised with a heavy sense of resignation that she was unable to force Mary's attendance.

That man, what's he shouting? In a car, out here along the beach road. Lives down our road. No, I don't want a lift. Never mind about husbands and children and their dinners. I'm not listening to his nonsense. The cheek of it!

Letitia acknowledged that Father Ingham was not another Father Reeves. She found him sterner than Father Reeves, less warm and accepting. His sermons too were, to her tastes, rather boring and his voice often flat and monotonous. He was tall and thin with a line of beard around his jaw that reminded her of the American president, Abraham Lincoln, in photographs that she had seen. But he nevertheless listened to her when she went to see him about Mary not wanting to go. He said many children often did not want to attend and that a little bit of discipline was sometimes necessary. As parents, he added, you sometimes had to be cruel to be kind.

As far as Letitia could make out, he had been trying his best. He had even taken the sensitive ones like Mary out to the little room round the side of the altar to talk to them individually. To Letitia, remembering how much she had loved Father Reeves when she was little, this seemed such a privilege. One that she had never had. And yet it seemed to get Mary into an hysterical state.

I'm not speaking to that silly man. I'll turn around right now and walk back to town. I've got the housekeeping. It's safe in my pocket. And the prayer book.

Sidney had been thirty-two when his call-up papers came through and only in the War six months when it happened. The rest of the family, Letitia knew, attributed what they later referred to as her 'down in the dumps' spells to the tragic loss of her loved, older brother.

They gave Sidney a medal after he died. They gave it to Edith. The family were told that his captain had been leading a charge up out of a trench and in to No Man's Land seconds before a shell hit them all. Sidney had been right behind him. Edith gave the medal to George and Ivy, who displayed it in the centre of the chimney breast above the range. Everybody was very proud of Sidney and also aware that they needed to stay strong to support Edith and the twins.

It was true, what her family believed. Letitia did struggle for many years with her sadness and with how much she missed her brother. But her sorrows were magnified many times over by other facts that she later learned about

Sidney's death, details that her younger brother, Bertie, sternly advised her never to mention to anybody ever again.

Some five or so years after the end of the war, Letitia was delighted to learn that Father Reeves, although very old by then, wished to come all the way down to her by train to impart some very important information. She got out her best china, tidied everywhere and welcomed the elderly, stooping clergyman into the house when he knocked on her front door. Although she had loved him when she was a child, Letitia had also been a little frightened of his imposing presence and loud, booming voice that filled the church. But that day, they sat together in her parlour as if he were one of the family. Just seeing him again after so many years, since Bertie's wedding in fact, brought back many memories, the most prominent of which was her little brother's severe illness and Father Reeves' prayers that, Letitia was sure, had saved his life.

But the story he had to tell that day, as they sat sipping tea, seemed unbelievable. So much so that Letitia had difficulty taking all of it in.

An old soldier, somebody who had served with Sidney, had apparently sought Father Reeves out. This chap was in a terrible state. Half crazy, Father Reeves described him as. But from his description it was obviously Sidney he was talking about. Sid, they had called him – a big man, strong from working at the smithy. His father worked there too. There was a wife and twins. Possibly a brother and sister or two, the stranger was not so sure what with his nerves and his memory after all that time. Father Reeves, however, was convinced it was Sidney and, if it was good enough for him, then Letitia was willing to believe it too.

What this wretched fellow had to say was that Sidney had not been gassed or shelled as the family had always been led to assume. He had been shot! And – this was the worst part of all – he had been shot by his own side! The men had all been huddling in a trench in the early morning and the captain gave the order for the men to prepare to go over the top, as they called it. This captain, they didn't think that much of him, always shouting at his men. They had had enough, and they just refused to go. So, he took out his pistol and started waving it at them, threatening to shoot one of them if they disobeyed him. Sidney got up to do as he was told and was right behind the captain when there was a shot. It was one of the men, lost all his senses and just shot the captain with his rifle. Point blank. The bullet – this is the awful bit – the bullet went right through the captain. And it passed on into Sidney and killed him too.

It's busy. People in the street, cars too. Down there on the beach. Bathing in the sea. All of them. Too busy. This lady, she knows my name. Haven't got time for stopping.

The fellow ran away, back along the trench. Ran for all he was worth. And just as well, because there was a huge explosion, a shell had hit them right where they were all crouched.

Father Reeves said the man was shaking and unable to give a full account of himself. He had been wandering for years – he was a tramp really, living off people's good nature and unable to settle.

Whatever next? 'Are you all right, Mrs Roberts?' Has her hand on my arm. Let go. Let go of me. How dare she. All these people. All this noise.

After this visit, Letitia's spirits went into decline. She felt deep despair after attempting to share the ghastly truth about Sidney's death with her younger brother. Bertie, for all his sweetness, would not believe what she told him. Or rather, he would not hear that the authorities could be wrong and told her not to speak about the matter again with him or with anybody else. Bertie was the perfect policeman, he was big and talked slowly to people and Letitia said that people knew where they were with him. If he said he would do something, he did it. He did not accept any nonsense. But he did not want to know the truth about Sidney's death and that was part of what brought her down so low.

Letitia struggled to buck up and put on a good show. She knew that if Hardington Hospital took somebody in for their nerves then it was anybody's guess when, or even if, they would be coming out again. Her neighbour, Flo's, husband had died in the war, had only been signed up for a matter of weeks before the whole lot of them were wiped out in one go. Flo was never the same and they had to take her in there even though she had children she was supposed to be looking after. When she came out, she had changed so much. It was like she was not all there, not just a bit absent-minded but really slow and vacant. Letitia never found out what they had done to her. She just knew she had to buck up and make herself presentable if it was not going to happen to her as well.

What's my name? None of their business. Leave me alone. Poking their noses in. Get out of my way. Need to get on, buck myself up. Get away from all these people

On top of all these memories and worries, Letitia was dreading another set to with Mary when Wednesday teatime came around. By Tuesday evening, Mary was complaining of tummy ache and feeling sick. She and Douglas would not answer when Letitia spoke to them. Even Clarry seemed

254

wary of her and had started to suck his thumb again, which he had not done for years. Every time any of them looked at her with a suspicious frown, Letitia felt a panic rising in her. William was away at his boat and Letitia spent the Wednesday worrying that Mary might run away again, properly this time, and even take one or both of the others with her. She tried to be firm with Mary about her going but could not understand the strength of her resistance. Nor how she seemed to have passed it on to Douglas, and maybe even Clarry as well.

Then, later that afternoon as Letitia was preparing a tea of toasted crumpets for her children, she noticed that the parlour had gone silent. Their voices were not to be heard. Neither, she found as she hurried out from the scullery, were they to be seen. All three were missing, their empty outlines hanging in the stillness of the room. There was no sign of them through the back window and the front door was still bolted. Letitia ran out into the back yard, pleading across blank walls and gardens. Then she heard shuffling and whispering from the privy. All three were in there, with Clarry grizzling and wanting to come out. Mary and Douglas were muttering, trying to console him and urging his silence.

Letitia tried the door, rattling it against the bolt. Clarry wailed, Douglas called out to her too.

'Mary, open this door!'

Two little voices, the younger ones, were calling now. Their crying was intensifying.

Crash!

Letitia threw her shoulder against the door. The pain happened somewhere else, to a stranger. The cries were now at a pitch, all of them in agitation.

255

Letitia could not speak, no words would form in her tightening throat. She could the hear struggles of tightly-packed bodies behind the door, feel the same rising panic as her children. Then her fingers were tearing at the door, a disembodied strength attempting to gouge the surface, to splinter fibre from jagged fibre. There was blood under her nails. She was trying to tear through the whole indifferent obstacle.

The money's in my pocket. There isn't any dinner. Wicked. I'm wicked. Haven't been to the shops. I must get on, hurry.

Letitia realised later that she must have blacked out as Mr Critchley from next door climbed over the garden wall with Mrs Critchley shouting something about waiting. The next thing she knew about anything, William was there, with Clarry clinging around his neck and Mary red raw in her face and cowering beneath one of his arms.

They told her later that Mr Critchley had broken the bolt at his second attempt, the force of the door swinging open and dealing Mary and Douglas blows to their faces. Clarry had been hunched in a bundle on the dirty, tiled floor at Mary's feet and had taken a sharp smack to his shoulder and hip. Letitia had fallen to the ground as the door finally crashed open, they said, with her legs unable to hold her. But she could not remember any of it. Douglas was on his knees beside her attempting to burrow his head into her as hard as he could, his cries of pain and desperation echoing around the yard. And Mary stood looking from William to Letitia and back again, full of silent tears and as lost as a discarded doll.

How they all slept that night, Letitia had no idea. William must have put the children to bed, must have seen to it that she too climbed the stairs and made some attempt to undress herself.

In the morning Letitia had difficulty getting up. She felt overwhelmed by the memory of her children clinging to each other. Instead of letting her comfort them about whatever it was, they seemed to be frightened of her, terrified. William sat on the side of the bed and held her hand. He just kept talking to her, in a gentle voice encouraging her to buck herself up. She had made him late for work and forced herself to get up and light the copper and then make the breakfasts. She was worried about William getting into trouble but he still stopped and ate with the family. The laundry had not been done from Monday. He had every right to complain, she felt, but he did not. The children got themselves ready for school. Douglas left with his shirt hanging out the back and his tie all skew-whiff. Letitia felt that they did not need her, that she could not do anything useful for them anyway.

The next one. I don't care. Anywhere. As far as I can. That train there. That one hissing steam.

The laundry pile looked huge, much bigger than usual. The breakfast dishes seemed stuck to the table cloth, it was difficult to lift them. The room was too small, there wasn't enough air. Letitia was feeling hotter and hotter and dropped the pile of washing in the doorway to the scullery. The smell of the laundry was making her feel sick. It was her own family's dirty clothes, some of them her own even, but she just kept smelling all the horrible things that come out of bodies.

It's ready to go. That one. A ticket for that one.

The more she kept moving, the faster she walked, the more she was able to keep the washing and the laundry from piling up behind her, to forget the children's frightened faces and to stop imagining William being torn off a strip at the dock.

It's all I've got. Anywhere. I don't care. As far as I can. Hurry.

Finally, she was at the railway station. Her elbows sawed through the air as she stood in the queue at the ticket office. She longed to be sitting confined to a compartment, rattling along the tracks and breathing in the sooty air through an open window.

Wicked. Too wicked to die.

16. THE TIDE AT FLOOD

Halfway up the hillside, where the track turned back upon itself, Letitia stopped and looked across the miles of farmland towards the sea. Above her a kestrel locked tight its position in a wind that ruffled the feathers of its breast. A tower at the top of the hill stubbed at the sky.

An early haze had evaporated as the morning sun struck the first chords of the day. Letitia struggled to remove her overcoat, anxious that the remaining section of the track, its red earth scattered with awkward flinty stones, might somehow conspire with the heat of the ascending sun to render her climb impossible.

'If they don't get – these sleeves – if these sleeves -' said Letitia, struggling and partly removing her coat and then, in an increasingly agitated state, managing to work her hand and arm back down into one of the sleeves.

She continued to the crest of the hill where she stopped. She touched the stone wall of the monument, its permanence and solidity a rebuff to transitory struggles, to achievements and failures. Away to the south was the town that had been her home for almost twenty years. All she could discern in the bright sunlight were the darkened patches of rooftops, almost liquid in texture, punctured by the clean, white, soaring spire of St Mark's.

They had doubted her, witnessed her despair and then turned their backs, the people of that town.

Her climb to this elevated patch of heathland had given her a perspective, a final view, of home. She had arrived as a young woman with an unwritten and unknowable future, excited and a little apprehensive among the elegant facades of the grand houses and unfamiliar streets. Within a year she had been anticipating a life with William, companionship and conversations, perhaps children who would grow in his strong likeness. These had provided more than adequate compensation for leaving her parents and brothers. Now, a sense of abandoning and being abandoned blew about her, like the hot indifferent wind that failed to cool her after the climb. She felt no excitement at the prospect of a destination, no slumping relief from a sense of departure.

A skylark's song held steady on the air despite the gusts. The kestrel meanwhile fell away on a long descending arc, its shadow racing across the heather as its body plummeted towards the lowest reaches of the scarp she had just ascended.

Somewhere further inland, there were villages where people spoke in warmer accents and with a reassuring lilt familiar from her childhood. Should she turn away from the coast and walk north, off into that interior? Or should she continue towards the edge of land that was only an hour or two away, towards the huge western horizon of the seascape?

She retraced her route back down from the hill, still stepping awkwardly to avoid the rounded flints. At the bottom, where the path met a wider lane rutted with cartwheel tracks and pitted with hoof marks, she found an old bench. The plank was grooved with a wet rot and one of the two supporting stumps was entangled with bindweed and inclined to one side. She sat on the opposite end, shivered once, then twice, as if with relief at being able to rest.

'Hello missus, are you all right, sat out here all on your ownsome?'

The farm lad surprised her, not so much by his sudden appearance from around the brambled corner of the lane as by his forwardness.

'Don't see many people, apart from them as from the farms, round here,' he added, as if undaunted by her silence.

Sidney, when he was this age, fifteen or sixteen, would not have approached strangers and commented on their appearance, on whether they belonged in this place or that.

'Young man, I – oh dear, what's it called – I only – ?'

'What is it?' he echoed, with a puzzled expression. 'Is it water, missus, you want? A cup of water?'

Sidney's manners had been a delight. His hands were always clean on a Sunday, his fingernails scrubbed. When they were both young, he had brought her posies before church, picked from the field opposite their cottage, celandines and buttercups in a froth of cow parsley. Unlike most of the boys from the village, he willingly complied when asked by their mother to accompany her along the lane for the morning service. On his arm, especially on Spring mornings when the warmth held such a prospect of renewed growth, she wondered whether she could ever love a husband as much? Friends of their parents would sometimes turn in their pews when brother and sister stepped in beneath the low entrance arch, heartened as they were by his quiet consideration.

'Be off with you and your water,' she said. 'I don't – I've far too much – '

When the lad had stumbled off, shaking his head and muttering to himself, she tried once more to remove her coat. And this time, having rested, her release came more easily. She folded the garment into her lap, nodded once to herself and began walking back towards the railway station from which her morning's walk had begun.

She had alighted from the railway carriage with the same sense of panic as she had boarded it in her home town some half an hour earlier. How long would it have taken her to walk this distance? More than a day certainly, even if she had been a man wearing tough boots like Sidney's. She was being driven by compulsions she could not name, first to climb to the hilltop tower, then to reach the sea. There had long since ceased to be any purpose to her wandering.

At the village church, she leaned against the high wall, shamefully aware of her slovenly appearance but also anxious that she might collapse otherwise. The voices of two men beyond the honey-coloured wall, gravediggers she assumed from their grunts and coarse accents, caused her to straighten her posture again, holding one hand against the warm, gritty stone.

Exhaustion burrowed further into her with each chime of the noontime bells. There would be a time to rest, a time not too far off now.

The road descended gently and became the main street through the village. A flagged pavement rose above the road, providing a wide frontage to the closely-cramped cottages. Before them, however, Letitia had to pass a double-fronted dwelling that served as a public house. She felt wary of the eyes, possibly even the enquiries, that would be directed towards her as a stranger. Some new, growing desire she could not restrain seemed to be driving her towards the open fields beyond the village and onwards again to the remote stretch of coastline. Despite the raw heat of the sun and the intensity of the light scouring every unshaded crevice and cranny, the open doorway to the drinking parlour exuded an atmosphere of fetid human energies – growls, slurs and laughter. Had Letitia glanced that way, she would have seen a deeply darkened interior, untouched by the brilliance of the early afternoon sun.

'Ere, missus, come in 'ere, don't just walk on,' came a voice supported by the conspiratorial chuckles of others, a swelling chorus of mockery and antagonism.

Letitia closed her fists tightly, tensed the length of her forearms, and stepped past the open doorway, the roar of a harsh camaraderie at her back as she proceeded. Once at a safe distance, she relaxed her arms and neck and felt a welling of despair, as if the past was slitting through the numbness shielding her from the everyday.

On the pavement ahead, a small child was playing with sticks outside an open cottage door. A woman, probably the girl's mother, called for her to come back into the house and to eat some item of lunch. The girl, three or four years of age, continued to scratch at a dusty groove between the flagstones with a twig. Her squat position with her knees tucked up almost to her chin, the curve of her knobbly spine visible through the stained muslin dress she was wearing, and her steady preoccupation with the small dust bowl she was creating, somehow stilled the increasing distress that Letitia was feeling. She saw that the child was attempting to cover a small group of ants with the fine silt that she had created with her scratching.

Letitia smiled, reassured by some old association that seemed temporarily to stay her sense of alienation.

'I used to have – I used to – but – ' she said, causing the child to turn and squint up at Letitia's shadowy form that eclipsed the burning sun.

Bertram had been about this age when the spirit had drained from his brown, wiry body, when his skin had faded to the colour of this child's muslin dress. His form had become so light that Letitia, older by only three years, had felt sure that she was strong enough to lift him from the bed and to cradle his head of tangled hair against her shoulder. But their mother had warned both her and Maud that they must never, ever attempt to lift or move him.

The little girl's mother, calling again, now appeared in the doorway and looked quickly away from her daughter and towards Letitia.

'Good day to you, missus,' she said, wiping down floured hands on her apron. 'Is our Beth getting in your way?' And then to the child, she added 'You let the lady pass instead of sprawling all over the place. Be a good girl now and give the lady some room'.

Letitia recognised elements of the mother's concern but struggled to give a voice to these feelings.

'Those ants – God's creatures – ' she said instead.

'My dear, are you unwell? Would you like to come inside, to sit yourself in our front parlour for a while? Perhaps the sun – you look like you have been walking in this heat for too long. Do you not have a hat? And you won't need that heavy overcoat today of all days. Come and rest indoors, in the cool. Let me bring you a glass of water'.

A bolt of sadness shot up into Letitia's throat. She searched the air in front of her eyes for words.

She saw the faces of her three children, the eldest no more than thirteen. She knew them so well, every eyelash and hair. But could not remember their names. She pulled more frantically at her coat, desperate to free a hand with which to pull them towards her. In one set of eyes and then the next, there was no sign of recognition. They regarded her with hardened gem stones, beautiful blue and green opals, cold as crystal.

*

'We should probably start,' said Marjorie, the social worker who had introduced herself to Sue and Janet in the corridor a few minutes earlier. 'Sylvia, she's the OT, she won't be long but in view of the time we had best get going. The purpose of this meeting, the reason we're all here, is to sort out what's in Avril's best interests at this point in time'.

'We'll do some introductions in a minute but first,' she added, turning towards Sue and Janet, 'can I say how grateful we are to you two for making the time to be here this afternoon. You've had long journeys, the both of you, haven't you?'

Sue felt the accusation straight away but was unsure whether Janet would have registered it.

The two sisters were seated next to each other in the conference room of the hospital's assessment unit. Behind them there was a large window running the length of the room and overlooking some small warehouses, storage yards and the other drab paraphernalia of a light industrial estate. Around the large oval table, in addition to Marjorie, there were two nurses, the ward manager, a speech therapist, the manager of Avril's residential home and two doctors. The last two were introduced by their professional titles, everybody else was encouraged to give their first names.

'First of all, can I just check something? Avril's been entertaining us all on the ward with stories about Weymouth and we were wondering, has she in fact ever lived there?'

'Oh yes, she certainly has,' Sue replied.

'I still do,' added Janet.

'Both our parents grew up and lived there until they moved here with our dad's job about twenty-five years ago'.

In fact, tales about Weymouth had been a constant source of conversation for their mother all through her life. Only latterly was Sue beginning to question whether this really was an inexhaustible 'topic for conversation' – or merely the stimulus for a set of monologues. After being widowed, when Avril started to shun friends and neighbours, she frequently walked into the city centre to talk with strangers on public benches for long stretches at a time. The reports her daughters received from neighbours who had observed these encounters often mentioned that Avril had seemed in full flow with accounts of her old home town and they had been uncertain about whether to intervene.

But that town by the sea, those characters and the tumble of anecdotes that connected them all, belonged not only to Avril. Sue too had always recalled her own early life there in colours that drenched her childhood days, with sounds reproduced in razor-sharp fidelity. But now, after forty or so years, that place and time were at last assuming an historical dimension and loosening their grip on her recall.

Other aspects of the past had also begun to lose their allure for Sue. Letitia and her family still seemed very close and intertwined somehow with her own life. But the expanding possibilities for obtaining far more facts and figures about her grandmother from the internet and other commercial facilities had grown less and less appealing. Sue had continued her research, and this had provided some undoubtedly exciting moments – the discovery of more brothers and sisters, glimpses here and there of their

266

marriages, subsequent addresses and employment, and the briefest outline of a war record for one of them.

Letitia, however, a soul and substance, had by now taken shape in Sue's imagination. The texture of her grandmother's childhood and early life, her brief adult years and her suffering had become palpable and Sue had a strong sense that tracking down other stray and distant descendants, a garage owner or a carpet fitter somewhere in the West Country, might rob her of the grandmother she had fashioned for herself.

So, Letitia would remain for her an imagined figure, an artefact perhaps but also a source for deep and real compassion.

*

'My dear, whatever is the matter? Come inside, come in here and rest'.

The woman placed a hand on one of Letitia's shoulders, her other arm around her back. Her daughter looked up at the two women, one bent as if in supplication, the other shepherding her to safety. A biblical tableau.

'No, I must – I have to –'

'Dear Lord, where is it you're wanting to go? Come inside. What is it that is bothering you so much? Where are you from, my dear? Can we get someone to come and look after you, to take you back home? Do you have a husband, some family, we can fetch?'

From behind them, from the doorway of the public house, three men emerged singing and stumbling, with the middle one supported on the shoulders of the other two. Letitia's shoulders tightened as the woman attempted to embrace her more fully. The child herself moved towards her mother grabbing bunches of her heavy skirt in her tiny fists, her eyes cast upwards observing the agitation across Letitia's face.

'Have these men alarmed you? Take no notice, dear, come inside away from their antics. Children they are, no more than children with the drink. Troublesome, wearisome children at that. Come in and rest with us'.

But Letitia could not be comforted, would not accept the invitation to rest, the simple hospitality of the concerned countrywoman. She pulled herself free as if from restraining hands with a force that so surprised the woman and her child that they both stepped backwards to demonstrate to Letitia that she was completely free to continue her passage. And this she did, on down through the village with a determined stride and without any acknowledgement of the kindly attention that had been shown her, talking to herself in a more insistent fashion as she quickened her already hurried pace.

At the end of the village, where the cottages ended and the fields began, she eased herself through the gap between a dilapidated five bar gate and the hedgerow. Blackthorn spiked at her clothes and skin. Carrying her coat like some oversized muffler, she proceeded among the deep shadows at the field's edge, among grasses still in places damp with dew.

At the next field entrance, she entered a cloud of midges rising and tumbling about her head in a buzzing spiral like gauze at an open window. She flinched and flicked at the side of her face, only managing to intensify their frantic motion. No sooner had she divested herself of them, stifling a cry of panic, than she almost placed her foot into one of the huge, crusted droppings deposited on the baked ground by idling cattle. The surface of one of these had split and in the darker, liquid mulch, hordes of orange-backed flies flitted and feasted. These reminded Letitia of spiced peel for Christmas plum puddings and she shuddered, icicles plunging down beneath her clothes despite the sun's continuing and uncompromising force.

The hedges grew more sparsely the nearer she came to the head of the lagoon. Through the gaps between the trees and bushes and over the tops of clumps of gorse, she could see the sand bar. There was a stiffening, a saltiness, in the breeze. The trapped, brackish water seemed unwashed by tides. A flock of sandpipers skittered across the sweet-smelling mudflat. Two swans beat their way towards her, black beaded eyes, soft-boned beaks and huge lumbering undercarriages behind their long, vulnerable necks. The sandpipers were thrown against the air by some invisible force, the sharp angles of their flight in perfect synchrony, and Letitia stared down at the lace-like pattern formed by their thousand footprints on the shore.

To an observer, Letitia would have appeared a small, stationary figure alone in an unfrequented stretch of land, a woman somehow lost at the water's edge. Beyond her, a bar of sand, devoid of both people and vegetation, rose up to separate the inland lagoon from the wastes of sea beyond.

Letitia picked her way along the firmer ground just before the water's edge, where a layer of decaying vegetation provided her best shoes with some protection from the mud. She noticed nevertheless that one had become smeared with the foul-smelling slime deposited by the wading birds. Although it could be easily cleaned with the correct materials, she became preoccupied by the blemishes as she began to climb the bank of sand and distressed by thoughts that she would never be able to restore the shoe to its original, unsullied state.

Her sadness threatened to overwhelm her.

*

'Well that's cleared that up. Thank you,' said Marjorie. 'We didn't think she could be making it all up but we weren't sure sometimes. Tricia, she's been with you now at Salisbury Court for, what, three or four years? Can you tell us how she's been in that time?'

Tricia was wearing a dark suit and was more formally dressed than the times when Sue had seen her at the care home. She had in front of her a bulging, tattered manila folder containing a jumble of documents. She glanced hesitantly, almost furtively, towards Sue and Janet before opening the cover.

'Avril was our first resident when we opened in 2002 so she had quite a bit of fuss made of her. Of course, she didn't find it so easy when we started taking others in and she once rang 999 and told the police we weren't looking after her'.

Reactions around the table varied – most seemed discretely amused, the speech therapist whose name Sue had already forgotten inclined her head slowly to one side presumably as an expression of sympathy, while Marjorie remained poised and attentive.

'Another time she managed to slip out through the front door undetected and got herself onto a bus to the city centre. She was there some time and didn't know how to get back so she went into the fire station. They rang around the care homes until they found us and then brought her home in a fire engine. She was sat up in the front by the driver, looking very pleased with herself'.

'Oh heck,' said Janet.

'That sounds like Mum,' Sue added.

'Was your mother always like this or has it just come on recently?' asked Marjorie. 'Can you give us a brief outline perhaps of how she was before she went into Salisbury Court?'

Sue and Janet looked at each other, batting the choice of who would answer between themselves with a succession of brief nods and raised eyebrows. Sue, by now, dreaded having to answer such questions. She had never been able to furnish a precise account of her mother's complexities, usually offering instead a roller coaster of examples and incidents that she hoped would illustrate the difficulty that any slick summation would pose. But she had learned by now that this approach could produce confusion and unease among those seeking only a thumbnail sketch. Brief, categorical descriptions though seemed far worse, like harsh and clinical dismissals.

So, Sue recounted just the most significant aspects of Avril's deterioration in the ten years since their father's death. The piles of unwashed dishes stacked in the bath and increasing in size each visit despite Janet's or her own efforts. Packets of out-of-date food swelling and exploding in cupboards and in the fridge, the mice extending their run of the bungalow even into her bedroom. Her mother's insistence that she would accept no intruders in the form of home helps, social workers or the rest. Practical and professional help seemingly impossible to arrange while Avril's continued ability to impress care and medical personnel through it all with her spunky resilience and astute engagement.

'Ally's a proper character and everybody loves her,' said Tricia. 'We'd be very sorry to lose her now after four years.'

'Ally? When had anybody ever called her Ally?' thought Sue, as she sensed stiffening postures around the table and the meeting moving towards some predetermined conclusion.

Tricia lowered her eyes towards her folder of papers then looked straight at Sue.

'But the thing is –' she said, ' – we just can't meet her needs any more. She requires more specialist help than we can provide'.

Around the table, Tricia's comments had elicited a nodding assent and Sue struggled with the rejection that she sensed beneath the affectionate tone.

Sue had already been briefed about the latest incident by Janet in the car park where they had met beforehand.

'We do fully accept that your staff can't be expected to put up with the violence,' she found herself saying instead of coming to her mother's defence. 'It's not acceptable for her to be striking out at staff with that walking stick of hers'.

Beside her, Janet seemed to choke on a sharp intake of breath and then lower her head while shaking it slowly from side to side.

'And other residents are getting distressed too by her wandering into their rooms at night and waking them,' Tricia added.

'We don't seem to have a current GP report,' said Marjorie, dissipating the growing stiffness around the table. 'Has she ever had a psychiatric assessment?'

'This has always been a bit of a grey area,' Sue said. 'She did attend a mental health hospital about six years ago as a day patient, about 1998-ish, but she stopped going and discharged herself after only a few weeks'.

'It's a pity we don't have any record of that,' observed Marjorie.

'And her old GP did say to me around the time of Dad's death in 1994 that he thought she sometimes suffered from psychotic episodes'.

Sue disliked the term 'psychotic' with its vague and menacing connotations. She had always challenged its casual use in conversations about certain youngsters when she had worked in the special unit half a lifetime or more ago. Today, though, she sensed an avoidance of eye contact and an embarrassed search by the others for a new tack to the conversation.

The opportunity of an audience for more examples of her mother's strangeness was creating an almost irresistible pull on Sue's dammed-up frustrations. But she judged that she should attempt to preserve some dignity all round and not mention, for example, their mother sitting in the road outside a neighbour's house while Janet was summoned by telephone all the way from Weymouth. Or, refusing to leave a tea shop in a neighbouring town one Sunday afternoon, settling herself with an unknown family and telling Janet and Trev to leave her there where she would be looked after by 'these kind people'. It felt more acceptable to mention the dangers – not locking her door at nights in a cul-de-sac that had known recent break-ins or informing callers at her door looking for casual gardening or tree felling jobs that she kept a ready supply of spare cash in a drawer in her living room.

'And did you never think about trying to move her closer to one of you?' asked Marjorie. 'Back to Weymouth perhaps?'

Without even looking at her, Sue was aware of the guilty panic that would be overwhelming her sister.

'We tried everything when she was going through one of her really bad spells', Sue interjected. 'We did manage to get a social worker to come and see her and Mum was insistent that she was not going to move from her house or from Portsmouth. They told us we had to respect Mum's wishes, that she was an impressive old lady who certainly knew her own mind and that we were not to impose our wishes on her.'

'So, how did she end up at Salisbury Court then?' asked Sylvia, looking up from her hectically scribbled notes.

'She just – one day they just – ' fumbled Janet.

'That was the craziest thing of all,' said Sue, immediately regretting her use of the word and sensing the disapproval of the paid professionals around her. 'The social worker had to do a review, she called it. There had been a furore about old cases or something and she'd come to make another assessment of Mum. Apparently, Mum had told her there and then that she was quite happy to go into Salisbury Court. After all the traumas we'd had with her it was just amazing that everything happened so smoothly after that'.

The more senior of the two doctors, a young Asian woman, quickly broke the silence that seemed to have gathered around the table.

'We've had all the various tests back now and I'm very pleased to say that your mother has a clean bill of health'.

The doctor was more fluid in her movements, more graceful, than the others and her widened eyes conveyed an

274

empathy that seemed deeper and more genuine than a mere professional demeanour.

'We can't find any physical cause for her collapses or vomiting'.

'That ties in with our observations,' said Audrey, the ward manager, speaking for the first time. 'She has behaved quite strangely sometimes while we've been observing her in the unit. Like this morning. I wanted her to get back into her bed and she said she didn't want to. Then she just sort of stiffened and slid from her chair onto the floor'.

'We had some of that sort of thing in Salisbury Court too,' said Tricia. 'That's why we were so keen for her to have a full medical assessment'.

The second doctor again remained silent while her colleague leaned forward, looking directly at Tricia.

'Everything from the tests is positive. Neurological, everything. There's no physical reason for her falls as far as we are able tell'.

Audrey shifted noticeably in her chair, her shoulders straightening and her cheek muscles tightening.

'Our view is that some of this is behavioural, perhaps a lot of it,' she said.

Sue assumed that by this she meant intentional and felt a massive sense of vindication whilst at the same time being unable to shake the feeling that many in the room were still judging her and Janet adversely. And seeing her especially, the one who did the talking, the mouthy one, in a far harsher light than her unassertive and visibly embarrassed sister.

*

Letitia reached the top of the ridge and looked down the sandy slope to the sea. Away to her right, a rocky promontory extended for some twenty feet or more out into deeper water.

She struggled to grasp her children, to tuck her fingers into their flesh.

'If you just let me hold you – you are too far away. Please. Please, you come closer,' she mumbled to herself.

The three stood side by side, flinching from her reach, the youngest staring at her in alarm while scrabbling for the hand of his sister.

*

'So, we have to decide whether Avril is able to make decisions in her own best interests', Marjorie said, pausing to look at each person around the table. 'I take this aspect of my job very seriously. I could effectively be depriving someone of their liberty'.

The conversation continued for another quarter of an hour or so covering, it seemed to Sue, old ground. Undercurrents of statutory responsibilities, diagnostic pronouncements, funding categories and placement options surfaced repeatedly with several around the table falling silent or pushing the expectation of a response onto one of the others. Eventually Marjorie declared that Avril should be classed as 'elderly mentally infirm' and that she would explain later to Sue and Janet the implications for her future care.

As the meeting disbanded and Sue was leaving to visit her mother on the ward, Marjorie stopped her and placed a hand on her forearm.

'You know you can always talk to someone about your mother, if you want to,' she said. 'You could talk to me if you thought it would help'.

'Thanks,' said Sue. 'It has been really – I appreciate the offer – but I have actually – '

*

Letitia stumbled down the bank towards the rocks. The deep, pulsing water, the regularity of daily tides and the vagaries of drifts and spray, seemed somehow to promise resolution to the insistent riddles and despair that had plagued her these recent weeks. At the water's edge, she put her coat back on and patted the hair at the sides of her head. Doing so, she noticed that she was still wearing her spectacles, so she removed them, folded them carefully and placed them in one of her coat pockets. She attempted to straighten the lower parts of her stockings, but they had become badly twisted and torn in places by twigs and brambles. Then she checked her hair at the sides of her temples one last time.

Sidney was the bravest man there had ever been. She was always aware of his gallantry, all through their growing up. She had known before anybody else, before even the King himself and all his ministers. Now the world must know too, and her quiet pride was nothing when compared to the sisterly love that she felt for him.

*

Avril looked small and withered but cosy when Sue found her in a big bed, one of four in the corner of a small ward.

'How are you, Mum? You look very comfortable in there'.

Avril stared back as if she didn't recognise Sue, her eyes two dark pits.

'It's me, Mum. Susan'.

Avril's eyes grew fiercer, burned deeper, and then a huge, slug-like tongue slithered out from between her lips, seemingly too big to have ever been accommodated within her stretched and collapsing cheeks.

'What are you doing, Mum? What's this tongue all about?'

She strained as if to extend it further, lifting her head from the pillow with the effort.

'Come on, there's no need – whatever's the matter?'

She swayed her head from side to side like a snake, moments before its attack. Then she withdrew her tongue back to where it had come from and opened her mouth into a rounded toothless hole, three dark spaces now staring up directly at Sue.

As she wriggled her head from side to side, still holding this pose, Sue backed away.

'This is silly, Mum. I'm going to come back when you're feeling a bit better'.

Avril's tongue re-appeared as Sue stared at her in horror while also attempting to shuffle around the end of the bed and towards the door. Her mother struggled to raise herself from the pillow, grunting and wheezing as she forced her tongue out even further, as if using it to prod and push her daughter from the room.

*

Letitia balanced out along the rocks as best she could, her feet unsteady on the patches of exposed and slippery seaweed. Very quickly, in only a few steps, the shingle floor of the seabed had become obscured beneath a gritty churn of water. The spine of rocks had ended, dropping away into sudden depths.

Sidney had been courageous, had shown a unique and exceptional bravery. He had not faltered for one moment.

Letitia stepped forward. Her breath and the trapped air from within the layers of her clothes bubbled upwards with the gaiety of carnivals as she sank beneath the surface of the water.

17. THE CENTRE OF THE ARC

Halfway up the hillside, where the track turned back upon itself, Sue stopped and looked across the miles of farmland. Above her, a skylark hovered some way from its nest crying in mock alarm. Although it was not yet mid-morning, the sun was already strong, and Sue was pleased she had chosen to wear no more than her khaki shorts and a T-shirt. She knew that, from the top of the scarp, the last fields of England would lie before her, fraying into the ancient margins of Wales. And the person who had been her steady support and companion these past years would be waiting, silhouetted against the sky.

Across the hillside, gusts of warm wind sent the grasses bending and bowing. Sue's hair swirled about her face. She laughed and attempted to clear it from her eyes, tasting mouthfuls as it flapped against her cheek. Although long and completely grey, her hair's lively independence for some reason flooded her with sensations from her youth. Her curls were momentarily back, blonde and bouncing at some art college disco. And so too was a sense of being temporarily free from responsibilities. The struggle to see where she was stepping and to stay upright on the uneven ground was for now her only concern.

The turbulence of recent years would subside. Despite the chaos and dislocation, older narratives would regain a rightful prominence. Love laid down and scattered over years, would bloom in a cleaner air, flourish against a clearer sky.

These were Georgina's gifts.

*

Sue's posture was stiffer than usual. She knew it but was unable to feel any more relaxed. She caught sight of her fingers, one hand kneading the other. There was no need for this stiffness. She was here voluntarily. It was long overdue.

The woman was saying something about preliminaries. A contract, charges, timekeeping, confidentiality. Sue nodded despite retaining little of what was being said, nodded too enthusiastically, assenting to everything, not waiting for explanations or elaborations.

'… unless, of course, I hear anything that should be reported to the police and then …'

Sue's eyes opened even more widely, her expression vigorously signifying even greater agreement.

The woman lifted her chin, pulled back her shoulders and flexed her elbows like a swan preparing for flight. Contemplating the huge power of her wings. She smiled.

Was that condescension, pity or just a honed professional manner?

Sue forced herself to respond in kind, as best she could.

'Now,' said the swan, smoothing her floral skirt across her thighs, 'tell me what's brought you here?'

'I feel like – it's going to sound like a cliché,' said Sue, 'but I'm just so angry. I thought it would go away, it would subside a bit by now. But it hasn't.'

The woman raised her eyebrows slightly but otherwise remained immobile. Sue took this as encouragement to continue but also wondered whether it might instead indicate surprise. Disapproval even.

'I don't know how to say it without sounding corny,' she added, looking down at the rush matting and then directing her gaze towards the small ornamental Buddha on the adjacent coffee table. She also realised that she was biting her lower lip and must look more anxious than she thought she really was.

'Just tell me in your own words. Don't worry what it sounds like.'

Sue looked back up, made eye contact and detected an acknowledging look – an acceptance.

'It's my husband – my ex-husband', said Sue, blurting the words out. 'Well, legally he's still my husband – we've never quite got round – but, no, he's my ex-husband'.

The widened eyes again. But there was also one slight nod.

'Giles. He's called Giles. It hasn't been good between us for a while. But I don't know if that's any different from anybody who's been married for as long as we have. Well, I say that but I know people – I've got friends – they don't – it's not as if I haven't – '

Sue stopped, the resentments that had simmered for so long bubbling and boiling over. A sticky mess of emotions, her words dissolving and shapeless. She swallowed and gulped in air.

'Take your time. There's plenty of time. Tell me about you and Giles if you want to'.

*

The Canada secondment. Giles had not pursued it the first time. Sue had been right. Both their children in their different ways and Avril with her distinctive neediness had required their attention. When the opportunity unexpectedly reappeared five years later, like a homing pigeon blasted way off course by storm and ocean, Giles had seized this second chance. He seemed unwilling to discuss his application with Sue. She felt reluctant, this time, to stop him.

'We can discuss how we are going to manage it if I get the job,' he said. 'It's pointless constructing obstacles and then worrying about how to overcome them when we don't even know that I'll get it'.

But Sue knew. He was competent. More than competent. He had a track record. He was a known pair of hands, and safe ones at that.

What she had not expected was that Grace would choose to follow her father and tear apart an assumed future, a web of anchoring, family connections.

*

'Why not start with how you two met and what attracted you to him'.

The quiet, level tone again. Steady, already almost familiar and predictable.

'It was the college climbing club. We were in Wales, Snowdonia. We had been out on a cliff face all day. In a huge mountain landscape. Mists below us. I needed to go to the loo in this ridiculous place. Half way up a bloody cliff. He even knew what to do in those circumstances!'

Sue grunted quietly and shook her thoughts and her head to one side. 'There was still snow on the ground. We were in his little tent that night. It was very romantic'.

A raised eyebrow. Just the one. But a definite communication.

'Romantic?'

'Yes, romantic!' said Sue, looking first defiant and then alarmed. 'Well I thought so'.

The silence pounded a missing beat. Then both women laughed. Giggles, a snort, then with shaking shoulders, the release.

'You were an adventurer'.

'Yes, I was. Well, I suppose I was. Can I call you Georgina?'

'Of course you can call me Georgina.'

*

Grace was every bit the adventurer that Sue had been. Only now it was planes rather than hitchhiking. It was power dressing, slick suits with pencil skirts, rather than kaftans and flared jeans. Careers rather than an ideological rejection of ambition. An easy confidence around check-ins and departure boards. Not the fantasy of a generation turning of its own volition down a dusty track, refusing to slot into the futures and histories prepared for them. Entitlement now, not enlightenment.

Callum, on the other hand, resembled neither his mother, his father nor his sister. He lacked Grace's drive and focus. Instead of her resolve, he had slumped into the beery camaraderie of other young men such as himself. But Sue felt increasingly reassured that he could earn a living. Girlfriends seemed to come and go, none of them staying long, but he had proved, at least, that he could hold down a job. Five years now it was since graduating, eight since his unsettled start at university. He had taken out a mortgage on a small flat near his office, he seemed happy and valued at his work and he had a set of friends whose activities centred around six-a-side football, pubs and video games. Sue felt an affection for this group of clever young men, still uncoordinated in their large lumbering bodies. Now that her children had left home, she experienced occasional but unexpectedly strong desires to receive the whole troupe of Callum's friends, to feed and water them while she washed and ironed their dishevelled, baggy clothes.

Giles. Giles was the problem. The focus of all her anger. The reason her family was falling apart. Giles and her own pathetic indecision, her inability to bite the bullet.

*

Sue made out the cheque for Georgina, tore it carefully from the book and handed it to her across empty space.

Why did this opening ritual never vary? Why no small talk? Was 'how are you' or some other civility really too much to expect?

'Thank you, Sue' said Georgina, like a robot. A kind, considerate robot but one with a clanking, mechanical script nonetheless. She wrote a receipt for Sue in silence and then tucked the cheque into a wallet.

And what am I supposed to do with a stupid receipt every week anyway?

Georgina sat back, folded her hands formally in her lap, then looked Sue directly in the eye. And remained silent.

It's always me has to fill this space, has to start it off. What about a bit of human contact? A bit of normal interaction?

'I've been wanting to ask you – um – but I don't know whether – ' began Sue and Georgina seemed to rise in her chair.

A friend of a friend had originally recommended Georgina to Sue and that had seemed enough at the time.

Sod it.

'What are your – I mean, for this job – what sort of training – ?'

Georgina's wide smile, not an aggressive or defensive one, reassured Sue that her question had been released safely into the room even if she had struggled to articulate it.

'Of course,' said Georgina and she reeled off a list of qualifications – an MA in something about therapy, an advanced diploma, a certificate. 'Gestalt' was in there somewhere. And 'Integrative'. Membership of an Association. And something about 'Supervision'.

Not swanky or irritated. Just a list, a simple matter of information.

'Is that helpful?'

'Yes, it's – it's very – I don't know why that was so hard,' said Sue, fumbling with her words and the bottom button of her cardigan. 'I've been working up to asking you that all week. I drove home after last week's session and I realised that my speedometer was up over eighty'.

Georgina gave her a long stare, boring deeply into Sue's disquiet.

'You were very angry'.

Sue discovered herself able to hold the gaze.

'Shall we talk about why that was so difficult for you?' asked Georgina in the gentlest of tones.

*

Perhaps Sue had never given Montreal a proper chance. She and Grace had joined Giles for a two-week holiday in the middle of his three-month trial period while Callum had shown no enthusiasm for the trip.

'Dad's crazy if he thinks I'm going over there. You both are. Why should I?' he complained when Sue told him – and told herself – that there was no harm in a visit, just having a look around. 'My mates are here. And my job. Why would I want to go to some place where I don't even know anyone?'

Grace, not one generally to express strong preferences or enthusiasms, at least to her mother, seemed nevertheless open to an initial visit. What neither of her parents had anticipated was that the city's wintry edifices, the sunlight that chiselled cold, clean contours onto the edges of buildings and the hiss and bustle inside small, steamy French cafes would captivate her so much.

What dreams and desires had her daughter been harbouring that found expression here? Sue realised, not for the first time, that Grace secreted away much that might have drawn them closer together as a mother and daughter – plans, excitements, intimacies. Callum, on the other hand, readily spilled anxieties into her lap, down the telephone line or through late night, drunken email rambles. He had exhausted her ability to reassure him only a couple of years earlier with his recurring panic about the 'Millenium Bug'.

'Everybody says there's going to be a crash. The government's left it too late,' he had said on a number of occasions.

'I'm sure it's not that bad,' Sue had replied, attempting to calm him. 'These people you work with, well they could be looking on the black side a bit,' she added, trying to reassure herself as much as him.

Disasters had not occurred. Planes had stayed in the skies. Grace had thoroughly researched the protocols for transferring for media work from England to Canada and, three years after her first visit, boarded a plane to join her father in their new home.

*

'What did you feel in your body when you told me that?'
What does she mean what do I feel?
'Are you aware of any sensations that seem different anywhere in your body?'
'Not really. I'm not sure if I know what you mean'.

287

Then, conscious of trying to provide whatever it was Georgina was hoping to hear, she added

'Do you mean like tension across my shoulders or something?'

'It could be. Or it could be anything else'.

'Well perhaps there's a bit of that,' said Sue, casting around for an answer, conscious of summoning up phantom symptoms because that was what was expected.

'Maybe my neck feels a bit stiff, sort of strained', she said without much conviction and then added, 'But nothing much really, I'm afraid. I'm sorry'.

Georgina pursed her lips slightly and Sue imagined a nursery teacher about to address a wriggly group of toddlers at her feet.

'Are you aware of your voice going very quiet just then?'

'Going quiet?' replied Sue, feeling – *feeling what was it? – tricked? – patronised? –*

'Maybe a bit but not much. Nothing dramatic'.

'It did. When you told me about your neck and then you apologised as if you hadn't given me the answer I expected. Your voice dropped, and you looked down at the floor. Your eyes dropped too'.

Nonsense. If it did, it was only by a couple of decibels. What of it? It's hardly the end of the world.

'I know you want me to say, I don't know, that I've got a dry throat or tightness across my chest. Something like that. But I haven't. I could try to invent something just to keep you happy but what's the point of that?'

'There wouldn't be any point. I just wondered whether you were aware of any different sensations in your body as we talked. That's all. You don't have to have any'.

God. Talk about mountains out of molehills!

'Well, I don't. And I really can't see the point of going over and over something like this!'

The space between the two women tingled.

'I think you are very angry with me,' said Georgina in a measured, neutral tone.

'I'm not angry with you,' snapped Sue.

'I think you are,' she said and then added, 'Do I remind you of anybody?'

*

Janet had borne the brunt of driving up regularly from Weymouth to Portsmouth to look after Avril for so many years. And Sue felt that this had added to the growing mountain of obstacles that blocked the two sisters' appreciation of each other. So, when the case conference at the hospital concluded that Avril required a greater level of care and in a more appropriate setting, Sue welcomed the opportunity to seek out an establishment close to her own home.

Avril, at eighty-six, was strapped into a wheelchair that was bolted to the floor up next to the driver of a specially converted van. Seated high up behind an enlarged windscreen she made the journey all the way up through England in the company of a nurse and the driver. Sue was waiting for them at the new care home at the predicted arrival time, fearful of the effect that such a prolonged journey would have upon Avril's frail, elderly frame.

She need not have worried. When the white van pulled up at the front entrance to Hill Crest Care Home, the stocky, red-faced driver hurled back his sliding door as if urgently needing to fill his lungs, even if with alien, northern air. The nurse too seemed to be escaping confinement, but in a cloud of cheery, professional bluster.

'Avril's been entertaining us all the way up with stories of her life in Weymouth,' she announced to the welcoming party – Sue, the home's manager and two of the care staff.

Sue could hear her mother's raised voice as the staff began to release the wheelchair from its bolts.

'Wherever are we now?' she was saying with the exaggerated intonation that Sue had known so well all her life. Exaggerated as in a stage performance.

A performance that was nonetheless almost complete. Avril, seemingly in full flow, was delivering her very last lines. The remaining tattered pages of the script were all completely blank.

*

'I think your mother was very ill at times,' said Georgina.

'I think she was too. But I was the only one who did, sometimes. Well, I felt like I was the only one'.

And Sue began to recount the incident with the doctor who had told her that all Avril required was more sympathetic attention and company.

'She pulled the wool over his eyes completely. The night before I called him she had been lying on her side in her bungalow, with her dressing gown tied around her neck like some huge, crazy scarf, trying to push herself along the carpet with a walking stick. As if she was lying in a punt or something. It was bizarre. Crazy'.

Sue stopped pulling at her chin with her hand and raised her eyes towards Georgina.

'It was very, very distressing for you'.

'You can say that again. What was worse though was nobody else saw it. They were all chuckling away. Oh, she's a proper character. We all love her blah blah. Makes us all laugh. And my Dad was just as bad most of the time.

Your Mum's just a bit eccentric or *They all love her, your Mum. They think the world of her.* Talk about propaganda. They were both at it all the time. Each of them the publicity agent for the other. Huddling their real selves away from the world. And I was 'the rest of the world' sometimes. Talk about Hansel and Gretel! But it never rankled with my sister so much. She just seemed to accept it a lot of the time. But me – I just – '

And before Georgina could tell her again that she was very angry or ask her whether she was experiencing any unusual bodily reactions or any of the rest of it, she threw herself head first into the past, splashing and spluttering. Avril swaying on tiptoes with a boiling kettle. Under a wave and back up to the surface. Avril sitting in the road. Mouthfuls of salt water. Avril not answering the phone. Gasping for air. Avril on the phone, unable to leave the room. Empty fists grasping the air and water. Her huge tongue.

Sue's forehead was damp with sweat and she could detect the smell of her armpits.

'I'm sorry, I couldn't stop,' she said and realised that she was shivering. 'I just couldn't stop.'

'That's all right. You have a lot to say'.

Georgina's voice sounded so composed. An indoors voice from a quiet room.

'I was afraid I couldn't stop. That we'd run out of time and that I'd be out on the street like this'.

'I won't let you leave until you are ready.'

'But I can't – I mean what's the use of just pouring all this stuff out. I know you are supposed to. But it doesn't go away. It's all still inside at the end. It's all still there'.

'I think you are very angry with your parents'.

'I am. I was. I still am. Sometimes I was so bloody – and Janet. Sometimes I could have – and bloody Trevor. Especially him – chauvinist pig. And Giles as well. Bloody Giles. Where was he when all this was kicking off? Canada, that's where. Or on his way. Or up to his neck in sodding application forms. Might as well have been there for all the understanding he showed'.

Sue eased the hair that had begun to stick to the side of her face back behind her ear.

'The whole damned lot of them! All of them. Sometimes, I really did, I wanted them all –'

She swallowed and drew in a staccato breath in time with the shuddering of her chest. She closed her eyes tightly, indicating that she was unable to continue.

'You wanted them all –?'

'I wanted them all – '

She exhaled uncontrollably.

'In – '

Silence.

'– In New Zealand! All that way away. The whole lot of them'.

Her tears broke out into the open.

'And bloody South Island as well while we're at it!'

*

Pine disinfectant and bleach. Sue was adjusting to these ever-present smells. She no longer hovered on the brink of retching during her weekly visits to her mother. She had, at first, concentrated on breathing in as shallow a manner as possible, giving more of her attention to this than to Avril. Not that her mother seemed aware of her presence most of the time, anyway. She offered the occasional 'Hello' when Sue arrived but otherwise sat in the day room or lay in her bed in silence with long periods of sustained and unsettling staring. Cold and metallic. Eye to eye.

Sue had soon adopted a regular visiting schedule and, when not talking to an unresponsive Avril, easily slipped into reverie, remembering her upbringing and the sometimes intense emotions associated with her mother and other family members that had been surfacing in her other weekly sessions – those with Georgina.

Some weeks she brought a sketch book and made pencil drawings of her sleeping mother, swift, sweeping lines in soft graphite. She worked with an urgency on the complexity of her mother's character. With an increasingly free hand and eye, she revelled in the speed of her actions, in her ability to freeze time, in the echo of light and carefree days back in art college in the nineteen sixties.

At other times she brought her box file of Letitia clippings and notes, wondering whether, now that she was teaching significantly reduced hours and about to retire fully at the end of the academic year, this might be the time to organise her material into some more coherent form. She re-read the 1927 newspaper report of the inquest and the various names, dates and locations gleaned from the county archives. And again, she felt irritation with the way all this information seemed to render Letitia less, not more, knowable as a person. A mass of data rather than a connection through blood, bone and ancestry to this tragic figure.

But predominant in her thoughts, as she sat beside her sleeping mother, was the ending of her marriage to Giles. After thirty three years together and almost eighteen months since he took up his post in Canada, Sue was admitting to herself that their experimental arrangement of living as man and wife – or, as she preferred, woman and husband – but on different continents, was unsustainable. Her anger with him had subsided considerably over the period of their separation. In their emails and during their half-yearly visits to each other, a muffled sadness seemed to permeate their conversations. Sue experienced a greater affection for him than she had known for years, the matter-of-fact severing of their marriage and the growing distance between them seeming to rekindle in her memories of the relative strangers they had once been to each other.

But she accepted that it was over.

He might well have a new romantic interest in Canada. Grace had been infuriatingly discreet, loyal or just plain insensitive to her mother's curiosity about such matters. And, anyway, perhaps in her own life there might one day be possibilities. Changes. Opportunities.

*

'We're going over and over my parents,' said Sue. 'They weren't that bad. Some of the kids I've worked with, they *did* have a rotten deal from their parents. Mine had a lot of good, admirable qualities'.

Sue was weary. The weekly sessions with Georgina had been going on for almost three years. She prided herself in her persistence. Her father's daughter she was, she kept going, didn't give up. But she also wondered whether Georgina might actually be a waste of time and money. Calm and supportive, yes, and she presumably knew what she was doing, but was this constant raking over the same old things really getting her anywhere?

'Tell me about those admirable qualities,' said Georgina.

Does she really have to say everything back to me? 'Reflecting' they called it on a course I went on – 'Talking with Troubled Teenagers'. And we always get back to my parents. If I'd come in here with an ingrowing toenail we'd still have to talk about my bloody parents!

'There were a lot', said Sue. 'My dad had an amazing faith in education. He'd had his stolen by the tragedy of his mum. But I never heard him complain. I remember feeling a burning sense of injustice on his behalf. But he just kept going. He was a provider. And a good one at that.'

'And your mother?'

'She was more complicated,' said Sue. 'But she was great. In some ways she was brilliant. When my kids were little she was such a lot of fun. They used to play games early in the morning when we stayed down there. Pubs. They loved it. Out in the kitchen before Giles and I were awake, a whole row of bottles lined up – pop, gin, sherry, my dad's home-made beer in a barrel. She was the barmaid and they were the customers. Or, their favourite was when she had to be a drunk'.

'The child in her came out,' said Georgina. 'She knew how to play'.

'Yes,' said Sue. 'That crazy side of her could be great. The piano, she could bash out a tune. Pub piano, that sort of thing. And painting. She wasn't that good, but she put everything she had into it'.

Sue ran out of words. Her parents felt very close, blurred presences in the room, just out of sight.

Georgina remained silent too, both locked in shared solemnity.

'So, why do we keep talking as if I had some sort of terrible childhood?' asked Sue, feeling a sudden surge of resentment. 'As if I've got some sort of major problem'.

She's going to ask me if I'm feeling something in my body. Any moment now. I can hear it coming.

'And before you ask, it's in my neck and my throat. An ache and a dryness'.

But Georgina did not nod or smile. Or show any other sign of approval.

'I think you do have a major problem,' said Georgina.

Harsh, callous words. Slashing out. Cutting through the closeness.

'I – you – '

'Your mother wasn't always there. Perhaps she was carrying some of your father's trauma for him. Trying to process it, somehow. And you were a very clever, little girl. You had to pay very close attention. Your mother swung through an arc from an out-of-control entertainer at one end to a slumped and unavailable being at the other. And as she swept through that curve you could connect with her just in the middle bit. You had to hang on to her for as long as you could. You never knew when she would be gone from you again'.

'Hmm, compared to what some people though – '

'Sometimes when children suffer a sense of unpredictable abandonment,' said Georgina, interrupting Sue for what seemed like the first time ever, 'that can have serious consequences. Not the same as abuse or other terrible treatment. But it's the longing for the parent the child knows can be there sometimes. Little Sue didn't know when or how – or if – she could get her Mum back'.

'I don't – I can't – ' mumbled Sue.

'And we've seen Little Sue in this room sometimes,' continued Georgina, firmly but kindly. 'She's been longing to have her mother back'.

Georgina paused.

'She still is'.

Avril at her wildest barged about the room. Georgina sat some vast distance away, staring. Sue battled, using her whole body, panic versus a crushing sense of pity, despair against an intense determination to survive.

'Breathe,' said Georgina.

*

It was only a small, local, exhibition Sue explained but Callum, for one, was having none of her modesty.

'Get off it, mother. These are great,' he said, looking over the sketches spread across the dining room table. 'This one's brilliant. It's Gran to a 'T'. I'd love that for my wall. To remember her by'.

After nearly three years at Hill Crest, Avril's death had been a muted and unsensational affair. During the preceding day, she had slept, as usual, for long periods and only been woken by staff for regular drinks, her liquidised meals and for turning. During a routine check at two in the morning, a nurse detected extremely shallow and irregular breathing and before she could summon additional help, Avril had silently departed.

Then, Sue's set of drawings of her mother became the family's most precious artefacts. Avril left little in the way of possessions, there was nothing that seemed distinctively or memorably 'her'. But she was captured so convincingly within the sketches, her contradictions, the fun but also the disquiet. Sue allowed each member of her family – Grace, Callum and Janet – to choose one. She even arranged to send a smaller piece, via Grace, to Giles in Canada. But before this collection was permanently dispersed, she was persuaded to display them at a public exhibition held at the local art college.

Ben, her tutor there at the evening classes she had been attending, had been less interested in the rendering of lifelike similarities and more impressed by the interpretations of character and natural environment that he felt she excelled at. He had encouraged her to extend her subject matter while retaining a focus on ageing and its institutions. So Sue had also drawn the empty corridors with abandoned meal trolleys or changes of bedding, the huge TV screens dominating the day room with its slumbering occupants, the brilliant and unspeakable hygiene of the sluice room.

'These have such life, such sympathy,' Ben said, staring at her work. 'They – they – '

He seemed to lose interest in his own words, as if admiration had flooded critical distance, washed away the necessity for the rationalisation.

'It's the humanity. Our humanity. These deserve a much, much wider audience'.

*

'I know what my parents went through,' said Sue. 'It was terrible – far, far more than I've ever had to. It feels so wrong sometimes to be here slagging them off every week'.

'Big Sue knows those things,' replied Georgina. 'But it's Little Sue we're trying to help. She's the one who's still frightened sometimes'.

And a little girl stood looking down at her mother. Round and round in the whirlpool she careered, one moment cackling with glee, the next reaching out a hand towards the girl who was watching from up behind the safety rail.

Help me – please – save me!

Then the cries and accusations. Discords crashing through the thundery air. The thick, grainy liquid sucked down into the vortex, the woman shouting and swirling around with both arms now extended. The girl immobile and frozen.

Georgina stood by Sue at the rail and they both looked down together.

'Little Sue needs her father to help her out,' said Georgina tenderly. 'But he can't do it. He has too many of his own worries.'

Sue tried to shake her head in an attempt to deny the thought and suppress a huge anguish. But instead she found herself nodding furiously, acknowledging the images and ideas.

'What could he have said that might have helped?' asked Georgina.

'I don't know,' said Sue, choking on her words. 'He could have – just put his hand on my shoulder – just sort of said 'let's go over here and do something else for a while. Your Mum – she's not feeling very – '.

And Sue's tears broke like a reservoir through a dam, a huge zig-zagging fault line splitting down through a lifetime's thoughts, excuses and redundant reassurances.

'So, what can we do?' asked Sue, forcing each word out through her deep distress.

'Our job is to find ways for Big Sue to help that little girl,' said Georgina reassuringly. 'Big Sue is clever and resourceful. She'll be able to help'.

18. THREE PAINTINGS

The hill was steeper than she had been expecting. Either that or all the time spent over the last year in her new studio, the day-long absorption in her creations, her canvases, had made her unfit. Once, Sue would have romped up this slope, thought nothing of it, but today she was breathing heavily and conscious of the pull in tendons and hamstrings. Unless, she told herself, it was normal to feel like this approaching one's mid-sixties.

Towering above her on the skyline was Ben. Ben, who had championed her painting, genuinely excited by its freshness and defiant disregard for convention. Ben, who could readily acknowledge, and without jealousy, that her work had a confidence and originality that his efforts had never really achieved despite a lifetime of trying. Ben, whose sympathetic eyes and welcoming face greeted her with an uncomplicated warmth, whose hand reached out readily for hers and whose lips she kissed with an unruly enthusiasm. She pulled back her wayward hair, laughed at the vast, open sky and accepted his embrace.

Above them a kestrel locked its position tight against the wind.

*

Sue had initially been hesitant about becoming Ben's lover. At her age.

He had been on his own since his wife died five years earlier. He had a son in London and a daughter, with children of her own, in Australia. The end of Sue's marriage had been such a protracted affair – rightly so, she felt, given the length of time she and Giles had been together and the children they had given birth to and raised. This process of disengagement had drained her and the new lightness of being she felt around Ben disorientated and unsettled her as much as it gave her a sense of joyous intoxication.

Things needed to settle.

Things needed to explode.

The difference between these two men was obvious to Sue. One was determined, single-mindedly ambitious at times and had been critical of her in a number of ways. The other was patient, seemingly content with his life's more modest achievements and admiring of her. But one was also adventurous, bold and assertive while the other took what life handed out in a relatively uncomplaining fashion. Sue was in no doubt that she felt more valued and authentic, more listened to, when she was with Ben.

But she was also aware that she herself had changed. She was now capable of valuing, accepting and, in equal part, creating this deeper and more satisfying relationship – Georgina's greatest gift.

One area where she had hoped for a new beginning after their mother's death was in her relationship with her sister. They had now lost their joint concern for Avril and their frustration with her, and Sue hoped that this might allow them some new beginning. But the reality had been that there was little now to draw them together, to merit lengthy phone calls – or any phone calls at all. Sue understood her own sense of loss but was now resigned to it more calmly than at any other period of her life.

Janet received the news about Ben in a non-committal fashion. *Was she pleased? Uncomfortable? Or disapproving even?* Sue held back the sarcasm that she would once have voiced, if only to herself. She no longer had need of it. She knew of sisters submerged intimately in the minutiae of each other's lives. Had envied them greatly and bitterly at times. Now, she could accept that her life contained other blessings.

Like Callum, who, since his new girlfriend had moved into his flat, had become an effusive advocate for love and togetherness.

'That's great, Mum,' had been his first reaction to the news. 'Really cool'.

Grace, as ever, was more constrained just as she was unforthcoming about possible romantic developments in her own life. Career, she could talk about that with energy and enthusiasm, but any men had to be coaxed and then finally dragged from the shadows by Sue in conversations and emails. Her daughter though, despite the reserved manner that Sue now understood far more fully, clearly did approve.

During their first year together, while Sue and her family rearranged their loyalties and sympathies around each other, Ben encouraged her to extend her art techniques, to venture into media – charcoal, chalk, water colour – that she had last dabbled with half a century before. Accordingly, she gathered together her old photographs, took new ones of clouds and skies, seas both tranquil and riotous, and ripped illustrations from magazines. She lost herself in a heavily darkened tableau of characters in period dress around a small child's sickbed, the face of a tall, angular clergyman catching the candle light and dispensing reverential piety. Another, in watercolour and with characters from a similar historical era, showed a family taking a makeshift meal in a partly-harvested wheat field. The dry edge of a row of elms stood out sharply against a rumble of clouds.

'It's good work. Very good,' said Ben. 'You have a feel for the medium. The electrical storm building, the anxiety about the crop. You've captured it. It's all there'.

Momentum carried Sue forward, there was no shortage of topics to hook her creative energies. She went back to an old sketch book and photographs she had taken decades earlier on her journey from Istanbul to Kabul. She revisited mountain landscapes where she had first met Giles and holiday destinations they had shared before the children were born.

But the subject that frustrated her, the scene that refused to tell its full story, was one from the trenches of World War One. She worked to evoke a dismal dawn with energy leeching into a lifeless horizon. A captain with his pistol waving. Men tired and cold and failing to stir, unable to rise from the stinking water. Mumbled insurrection. The captain's desperation, his arm readying, his point-blank aim becoming sure. The smoky discharge from a weapon hurrying along the passageway in the pale light, fondling the tattered uniforms of the men.

'It's no good,' complained Sue. "It's too – static. Too much is left out'.

'It's got life and atmosphere,' said Ben, paying attention to details. "Perhaps you have too much in your head for just one picture. What about a series? When we have our week away, you should do a related sequence. And this subject, this intensity, it needs oils. Oils or acrylic. We'll set you up in Shropshire and you'll be away!'

*

The strip of beach, with the lagoon behind and the huge surface of sea in front, itself seemed precarious and vulnerable, the lone person, tiny, lost and irrelevant amongst Nature's huge menace. Sue had used a palette knife to scrape a handful of sky, brilliant blue with streaks of white, across her canvas. The gritty sweep of her beach dissolved in the distance, claimed by the tussle between sea and sky. The figure she added later with a small, stiffened brush. A few swift marks, a coat, possibly a hat, most definitely a woman. Sue brought her face up close to the canvass, gauging the relative sizes of the figure and the bay, gave a small grunt of satisfaction and rubbed her hands vigorously against her thighs. Then she threw herself into the sea again working to elicit its unknowable depths, gouging out spray and foam with her knife and a stick. She forced the whole scene to belittle and then crush the tiny figure on her steady plod towards nowhere.

She stepped back from the painting, aware that her intense concentration had claimed and suppressed her breathing. She straightened her back and adjusted her focus back to the room's proportions and timescales. It was past midnight and the cocoa that Ben had made her more than an hour earlier had shrunk and stuck in a sullen circle around the inside of the mug. She was aware of the insistent pull of her canvas but, with one last, reluctant look for that night, turned and made her way towards the stairs.

The next day Sue divided her energies, her heightened, rampant energies, between additional but minor modifications and a new piece. To her ear, Ben was a silent presence in the building. She smiled at the thought of his sensitivity to her work habits, he seemed to know when to engage her in conversation or silent embraces and when to leave her completely undisturbed. In fact, he seemed a far better judge of her requirements in this respect than she herself.

The second painting was part of the series. She knew that even though, at this stage, she was unable to say how many would constitute the complete set nor what these pieces would depict. The landscape that had haunted her in the previous days, the vastness and the despair, still hung in the air all around her but her composition this time was strikingly different.

Huge bodies filled this new frame, part underwater, part above, gasping beneath the fierce pigmentation of a huge, empty sky. Two young men with boots and huge limbs were thrashing beneath the water. Sue gave them muscular substance, frantic movements, as they grappled, like submerged dancers, with a woman's shoulders, her heavy skirt and coat that pulled with the tide and currents. She bit back her own breathing and frowned intensely, as the heads of her three figures broke the surface, an addled chorus coughing and spluttering in a crosswind.

Later Sue remembered their week in Shropshire as the time when style, purpose and commitment had all crystallised in her work. Her love for Ben deepened during the holiday partly because he made no demands on her time and tolerated her absences even when they made a conscious effort to be together on occasional walks or visits to the local pub. The least alert and engaged parts of her accompanied him on these rambles and around contrived, rustic fireplaces. Her imagination was firing elsewhere, and she often felt unable to dampen or disguise her desire to be back in the outhouse that had been designated her studio for the week. Ben seemed to accept all of this, to be content with his own company, reading, pottering, preparing their meals.

But mainly her feelings for him were growing because of his reactions to the paintings she was producing. He had always been encouraging. That was part of his role as a tutor, she told herself. This week, however, he seemed profoundly moved by her work and was supporting her because of his own intense desire for it to be born and alive within the world.

Sue began her third canvas while still making additions or alterations to the other two, as if thoughts about any one of them inspired extensions to its companions. This time there was a group of figures in the foreground, viewed from an elevated position. A strong sun beamed down on them. A blue sky, void within void, surrounded and encased the little group.

A woman had been dragged up the beach leaving a furrow in the sand. Salt and grit had matted the hair on the back of her head. Awkward, bony fingers were digging into her waist. Steam was beginning to rise from her sodden coat and skirt, the sun burning away that which did not belong on land.

Sue gazed down from her vantage point, anxious to guide the party's actions. She made the sand hot and golden. The two young men she caused to stumble and sigh, breathing drunkenly as if in competition for a whole sky full of oxygen. A man in a uniform like that of a naval officer or a coastguard was instructing the small group to move back, to allow some light and air. The woman who had been dragged from the sea was retching and attempting to sit up.

She was alive. Her forehead was being stroked by a village woman. Skin on skin.

Sue delicately added a crust of salt to the woman's cheek and nose.

She finally stood back, knowing that at last it was finished. She stared at the painting there before her on the easel, unable to understand how it had come into being. She looked down at her own gloriously stained hands, marvelling at their complicity.

She called to Ben who came and stood in silence for many minutes beside her.

Her hair contained a streak of paint, a patch of similar colour was smudged across her cheek and forehead. She was so exhausted her chest and shoulders began to shudder.

'Come to bed,' Ben said, placing a hand gently on one of her arms. 'You need some sleep'.

She reached for his hand.

'Come on,' he added. 'It will all still be here in the morning'.

Acknowledgements

The late Carole Blake, from Blake Friedmann, and David Duncombe read early drafts of this novel and their detailed feedback significantly aided its later development. Paul Anderson, Angela Barton, Gaynor Backhouse, Megan Taylor and Frances Thimann, from Nottingham Writers Studio, provided detailed critiques during its completion and the cover artwork and design were created by Vally Miller and Bill Bevan.

I am deeply indebted to them all for their skilled help and encouragement along the way.

Printed in Great Britain
by Amazon